Also by Adam Rubin

Tales from the Multiverse: Volume One

THE ICE CREAM MACHINE

ADAM RUBIN

illustrated by

DANIEL SALMIERI   EMILY HUGHES

CHARLES SANTOSO   NICOLE MILES

LINIERS   SEAERRA MILLER

putnam

G. P. Putnam's Sons

G. P. Putnam's Sons

An imprint of Penguin Random House LLC, New York

First published in the United States of America by G. P. Putnam's Sons,
an imprint of Penguin Random House LLC, 2022

Library of Congress Cataloging-in-Publication Data

Names: Rubin, Adam, 1983- author. | Salmieri, Daniel, 1983- illustrator. | Santoso, Charles, illustrator. | Liniers, 1973- illustrator. | Hughes, Emily (Emily M.), illustrator. | Miles, Nicole, illustrator. | Miller, Seaerra, illustrator.
Title: The ice cream machine / Adam Rubin ; illustrated by Daniel Salmieri, Charles Santoso, Liniers, Emily Hughes, Nicole Miles, Seaerra Miller.
Description: New York : G. P. Putnam's Sons, [2022] | Audience: Ages 10 & up |
Summary: "A collection of six short stories in a variety of genres and settings, all featuring ice cream"—Provided by publisher. | Identifiers: LCCN 2021018388 (print) | LCCN 2021018389 (ebook)| ISBN 9780593325797 (hardcover) | ISBN 9780593325810 (epub)
Subjects: CYAC: Ice cream—Fiction. | Humorous stories. | LCGFT: Short stories. | Humorous fiction. | Classification: LCC PZ7.R83116 Ic 2022 (print) | LCC PZ7.R83116 (ebook) | DDC [Fic]—dc23
LC record available at https://lccn.loc.gov/2021018388
LC ebook record available at https://lccn.loc.gov/2021018389

Printed in the United States of America
ISBN 9780593325797

1   3   5   7   9   10   8   6   4   2

LSCH

Design by Eileen Savage. Text set in Skolar Latin.
Geometric background image courtesy of Shutterstock.

For T, la estrella fugaz de mi cuento favorito. Te amo.

Any object observed from a fixed viewpoint offers infinite possible interpretations.

—Professor Kokichi Sugihara,
doctor of engineering, Meiji University

Writing Is Magic

H owdy! It's me, Adam. I wrote this book.

Well, technically, I typed this book into a laptop, but all the same, here we are now, you and I together, on this very *word*.

Strange, right? It's almost as if these sentences have formed some mystical, telepathic connection directly from my brain to yours. You are reading my mind right now, and I, in turn, have you hypnotized.

I can prove it: Imagine a dog eating a diaper.

You couldn't help it, could you? As long as you're reading my words, you're under my spell. That's the thing they never mentioned when they made me practice lowercase z's between the dotted lines. Back then, I thought writing was boring and useless and difficult, but now I know better.

Writing is magic.

For example, imagine you recently painted a bench in the middle of the park and you need to make sure no one sits on that bench before the paint dries.

You could stand there all day, shooing people away, or you could write *Wet Paint* on a big piece of paper, gently set your writing on the bench, and saunter off to get a snack.

Booyah! You cast a no-sitting spell on that bench. This particular anti-butt spell is so powerful, it can prevent people from sitting someplace even if that place has *not* been painted recently . . . but I would never suggest you use your magical powers for mischief.

Here's a good one: Write *I love you* on a piece of paper, sign it, and slip it into your mom's coat pocket when she's not looking.

Blammo! You just traveled into the future. Someday (no one knows exactly when), your mom will find that paper, open it up, and melt into a jiggling puddle of warm fuzzies while she thinks about how sweet and considerate you are. I promise she will let you know when she finds that note and she'll tell you how happy it made her, and if you ask for a present that day, you'll very likely get it.

I'm telling you: *Writing is magic.* It allows your thoughts to escape your body and go venturing off into the world on their own. Writing lets you capture an idea like a genie in a lamp. It sits there, waiting until someone comes along to read the words, then—boom—your idea explodes in the mind of a total stranger!

This is an ancient kind of magic. There are writers who've been dead for centuries and we're still talking about their ideas to this day.

For example, more than twenty-five hundred years ago, a Chinese writer named Lao Tzu said: "A journey of a thousand miles begins with a single step."

Pretty deep, right? That's an idea that stands the test of time. I mention it here because it's as true about writing as it is about walking.

Staring at a blank page has stopped many would-be writers from ever getting started. Even for me (professional writer guy), a blank page sometimes scares me into thinking I'll never have another idea in my life.

But the truth is, everybody has ideas. Not just writers. Firefighters, doctors, shoemakers, treasure hunters—it's hard for any human being to go through their day without having at least one idea. The tricky part is giving yourself permission to think that *your* idea is a *good* idea. Some people have the opposite problem: They think *all* their ideas are good ideas. These people often go into politics.

Maybe I can help eliminate the pressure of coming up with a "good idea" the next time you feel like writing a story. An idea is really just an excuse to get started anyway. It doesn't need to be some groundbreaking concept like electromagnetism or democracy or SpongeBob

SquarePants, it just needs to be something that tickles your brain. Something that makes you go "Oooh."

Look at the words on the front of this book: *The Ice Cream Machine*.

Doesn't that sound like a good idea for a story? I thought so. I thought it sounded like a good idea for lots of different stories frankly, and to prove it, I wrote six. Each story is totally different. The only thing they have in common is their title. Actually, they have a half a dozen little wormholes in common too, but I'll let you discover those on your own.

I had a lot of fun writing these stories, and I hope you'll have fun reading them, but my real hope is that this book might serve as encouragement for aspiring young writers to create their own versions of "The Ice Cream Machine."

If so, I left a few tips in the back of the book for how to get started. I've also included my mailing address. Someday soon, it could be *me* reading *your* words.

Write whatever you want. Anything you can imagine, you can put in your story. If you want to eat ten thousand pizzas, you can. If you want to play basketball on the moon, you can. If you want to turn into a giant monster or ride an octopus or travel back in time, you can do that too.

And here's the most magical part: No matter how ridiculous, how outrageous, how downright impossible the things you make up are, once you put them in writing, they become real for whoever reads them. The people, places, and things that you plucked from thin air suddenly *exist* in someone else's imagination.

So here we go. You're about to enter a universe of my own invention. Multiple universes, in fact. If things go well, the time you spend in my multiverse might make you smile. If things go very well, you might laugh or gasp or even cry!

How incredible is that? Little black squiggles on paper, when placed in a certain order—when "spelled" correctly—gain powers. Writing enchants you to see things and feel things that don't really exist.

What else can you call it but magic?

Contents

THE ICE CREAM MACHINE

(the one with the five-armed robot)

illustrated by

DANIEL SALMIERI

A glimmering blue streak rocketed through the air above Megalopolis, weaving between skyscrapers, ducking below streams of flying hoverpods, and blasting through holographic advertisements just for fun. Excitement spread throughout the city as ordinary citizens identified the flying object overhead.

"Hey, look! It's Shiro and Kelly," said a man selling digital tacos on a street corner. He waved up at the sky to greet the famous duo.

"Shiro and Kelly." An old woman on a park bench chuckled as she adjusted her cybergoggles. "Off on another exciting adventure, I bet."

"I wish I had a superbot," said a kid staring out the window while feeding his dead goldfish.

Before long, Shiro Hanayama and his robot best friend/tutor/bodyguard, Kelly, reached their destination: the Hanayama Robotics Corporation, a two-hundred-story building covered in lush bioluminescent greenery, which towered over the sprawling cityscape that had once been known as Los Angeles.

A landing pad extended from the building, and Kelly touched down gently in the center. Shiro climbed out from inside the robot, yawned, and brushed the jet-black hair from his forehead. He was pale and chubby but had his father's handsome features and his mother's fierce, intelligent eyes. He wore a flight suit with a helmet, bright-pink sneakers, and a backpack.

Shiro stretched his arms over his head. "It's getting tight in there."

"If you don't like it," replied Kelly, "stop growing."

Kelly adjusted her configuration. In flight mode, she resembled a squid: five thin arms positioned at the bottom of her squat, egg-shaped body, ionic thrusters blasting from the tip of each three-pronged claw.

In casual mode, four of her limbs reconfigured into more traditional arm and leg positions, while the fifth moved around according to her mood: Sometimes it sat coiled atop her head like hair, sometimes it swished behind her back like a tail, and sometimes it moved to the front of her body to assist with tasks that required three hands.

Kelly's limbs were dark and dull in color, but her body was iridescent, like the glimmering wings of a blue butterfly.

She was built from indestructible bioengineered materials, covered in armored scales (like a pineapple), immune to microwave attacks, and completely bulletproof (unlike a pineapple).

A series of quantum processors gave her the capacity for independent thought. She was bubbly, funny, and kind, with an IQ of 250.

Kelly was famously considered to be the most advanced robot on Earth. Her groundbreaking technology was highly coveted by government spies and rival corporations, but despite their best efforts, the superbot's mysterious power source remained top secret.

Shiro's mom, Professor Hanayama, had designed Kelly to help care for and protect her son.

The professor was tall and thin, with big, penetrating eyes, a small mouth, and an asymmetrical haircut that had been dyed snow white. She always dressed in gray from head to toe, with a single fresh-cut flower tucked into her lapel for a touch of color.

Professor Hanayama ran one of the largest corporations in the solar system, leading the innovation of bio-quantum technology and working tirelessly to protect what little remained of Earth's natural resources. It was a very demanding job, which meant she didn't get to spend much time with Shiro. They had planned to have breakfast together before she left for work that morning, but Shiro had overslept. Again.

When Professor Hanayama noticed her son and his

robot outside her office on the landing pad, she paused her presentation and glowered at them through the window. Shiro pleaded with his hands, miming an apology. His mother turned back to the national ambassadors gathered around the table in the conference room, excused herself, and stepped outside.

"Good morning, Professor," Kelly said, bowing.

"Good morning, Kelly," said Professor Hanayama as she gave Shiro an angry hug.

"Good morning, Mom," Shiro mumbled with his face smooshed against her chest.

"It would have been a better morning if you had shown up for breakfast like we'd planned."

"Ow, Mom, you're squeezing too tight!" Professor Hanayama let go, and Shiro breathed a sigh of relief. "I'm really sorry. I was up late, and I couldn't find my new sneakers this morning, and—"

"Save it, Shiro," said Professor Hanayama. "I'm giving you one last chance. But if you dare break your poor mother's heart again tomorrow, I swear I will send you to the Mars colony to live with your father."

"But the only reason I—"

"I don't have time for any more excuses." Professor Hanayama adjusted the orchid in her lapel and walked back inside.

"You should have woken me up," Shiro muttered under his breath.

"You made me pinky-promise not to!" Kelly protested.

"I believe your exact words were 'I don't need you to babysit me; I can take care of myself.'"

Shiro grumbled, "I can, you know."

He pulled a kendama from his backpack.

Kendama is an old Japanese skill game involving a ball attached by a string to a handle shaped like a cross. The handle has three small cups for catching the ball and a single spike that perfectly fits the hole drilled into the ball. Kendama is a great way to demonstrate dexterity and coordination.

Shiro liked the game because it was one of the few amusements left in the world that didn't require any electricity. He whipped the red ball on the string around in his hands.

FWIP, FWIP!

He flipped the kendama around his back, under his leg, and into the air. He spun in a circle, caught the handle, and speared the ball on top.

FWIP, FWIP, FOOOOWIP, TOK!

It almost looked like an ice cream cone.

"Hey," Kelly said, impressed, "that gives me an idea. Let's call JoJo."

Shiro smiled. "You always know how to cheer me up."

The robot sent out a beacon, and they both sat down, legs dangling over the edge of the landing pad, to wait for the ice cream man to arrive.

THOUSANDS OF FLYING vehicles zipped through the smog that blanketed Megalopolis and obscured Shiro and Kelly's view of the ground, two hundred stories below. In the distance, a single wobbling object appeared to disrupt the orderly streams of automated shipping drones and robo-taxis that glided along in perfect harmony.

"Watch your butts, you dang auto-pods," yelled JoJo as he shook his fist. JoJo's was one of the few manual vehicles still in operation in the city. Across the side of it was painted JOJO'S OLD-FASHIONED ICE CREAM. The pod hovered up the side of the building and landed with a crunch behind Shiro and Kelly.

JoJo was a gruff man with a thick neck and a heavy mustache. He lifted his cap to stroke his bald head.

"All righty, then." JoJo grabbed his ice cream scoop with a meaty hand. "What can I get my two favorite customers today?"

"I will take three triple cones," Kelly said. "Chocolate/strawberry/peanut butter, hazelnut/vanilla/pistachio, and cherry/coconut/fudge chunk." Kelly's display visor flashed with excitement. "Please."

"You got it, boss." JoJo popped open the cooler.

Shiro retrieved the tablet from his backpack and consulted a detailed chart as he considered JoJo's colorful menu board.

"Hmm," said Shiro. "I've tried all of these flavors at least three times."

"Yeah," Kelly said as she held up a triple-scoop cone. "That's because JoJo makes the best ice cream in Megalopolis." A hole in her hull whirled open like the shutter of a camera, and she tossed one of the frozen treats inside. Her display visor sparkled with delight.

"Thank you, Kelly," said JoJo as he tipped his hat. "Take it from the superbot, kid."

"Yeah," Shiro said, "but there must be thousands of kinds of ice cream out there, and I've only tried three hundred forty-seven."

"What about freeze-dried astronaut ice cream?" Kelly reached inside her hull and pulled out a silver foil package.

"I keep this for emergencies. It's what they eat in the Mars colony."

Shiro opened the package and pulled out a gray paper cone with a limp string hanging from the tip. He pulled the string, which triggered a balloon-like mechanism inside the cone. Once fully inflated, the "ice cream" resembled a tie-dyed ball made of Styrofoam. Shiro sniffed at it and tried to take a bite. The texture was like chalk, and the taste wasn't much better.

"Bleh." Shiro stuck out his tongue. He tossed the astronaut ice cream into JoJo's trash can. "That's not what I'm talking about." He poked at his tablet and scrolled through pages of frozen confections from around the world.

"Oh!" JoJo pointed at the screen. "That there is gelato. It's Italian ice cream. Very delicious."

Shiro turned to Kelly. "Hear that? We've got to try gelato."

"Gelato, eh?" Kelly ran a search for *gelato* and projected a hologram from her display visor. A 3D map of Megalopolis floated in the air.

"Nah." JoJo shook his head. "You won't find any good gelato here in the city. You gotta go to Italy for that."

"I've never been to Italy," said Shiro.

Kelly turned to the window and looked inside the conference room. "Didn't your mom say something about taking a break from our 'impetuous escapades,' since they keep turning into 'geopolitical incidents'?"

"What's 'impetuous' about flying to Italy for a few hours?"

Kelly projected the text of the dictionary definition in the air: <<Impetuous: adjective, characterized by sudden action or emotion>>

"Oooh." JoJo snapped his fingers. "Good word."

Shiro waved his hands through the holographic text, and it disappeared. "What's the worst that could happen?"

Kelly's display visor narrowed. "The last time you said that, we got kidnapped by space pirates. They almost discovered my power source."

"That was a total fluke."

"The time before that, we got stuck on a submarine for three days." Kelly folded her arms.

"Those Koreans were so nice!"

"And just last week, we had to fight a gang of laser ninjas to save the crown prince of Dubai."

JoJo pointed. "I saw a video of that one on the news."

"It was awesome," Shiro said. "I got a medal." He rummaged through his backpack for a while. "Well, I *had* a medal."

Kelly put her hands on her hips and looked to the horizon. "Every time we fly off on some crazy boondoggle, you wind up getting us into trouble and I wind up having to save your butt."

"The robot's got a point," said JoJo.

"What?" Shiro threw his hands in the air. "Kelly needs me *way* more than I need her."

"Is that right?" asked Kelly.

"Sure." Shiro smiled. "Without me, you'd be so bored!"

Kelly's display visor brightened.

"The kid's got a point too." JoJo laughed. "He's an entertaining little rascal." He wiped his hands on a towel. "But I do have other stops to make today, so what's the deal? You want a cone, or are you too bored with my menu? Three hundred forty-seven flavors is more than enough for most people, you know."

Shiro looked at Kelly with puppy-dog eyes. "What else do we have to do today? Mom is busy, I finished all my homework, you're fully charged . . ."

Kelly paused, calculating risk factors and timetables. "Okay, fine."

Shiro did a clumsy cartwheel, jumped in the air, and pumped his fists.

"But this is not a boondoggle," Kelly cautioned.

"No, of course not," Shiro said.

"This is not an 'impetuous escapade,'" Kelly added.

"Clearly not." JoJo rolled his eyes.

"This is a valuable cultural experience and a perfect opportunity to practice your foreign-language skills." Kelly sounded quite convincing.

"Exactly. That's what I'll tell Mom." Shiro recorded a holographic message on his tablet: "Hi, Mom! We're going to Italy to learn to speak Italian. Be back soon!"

"Andiamo," said Kelly with a perfect Italian accent. A holographic subtitle hung in the air and displayed the definition in English: <<Let's go.>>

"Andiamo!" Shiro shouted.

"*Molto bene!*" said JoJo, laughing. "That means 'Very good!'" He watched as the robot converted into flight mode and the boy climbed inside.

Kelly's ionic thrusters began to glow. She lifted off from the landing pad and pierced the dirty brown clouds of the city to reach the bright-blue sky above.

Scrunched inside her hull, Shiro reviewed Italian vocabulary on his tablet. "*Vorrei un gelato, per favore.* I would like some gelato, please."

"Nice pronunciation," said Kelly. She set a course and ignited her thrusters, and the two friends rocketed across the western hemisphere at twice the speed of sound.

SHABOOM!

WHEN THE RESIDENTS of the small Tuscan village saw the flying blue robot appear in the distance, they started shouting and gathering their families.

"*Guarda quello! Sono Shiro e Kelly!*" Which means "Look at that! It's Shiro and Kelly!"

The robot landed in the town plaza, the boy hopped out, and all the children came running up to give the two of them high fives.

"Buongiorno!" said Kelly, which means "Hello!" in Italian.

"*Buongiorno!*" said Shiro, which also means "Good afternoon!" in Italian. "*Vorrei un gelato, per favore.*" He was a quick study. Kelly nodded with approval.

"Gelato!" A little girl pointed to the best gelato shop in

town, Gelateria Madre Mia. "Molto bene!" She rubbed her belly.

A friendly grandma behind the counter carefully sculpted petals of pastel-colored gelato perched on long, pointy cones. She set them in a special stand while she worked. Once she'd finished scooping and smoothing, the creamy confections looked like multicolored flowers. She proudly handed her creations across the counter for Shiro and Kelly to enjoy.

"Oooh," cooed Shiro.

"Mmm," hummed Kelly.

They thanked the gelato grandma and sat down on a bench outside to enjoy their treats in the sunshine. Shiro put on his sunglasses, and Kelly darkened the shade of her display visor to match. They quickly finished eating.

"According to my database, that was the most delicious ice cream I have ever tasted," Kelly said.

The grandma from the gelato shop came out to ask for a picture. They all posed in front of the store. Kelly scooped up the grandma and held her gently in her arms. The woman squealed, and her grandchildren giggled as they snapped holo-captures.

"Formaggio!" said Kelly, which is Italian for "Cheese!"

Shiro pinched his fingers together and kissed them, which is Italian for "Wonderful!"

Word of the famous visitors had spread throughout the town, and a large crowd began to form outside the gelato shop.

"Time to say goodbye," said Kelly as she shifted back into flight mode.

"Arrivederci," said Shiro before climbing inside.

The robot flexed her five powerful limbs and jumped thirty feet into the air before activating her ionic thrusters (so as not to incinerate their Italian fans).

"Arrivederci," said the townsfolk, and they waved at the sky as they watched the boy and his robot soar off into the distance.

"WHERE TO NEXT?" wondered Shiro.

"You want more ice cream?" Kelly laughed.

"Always," replied Shiro, totally serious.

"Well," Kelly said, "let's take a look."

Thousands of images of ice cream varieties popped into view, too many for Shiro to comprehend. Four hundred geotagged video windows ran simultaneously.

"What's that one?" Shiro touched an image of a long, thin treat on a Popsicle stick.

"It's an Indian dessert called kulfi." A map of the Indian subcontinent appeared. Kelly cross-referenced online reviews and press clippings to determine a specific location for their visit.

"They speak Hindi in India, right?" asked Shiro.

"They speak at least twenty-five different languages in India," replied Kelly, "but Hindi is one of the most common ones, yes."

She adjusted her trajectory and looped through the sky, leaving a long swooping trail of white steam behind her.

THE SUPERBOT LANDED gracefully in a small park in Bhopal, and a nearby cricket game paused as the players greeted the international celebrities who had unexpectedly dropped from the sky.

"Shiro and Kelly!" shouted a little boy. Shiro leapt from Kelly's hull, whipped out his kendama, and flipped it around acrobatically. The cricket players applauded.

"Kulfi?" asked Shiro.

Some kids in the crowd giggled and whispered.

Kelly put her hand on Shiro's shoulder. "I think you meant, *Hum ko kulfi kahaan mil sakatee hai?*"

Shiro laughed. "Yes, that *is* what I meant. Where can we find kulfi, please?" Then he gave it a shot in Hindi, repeating what Kelly had said.

"Your pronunciation is excellent," said a boy wearing a ball cap and a leather jacket.

"They speak English," Shiro whispered to Kelly.

"Yes." Kelly nodded. "But that doesn't mean you shouldn't make an effort to learn *their* language as well."

"Fair enough," admitted Shiro.

The kids led the two visitors to a nearby kulfi stand, and they happily signed autographs while the kulfi man prepared their frozen treats. He pulled two sticks of cone-shaped cream from the freezer and rolled them through a bowl of chopped nuts. The kulfi man's wife recorded a holo-capture of the boy and his robot posing in front of the stand.

"Wow, this is really good!" Shiro smiled at Kelly. The kulfi had a caramel-mango taste unlike any other ice cream Shiro had ever tried.

"Mazedaar!" shouted a little boy who was also eating kulfi. "Delicious!"

"*Mazedaar!*" repeated Shiro as he pumped his kulfi in the air.

The crowd cheered and started singing. Street musicians played, and a celebration began.

"You know," Shiro shouted to Kelly over the music, "this has got to be our tastiest adventure ever."

SHIRO AND KELLY crisscrossed the globe. They tried silky ribbons of xue hua bing in Taiwan, colorful, fruity paletas in Mexico, and wild concoctions of halo-halo in the Philippines. They were quickly discovering that ice cream came in many shapes, sizes, and flavors. Plus, Shiro was expanding his vocabulary in several different languages, so Kelly was confident the whole trip could be considered an "educational experience" by Professor Hanayama.

Lying in the shade of a cherry tree later that afternoon, Shiro couldn't have been happier. They had come to Turkey to sample dondurma, a remarkably chewy variety of ice cream that some people eat with a knife and fork.

KAKIGORI

"We're like intrepid ice cream explorers," said Shiro as he finished the last bite and licked his fingers.

Kelly was scanning the "Around the world" section of the "Ice cream" article on Wikipedia. She had spread her arms between two trees and was swinging lazily like a hammock.

"We're missing kakigori, from Japan." She projected a holographic image. "But I'm not sure if it's technically ice cream or not. It doesn't have any dairy in it unless you pour condensed milk on top."

"So it's more like a fluffy snow cone?" Shiro asked.

Kelly magnified the image ten thousand times to study the molecular composition of the dessert. "I guess so," she replied.

Shiro's tablet buzzed loudly in his backpack. It was an incoming video call from Professor Hanayama.

"Hello, dumpling," she said. "Where are you?"

"Um." Shiro looked around.

"We're in Turkey, Professor," Kelly chimed in.

"Ah, thank you, Kelly." Someone off-screen asked the professor a question. "Yes," she replied, "one minute. Shiro, I have to fly to Montana tonight to prevent an ecological emergency. Some maniac is trying to harvest the Blackfoot Glacier to make luxury ice cubes for billionaires." She rubbed her temples with her fingers. "I'll be back first thing tomorrow, but we're gonna have to make it a late breakfast, okay? Kelly, set Shiro's wake-up for ten a.m."

"Of course, Professor," Kelly replied.

"Hey," Shiro objected, "I can take care of myself, you know."

"Oh, really?" Professor Hanayama looked dubious. "Okay. Well, then I will definitely, one hundred percent for sure, see you at breakfast tomorrow."

"Yes. You will." Shiro nodded.

"Promise?"

"Yes, Mom."

"Pinky-promise?"

"Yes, Mom."

"I love you," she said. Shiro looked around to make sure no one else was watching.

"I love you too," he said quietly, and ended the call.

"So you don't want me to set an alarm to wake you up tomorrow?" asked Kelly.

"I can set my own alarm, thank you very much." Shiro poked at the touch screen of his tablet.

Kelly projected a holographic display of a rotating globe tagged with the locations and images of all the different ice cream varieties they had consumed that day.

Shiro felt twitchy and hyper. He couldn't concentrate on the map, so he got up and started skipping instead. "Do you think there's any type of ice cream that isn't listed on the internet?"

"Hmm." Kelly ran some calculations. "Ice cream production requires either naturally cold temperatures or refrigeration technology. The chance of some unknown persons having created an undocumented variety of ice cream seems extremely unlikely."

Shiro raised an eyebrow.

Kelly's display visor narrowed. "I calculate the probability at ten point six trillion to one."

"So you're saying there's a chance."

"Not really," clarified Kelly.

Shiro started pacing back and forth. "What we need to do is find a group of people that don't have internet access."

"There are only a few hundred hectares without internet access left on Earth. Most of that land is preserved wilderness."

Shiro snapped his fingers. "What about an anti-tech tribe in the jungle? What if it turns out they've created their own totally unique version of ice cream?"

"Without access to electricity?"

"It could happen." Shiro's teeth started chattering.

"I think you've had too much sugar to think straight. You need some nutrients. All you've eaten today is ice cream." A hole in Kelly's hull whirled open, and she pulled out a fresh steamed sweet potato. "Here, eat this."

"I don't want your stupid root vegetables." Shiro backed away. "I want to go find a new kind of ice cream in the jungle!"

"There is no ice cream in the jungle, Shiro."

Shiro gasped. He climbed up on a rock and posed with one hand on his hip and the other pointed to the sky. "Certainty is the enemy of discovery!" he intoned.

"Oh. Now you're going to quote your mom at me?"

"She's a very smart lady." Shiro smirked without breaking his pose.

"Fine." Kelly reluctantly shifted from hammock mode to flight mode. "But I'm only doing this to prove you wrong."

KELLY ACCELERATED FROM subsonic to supersonic to ludicrous speed. The velocity flattened Shiro against the wall of the hull and stretched his chubby cheeks back to his ears. The boy and his robot traveled halfway around the world in less than two hours and didn't decelerate until they reached a preserved wilderness zone in Peru, the only remaining section of what was once a vast rain forest known as the Amazon.

Shiro had never seen a jungle before. The trees stood as tall as skyscrapers and were packed so tightly together, it was impossible to see through the leaves as they flew overhead.

Kelly attempted a thermal scan, but the jungle was too hot to get a good read.

"We're gonna have to go down and search on foot," said Shiro.

"It's one hundred degrees down there," said Kelly. "There's no ice cream, trust me."

"Only one way to find out," sniffed Shiro.

"And what do I get when I'm right?"

"The greatest prize of all: me admitting I was wrong."

"Now *that* I would like to see." Kelly found a narrow path through the branches and carefully descended to the ground.

Shiro marveled at the untamed wilderness. The jungle was dense with giant trees, and he couldn't see more than a few feet in any direction. Smaller trees crowded into sunbeams, waiting patiently for a giant ancestor to fall. Huge roots snarled through the undergrowth, fuzzy with moss. Bright tropical flowers decorated the canvas of green and brown with bursts of yellow, purple, and pink.

He vaulted over a massive log dotted with orange mushrooms. A tantalizing melody from unseen birds kept Shiro's head on a swivel, searching for the singers. Frogs hopped from leaf to leaf. Butterflies fluttered in clusters, and for a moment, the rain forest felt like paradise.

"Ouch!" cried Shiro. A mosquito had bitten his neck. "Oooh!" Another had gotten him behind his ear. "Yow!" A cloud of hungry bloodsuckers had him surrounded.

Kelly raised her fifth arm and spun it in place like a fan, faster and faster, until the bugs dispersed.

"How did you do that?" Shiro was amazed.

"The high-frequency vibrations confuse the insects," replied Kelly proudly. Her propeller arm was spinning so fast that all Shiro could perceive was a slight blur around the edges, like the blades of a helicopter. "It's a waste of energy, but we shouldn't be here long. Unless we happen to find a secret jungle ice cream shop."

"You never know," insisted Shiro.

A mysterious growl rumbled from somewhere in the treetops above.

"Yikes. That sounded like a jaguar," Kelly whispered.

"Cool!" said Shiro.

"Not cool," said Kelly. "If you get eaten, your mom is gonna be pissed at me."

Shiro felt his shirt sticking to the sweat on his back. He could almost see the heat hanging in the thick jungle air. "You know what?" He shrugged. "I don't think we're gonna find any ice cream here."

"That's what I was trying to tell you seven thousand miles ago!"

"Don't you ever get tired of being right?" Shiro crossed his arms.

"I'm a robot," said Kelly. "I never get tired. I only run low on battery. Speaking of which . . ." She ran a diagnostic check and displayed her power meter. It was down to 20 percent. "That flight used a lot of fuel. I could use a snack. Can I have that freeze-dried ice cream I gave you?"

"I threw it away," said Shiro.

"Oh," said Kelly, recalculating. "Dang. Well, I should have enough power left to get us to the nearest city, which is . . ." She projected a holographic map in the air, but as she zoomed in, the information became pixelated. "Double dang. I'm not getting a signal out here, are you?"

Shiro checked his tablet and shook his head.

"My cooling systems are draining my battery faster than I thought."

"I wish I had cooling systems," said Shiro. "Even my knees are sweating."

"Sorry, but I gotta turn off the fan to conserve power."

Kelly stopped spinning her arm, and the mosquitoes swarmed Shiro once again. The robot rose high on two legs to look around.

"I've got an idea." She lowered and opened her hull for Shiro to climb aboard. "Get in. Maybe we can get a better view from above."

Shiro held on tight, ping-ponging from side to side, while Kelly scuttled up into the jungle's understory like a crab. The tree branches were just as difficult to navigate as the forest floor. Vines tangled every path, and ferns sprouted from mounds of fallen leaves that had collected in the elbows of massive trees. Shiro wiped the sweat from his chin, pulled his water bottle from his backpack, and tried to take a drink without spilling all over himself.

"Can you hold up for a second?" he asked.

Kelly paused, and Shiro took a long swig of water.

"Ahhh!" he said. "Hey, I wonder if anyone has ever done kendama in the rain forest."

He swung the bright-red ball around his head and caught it on the spike. "First!" he announced.

"We really don't have time for this," Kelly scolded.

Suddenly, there was a rustling in the trees and Kelly's display visor went into red-alert mode. A troop of angry monkeys emerged from the canopy, surrounding the boy and the robot. The monkeys shrieked and shook the branch that Kelly was clinging to.

"Whoa!" Shiro held on tight. "What are they so mad about?"

"Don't make eye contact," Kelly warned. "If they don't think we're a threat, maybe they'll leave us alone."

Shiro averted his eyes and crouched inside the hull as Kelly scuttled away. The monkeys chased after her, expertly swinging from vines and branches. Kelly then copied them, moving her fifth arm behind her and using it like a prehensile tail.

VOOSH! SWOOSH! SCHWING! FLING!

Kelly spotted a rocky clearing on the jungle floor up ahead.

"I'm gonna head down," she said. "These monkeys are too curious for comfort."

She quickly changed course and descended from the branches. Shiro hopped out to look around. Kelly reconfigured and stood on two legs.

"I think we lost them," said Shiro just before a monkey leapt from a tree and landed on his head.

In Kelly's robot brain, the scene unfolded in slow motion. Strands of spit stretched between Shiro's lips as he slowly opened his mouth and began to scream. Meanwhile, Kelly took a full 3D scan of the clearing, located twelve potential assailants in the branches above, and identified the primates as capuchin monkeys specifically. She ran a full confrontation analysis, then cross-checked it against a probability vector based on the statistics of all recorded Amazonian capuchin attacks. As a safety precaution, she sent out a radio distress signal in an attempt to reach any nearby aircraft. Finally, she calculated a nonfatal plan, which would fully protect Shiro yet inflict minimal injury to the animals. By the time she had finished her computations, Shiro had barely realized there was a monkey on his head.

"*YAHHH!*" he screamed. The monkey grabbed two fistfuls of Shiro's hair and pulled hard.

Kelly plucked a python from a nearby tree. She stretched the snake between two of her arms and whipped it back and forth through the air, spinning it in circles like nunchucks. The monkeys paused, confused by the scaly blue egg wielding a serpent as a weapon.

"Get him off, get him off!" yelled Shiro as he tried to shake the monkey from his shoulders.

The capuchin reached for the shiny red kendama in Shiro's hand. Kelly whapped the monkey halfway across the clearing with a quick slap of her python nunchuck.

"*EEEEEEAAAAAAHHH!*" screeched the monkeys in the treetops. They all leapt down into the clearing to attack.

"They want the kendama," Kelly shouted to Shiro. "They must think it's some sort of fruit." She smacked, whacked, and cracked the angry monkeys as they attempted to snatch the bright-red ball.

Monkey reinforcements arrived, and the battle intensified. Capuchins launched themselves from all directions at the intruders. Shiro stumbled across the clearing with a monkey clinging to each of his legs. He swung his kendama and knocked one of the monkeys in the head with the wooden ball.

Kelly jumped high into the air, plucked a second snake from the branches, and started fending the monkeys off with double-snake nunchucks.

WHAP! SLAP! SNAP! BA-DAP!

"*WOO! WOO! WOO!*" The capuchin leader sounded the retreat.

Shiro managed to shake the remaining monkey from his leg, but it swiped the kendama from his hand before climbing into a tree. Shiro fell onto his knees and rubbed his scalp.

The monkey with the kendama let out a victory cry, then settled in to enjoy his juicy prize. But when he tried to take a bite, he realized the bright-red bauble was made of wood, not fruit. Furious, he hurled the kendama at his enemies below. Fortunately for Shiro, the monkey missed. Throwing things accurately is one of the skills that separates humans from other primates.

"What the heck did we ever do to you?" Shiro yelled.

Kelly scanned the perimeter to be certain there were no additional threats. She dropped the two snakes and apologized as they slithered away in dizzy zigzags.

"We're trespassing." Kelly's visor switched from red alert back to normal. "This species of primate is highly territorial."

"Let's just get out of here." Shiro retrieved his kendama. It was covered in bite marks, dirt, and monkey spit. "Gross."

He wiped away the grime with a towel from his backpack. "All right," he admitted, "I was wrong. You were right, and I was wrong. Again. Are you happy now?"

Shiro heard a loud thud.

He turned around to find Kelly collapsed on the ground.

"JANGUS!" SHIRO RAN to Kelly and put his hands on her chest. The robot's five arms were splayed out to the sides, and her visor had gone dark. A tiny error message blinked faintly in her display: POWER-RESERVE MODE.

"Kelly! Wake up!" begged Shiro. He shoved the robot's round blue body with all his might, but she barely budged.

Shiro became frantic. He ripped off his backpack and spilled out the contents: water bottle, sunglasses, Rubik's cube, dirty towel, rejected sweet potato. His tablet had been smashed in the monkey fight.

"This is all your fault, you stupid, stinking monkeys!" screamed Shiro to the treetops. He was so mad, he was spitting.

Rotten figs rained down from above. One splattered right in his face. Though monkeys are not good at aiming, they do sometimes get lucky. The capuchins hooted with delight.

Shiro uttered some colorful Italian words he had learned earlier that day. He wiped the fruit from his face and knelt next to Kelly.

"Don't worry, buddy. I'll go get help." Shiro patted the

robot reassuringly. He stuffed his belongings back into his backpack, stood, and sprinted to the edge of the clearing.

Two steps into the dense jungle, he paused. Thinking better of it, he turned and ran to the opposite edge of the clearing. He paused again. Which way had they come from? And, more importantly, where was he trying to go? He searched his surroundings for a clue but found none.

He was lost.

Shiro returned to where Kelly had fallen and sat down on top of the robot to think. He rested his head in his hands and whimpered. Sweat dripped behind his ears. He felt just as power-drained as Kelly.

The sun began to set, and the jungle grew dark. The air seemed thick enough to drink. Shiro's teeth started to tingle. The tingling spread to his hands, and his head felt both light and heavy at the same time. Soon, his eyelids fell closed and his body slumped forward. He was asleep.

NIGHT FELL ON the jungle, and mysterious sounds filled the air.

"*HOOO HOOO HOOO*," said something.

"*ROBBA ROBBA ROBBA*," said something else.

"*SCREEE SCREEE*," said several flying somethings.

Shiro woke with a start and blinked his eyes in the darkness. He felt a tickle on his nose. He felt an itch on the top of his head. He felt something wiggle in his armpit.

"*AIIIEEEEEE!*" he shrieked as he shook millipedes,

moths, and spiders from his body. He hopped in a circle and brushed the creepy-crawlers from his hair. He kicked his feet and waved his arms until every last critter had skittered away. *"I HATE THIS JUNGLE!"* screamed Shiro at the top of his lungs.

Everything went quiet, and Shiro heard something curious in the distance. It didn't sound like an animal.

The nocturnal chorus of the rain forest soon resumed. Insects called out for their friends. Frogs croaked in secret code. Shiro cupped his hands behind his ears to try and hear better. In between the squawks and chirps, he heard a trickle. A trickle that sounded like water. A stream!

"Don't worry," he whispered to the sleeping robot. "I'll follow the water downstream to the nearest village." He looked up to the starry sky and wondered what time it was. "Gotta get back home for breakfast tomorrow morning." His stomach let out a pathetic growl.

Shiro pulled the semi-squished sweet potato from his backpack and considered it skeptically for a moment. He took a bite. It wasn't half bad.

"All right," he said, chewing. "It's about time I saved *your* butt for once, huh, robot?"

SHIRO WADED CLUMSILY through the underbrush toward the sound of the rushing water. He stumbled over vines, scratched himself on thorns, flung curious creatures from his sneakers, and got bitten by mosquitoes on every exposed piece of flesh. Sweat soaked his underpants. Even in the middle of the night, the jungle was stifling.

Eventually, he was able to find the stream. A weak trickle at first, it grew bigger as Shiro followed it downhill. The sound of the water got louder and louder until finally, he found the riverbank.

He knelt to splash cool water on his face. *If I follow the river, I should be able to—*

Shiro didn't get to finish his thought. He was distracted by something wet. The wet thing was the river he had fallen into after slipping on the mossy bank.

SPLOOSH!

He plunged in headfirst and tumbled under the surface, caught in the powerful churn of the current. For a second, he wasn't sure which way was up. Shiro kicked and paddled frantically, managing to get his head above the water. He gasped for air.

The river quickly swept him downstream, away from his stranded friend. He worried about leaving Kelly alone in the jungle at night but took comfort in the fact that even the hungriest wild animals do not eat robots.

They do, however, eat little boys.

So when glowing eyes appeared in the shadows, Shiro was filled with terror. The clouds parted overhead, and the pale moonlight revealed that the menacing eyes belonged to Amazonian alligators. The giant reptiles wallowed into the river and started swimming toward him.

Shiro turned the other way and swam as hard as he

could, but the current was too strong. He couldn't reach the riverbank, and the razor-sharp teeth of the hungry alligators were fast approaching.

"Help!" Shiro cried desperately, swallowing a mouthful of water. He spun around and tried his best not to panic.

A low branch drooped over the river ahead. It seemed too high to grab—just out of reach—but Shiro felt a burst of inspiration. He snatched the chewed-up kendama from his tattered backpack, kicked his legs hard, and whipped the ball above his head. The string wrapped around the tree branch like a grappling hook. He yanked himself out of the water.

SNIP, SNAP, SNORP!

The powerful jaws of the alligators missed by inches.

They circled and prepared for another attack. Thinking quickly, Shiro unbuckled his backpack and shook the contents out into the river below. The gators went into a feeding frenzy, chomping the tablet, the towel, and the Rubik's cube to bits. The luckiest gator got a chunk of sweet potato.

SHIRO CLUNG TO the tree branch, sopping wet, exhausted, and out of supplies. Just when he thought things couldn't possibly get any worse, he smelled smoke.

"Fire!" He climbed higher into the tree. Forest fires were common where he grew up, and very dangerous. He searched the darkness for a blaze but couldn't spot any flames. He sniffed the air. It was a familiar smell—but not of a forest fire, of barbecue smoke.

"Hello?!" called Shiro.

There was no response.

He climbed down from the tree and followed the smokey aroma through the jungle.

It started to rain.

The drops were fat and heavy. The curtain of water obscured his view. He slipped through the mud and tripped over sneaky, jutting roots.

It wasn't long before he spotted a wooden shack with smoke rising from the chimney. Someone inside was grilling fish, and it smelled delicious. He wondered if they might be friendly enough to share. He wondered if they might have a dry towel.

As he approached the dilapidated shack, he heard ominous music coming from within:

Fa-fa-fa-fa-fa-fa-fa-fa-fa-far better
Run, run, run, run, run, run, run away, oh oh oh OH!

A small light was on inside, and Shiro spied a tall, bedraggled man through the window. His eyes were bloodshot and wild. He wore a jaguar-fur vest and snakeskin pants. His long, greasy blond hair was decorated with animal bones and bird feathers. He was a poacher.

Shiro froze.

The man grabbed a giant knife from his boot and burst outside. "Do I hear dinner?" he sneered. "I skin you alive!"

"I'm sorry!" Shiro put up his hands and fell back into a puddle.

"Who are you, boy?" The poacher raised his gleaming knife and glared.

"I'm Shiro. I'm just a kid! Don't skin me, please!"

The man lowered his knife. "Shiro Hanayama? I am knowing who you are."

"Oh, good! I need help."

"Where is Kelly?" The poacher looked around.

"She's stranded in the jungle." Shiro scrambled to his feet.

"World's most famous superbot is being stranded in *my* jungle?"

"Your jungle?" asked Shiro. "I thought this was a preserved wilderness zone."

The poacher threw back his head and laughed until he started choking. Shiro tried to smile politely. The man hacked and coughed, then hocked a loogie over his shoulder. It was jet black.

"I am Svensen," he said, holding out a hand covered in fish guts. Shiro shook it reluctantly. "Come inside." Svensen grinned. "Is a jungle out there."

Shiro followed him into the shack. It was set up like a store. The walls were covered with animal pelts, the shelves stacked with jars of dead reptiles and insects. Svensen flipped the fish on the grill and tossed a bag stuffed with colorful birds into a corner.

"So . . ." He licked his palm and slicked back his greasy

hair. "How can I be of helping? You name it, I have it. Flares, bait, batteries, water purification tablets, *Mad Magazine* from 1993. Are you wanting to buy a machete?" The poacher held up a huge blade.

"Um." Shiro backed toward the door. "No, thanks."

Svensen began to pluck the meat off the fish with his fingers. "So the bot is *brukket*, and now you are alone?" He popped a big chunk into his mouth and talked while he chewed.

"Actually . . ." Shiro's eyes darted around the room. A person who had killed so many endangered creatures was not to be trusted. "Everything is fine," he lied. "I just dropped by to see if you have any ice cream is all. Kelly . . . fell asleep, and I was really in the mood for ice cream, and everyone told us that if you need anything in this jungle, you've got to go see Svensen. Svensen's the man, they said." Shiro looked to see if the poacher was buying it.

"Who is telling you that?" Svensen pounded the table. Shiro struggled to think of an answer, but Svensen continued. "Someone smart is who!" He laughed. "My reputation is preceding me." He took a bow.

Shiro nodded. His mother had warned him many times: Flattery is the easiest kind of lie to believe.

"Ice cream." Svensen whistled. "That is a tough one." He wiped his oily hands on his snakeskin pants. "Most of the frozen stuff is fish meat or snake meat." He lowered his voice. "I do have a couple of monkey brains on ice if you are happening to be interested."

Shiro gagged.

"Maybe not, then." Svensen slid open the lid of the freezer. "Some people are considering it a delicacy." The poacher reached inside and rummaged around. "Bread, vodka, Hot Pocket?"

Shiro shook his head.

"Hey, what's this?" Svensen tried to pull something out, but it was frozen in place. He tugged at it while cursing in Norwegian. He grabbed the knife from his boot and began hacking away at the ice.

THWUCK!

Svensen dropped a container on the counter. It was a one-gallon cardboard tub caked in a thick layer of frost.

"*Et voilà*—ice cream." The poacher sheathed his knife. "Must have been in there when I stole the freezer. I mean, it must have been in there when I *bought* the freezer . . . used." The label on the container said HELADO DE GUINDÓN. "I think it is—how you say—*prune*-flavored ice cream." Svensen stuck out his tongue.

Shiro swallowed hard and tried to play it cool. "Sounds pretty good. I'll take it."

"To eat?" Svensen pulled the carton away from Shiro's grasping hands. "Probably is expired and will make you do the vomiting . . . I give you discount. Five percent off."

Shiro noticed a map tacked to the wall. "Hey, is that us, here?" He stabbed his finger at a red X by the river bend.

"Smart kid," muttered Svensen.

Shiro studied the map and tried to retrace his steps. "I

followed the smoke smell after I escaped from the alligators after I fell in the river after I fell asleep and got covered in bugs after I escaped from the monkeys in the clearing, which should be . . ." He didn't realize he was thinking out loud.

Svensen knelt and put a grubby hand on Shiro's shoulder. The poacher's breath smelled like rotten cigarettes and fish guts.

"Well, that clearing could be anywhere." Svensen frowned. "Doesn't superbot have GPS, homing beacon, location tracker?"

Shiro didn't answer.

"Do you know what I am thinking, boy?" Svensen flashed a wicked smile. "I am thinking that you have made a mess-up. I am thinking you are lucky Svensen is such a Mr. Nice Guy. Someone bad guy might take advantage of world's most valuable robot lost in the jungle."

Shiro shuddered.

"Me? I just want to help." Svensen tossed the heavy carton of ice cream to Shiro. The rain slowed to a drizzle. Svensen seemed pleased.

"Ice cream is free now. I am feeling generous mood tonight. In fact, I can be helping you to finding precious robot."

Svensen led Shiro out to a shaky dock on the river. There was a strange sort of raft tied up there. It had a giant fan attached to the back and a bench in the middle.

Soon they were skimming across the surface of the

water, zooming down the river. The boat was fast, but it was not smooth sailing. Shiro held on to his seat with one hand and hugged the ice cream carton with the other.

Just when Shiro was starting to feel sick from the bouncing boat, Svensen shut off the engine, and the roar of the fan died off. The poacher grabbed ahold of some vines and pulled the boat up against the shore.

"There is your lift." He pointed.

A few hundred yards away, small lights flashed in the darkness of the early dawn. A large shape loomed above them, but Shiro couldn't make out what it was. He realized the lights were headlamps when they all turned in the same direction, illuminating the face of a square woman with gray braided pigtails. She was waving her arms around, gesticulating wildly. Shiro couldn't hear what she was saying, but it seemed clear that she was the leader of the group. She pointed over her shoulder, and the headlamps tilted upward to reveal a huge blue balloon.

Svensen nodded to Shiro. "Maybe you can be spotting your robot from above."

"Is it a hoverpod?" asked Shiro.

"Something like that." Svensen chuckled to himself. "Go. Go without me. I am too busy. Plus, Mrs. Piggy Tails is very upset about which creatures I can be killing and which ones I cannot." Svensen smiled. "But I say, 'If it bleeds, I can kill it.'"

Shiro took that as his cue to get out of the boat. "Thanks for the ride, I guess."

Svensen tried to light a soggy cigarette.

"And thanks for the ice cream too."

"Consider it a trade." Svensen winked and fired up the engine.

"A trade for what?"

The poacher pretended not to hear him over the roaring fan blades. The boat sped away, and Svensen snickered to himself. "I will be taking good care of your robot, stupid boy."

Shiro turned toward the hot-air balloon and started running.

Two elderly couples wearing safari clothes huddled together, sipping tea from travel mugs. High-powered binoculars were draped around their necks. They were bird nerds—or, as they called themselves, avian aficionados— who had signed up to experience a once-in-a-lifetime sunrise balloon ride and bird-watching expedition with their hero, Dr. Daniela D'Lima Caravaca.

"All right, everyone," announced the famous bird scientist, "into the basket. Vámonos. Let's go." She put a stepstool on the ground and helped the birders climb aboard. "Luis will be waiting for us when we land to give us a ride back to the hotel." A young man with a soul patch and a Yankees hat patted his van proudly.

Dr. Caravaca lifted one of her thick legs to climb into the basket, but suddenly she paused, dropped into a crouch, and cupped her field guide behind her ear.

"Shhh!" she hissed. "Is that the call of a wool-footed warbler?"

The birders went silent. Luis tilted his head and listened carefully.

"It might be a redheaded tea-tickler!" whispered the doctor.

The birders lifted their binoculars and craned their necks to the treetops, hoping to catch the first glimpse of a rare specimen.

"Or maybe a double-crested cowabunga." Dr. Caravaca flipped through her field guide, looking for clues.

"*Hey!*"

"It's a very unusual call," admitted Dr. Caravaca.

The call grew louder. "*Hey!*"

"It almost sounds like someone saying 'Hey,'" noted Luis.

"Hey!" shouted Shiro as he ran to the launch site. He waved one arm over his head and carried the ice cream carton under the other. When the birders saw that the sound was coming from a breathless boy rather than an exotic bird, they lowered their binoculars, disappointed.

"Hey," said Dr. Caravaca, closing her field guide, "aren't you Shiro Hanayama?"

"Yes." Shiro panted. "Can I come with you, up in the balloon?"

Dr. Caravaca clasped her hands together. "I am such a huge fan of your mother's environmental preservation efforts. Her generous donation helped save the majestic floogle bird from the brink of extinction!" The birders in the basket applauded politely.

"But . . . what are you doing out here?" She looked around. "Where's Kelly? And what are you holding?"

"I'm . . . She's . . ." Shiro started to get teary-eyed. "Can I just come with you? I'll explain later. We've got to hurry."

"Calm down, young man. *Cálmate.*" The doctor turned to the birders. "Would anyone mind having a special guest star join our expedition this morning?"

The birders all shook their heads.

"Well, then"—the doctor extended her hand—"welcome aboard, muchacho. I am Dr. Daniela D'Lima Caravaca, bird scientist and balloon-a-neer. It's a pleasure to meet you."

Shiro ignored her handshake and gave her a hug instead. Dr. Caravaca blushed and smoothed her braided pigtails. Shiro climbed into the basket and set the frozen carton of ice cream at his feet.

Dr. Caravaca followed him aboard. "¡Bienvenidos a todos! Welcome, everyone!" She adjusted the burners, which controlled the hot air shooting into the big balloon. "Hands and binoculars inside the basket. Away we go!"

KAVOOSH!

Down below, Svensen rumbled through the jungle on a souped-up four-wheeler. He dodged trees and splashed through streams at top speed. His greasy hair glistened in the light of dawn.

Back in the shack, when Shiro had accidentally let slip that Kelly was stranded in a clearing upriver, Svensen had known the location immediately. His plan was simple: send the boy up in a balloon to get him out of the way, then zoom through the jungle to steal the superbot and sell it for parts to the highest bidders. Svensen admired the devious brilliance of his own plan. He cackled with greed and revved the engine.

RAAA-VAVAVAVA!

MIST ROSE FROM the trees, and the big blue balloon floated lazily over the jungle. Dr. Caravaca opened her field guide—which was titled *For the Birds: Stop Watching, Start Seeing*—and pointed out some labeled diagrams to her passengers.

"This morning, we will be observing the murmuration patterns of a drift of Andean swifts as they engage in their crepuscular feeding activities," explained the doctor.

Shiro looked confused.

Dr. Caravaca lowered her voice. "We've come to watch the birds eat at sunrise." She continued: "Swifts are commonly misidentified as bats due to their erratic flight patterns and unusual wing profile . . ."

As the scientist droned on about birds, Shiro worried about Kelly all alone in the jungle. Normally, it was Kelly who worried about him. Shiro had never realized how big a responsibility it was to have to protect someone.

"Oooh! Look at that." Dr. Caravaca pointed to an enormous cloud of birds swirling and swooping like embers rising off a campfire. The birders jostled for position to get the best view.

Shiro borrowed a pair of backup binoculars from one of the birders. "Wow!" he said as he scanned the jungle below for signs of his lost robot. But it was no use. The balloon was hovering just above the treetops, and all he could see were leaves.

"I didn't realize you shared our enthusiasm for avian

aeronautics!" Dr. Caravaca slapped Shiro on the back. "They're eating mosquitoes, you know."

Shiro rubbed his bugbites and felt a sudden appreciation for the flock of birds. Still, he was growing impatient. "Excuse me, but can this thing go any faster?"

"Ha!" Dr. Caravaca laughed, and the birders giggled softly. "This vehicle is lighter than air." She smiled and rubbed the basket. "We go up, we go down, but through it all, we merely follow the wind. It's a lot like life, you see—"

The scientist dropped her binoculars. "*¡Piña!*" she

blurted. The bottom of the basket had brushed against a jutting branch and jostled the passengers. "My apologies, everyone. I was distracted by the natural splendor."

The birders gathered their hats and glasses from the floor and grumbled. Dr. Caravaca turned up the heat on the burners above her head to lift the balloon.

KAVOOSH!

SVENSEN DIDN'T HAVE any trouble finding the stranded superbot. He drove his four-wheeler into the clearing and circled Kelly twice before pulling to a stop and hopping off the vehicle. He rubbed his hands together.

"Now I will be getting rich." He chuckled.

Svensen looked up into the sky. No sign of the balloon. Still plenty of time.

He kicked the robot lying on the ground. "I am thinking you are not so tough as they say."

He didn't notice the faint message that flashed across Kelly's display visor: POWER-RESERVE MODE: THREAT DETECTED.

The poacher leaned down to hoist the robot into the back of his four-wheeler, but when his hands touched Kelly's hull, it triggered an emergency self-defense counter-measure.

An electric shock blasted through Svensen's palms, surged through his arms, stiffened his neck, and sent his teeth chattering. He made a sound like a vibrating spring, his eyes rolled back into his head, and he crumpled to the ground, unconscious.

SOMEWHERE ABOVE, BUT not too far away, Shiro was trapped in the basket of the balloon. He peered over the side and tried waving his arms through the air to turn the thing even a little. It was no use. He slumped onto the floor and kicked the quickly melting carton of prune-flavored ice cream.

"Is there really no way to steer this thing?" he complained. "How is this an actual form of transportation?"

"Well"—Dr. Caravaca sounded defensive—"a good balloonist analyzes the air currents at varying altitudes to subtly adjust course."

Shiro looked up. "How high can we go?"

The doctor swooped her braids behind her head and rolled up her sleeves. "Let's find out, shall we?"

She ignited the burners to full blast.

KAVOOSH!

WHEN SVENSEN REGAINED consciousness, he realized he had wet his pants.

"*Uff da . . .*" He stumbled to his feet. The hair on the backs of his hands had burned off, and his arms were numb.

Meanwhile, the robot's five limbs had dug deep into the ground, securing her body in place.

"You play dirty, robot." Svensen limped over to his

vehicle and threw open his toolbox. He picked up a chain saw and yanked the starter cord. The razor-sharp blades slashed and flashed. "Now is my turn."

THE BALLOON FULL of birders had flown so high, they were able to observe their beloved murmuration patterns from *above*.

Dr. Caravaca was thrilled. "What a fabulous idea, Shiro." She peered through a pair of binoculars and made notes in her field guide. "I've never made observations from such a high altitude!"

Shiro was too busy scanning the jungle below to enjoy the spectacle. He spotted a glint of blue metal in the distance. "There!" he shouted.

Dr. Caravaca turned to the other passengers. "It looks like the boy's been bitten by the birding bug!" The birders laughed and nodded.

"No, you don't understand," said Shiro. "It's Kelly!" He held up his binoculars for the doctor to see.

"Hold on." Dr. Caravaca pulled out a truly enormous pair of binoculars from her pack. She peered through them carefully. "It *is* Kelly," she announced. "And there's someone else there with her."

SPARKS FLEW FROM the blade of the chain saw as Svensen struggled to cut through Kelly's armor. Sweat poured down the poacher's back. He had been hacking at the robot for ten minutes and hadn't made a single dent. He figured that if he could get even one of the arms off and sell it, he'd be a millionaire.

The chain saw sputtered and started smoking. "What is this thing made of?!"

"STOP!" SHOUTED SHIRO. "Leave my friend alone!" But the poacher was too far away to hear his cries.

Shiro grabbed Dr. Caravaca's field guide and hurled it at Svensen. The book sailed through the air and landed in the trees, short of the clearing.

"Hey!" shouted Dr. Caravaca. "I had all my notes in there!" She grabbed the kendama from Shiro's back pocket. "I should throw your toy over the side and see how you like it!"

That gave Shiro an idea.

"We've got to go lower," he demanded.

"First you want to go up, then you want to go down." Dr. Caravaca shook her head, and her braids whapped the birders. "We're staying right where we are. Besides, the acrobatics have only just begun!" She gestured at the thousands of birds swirling and pulsing like crashing ocean waves.

A hungry hawk dove through the cloud of swifts and plucked one from the air to eat for breakfast.

The birders oohed and aahed. They were enthralled.

"That poacher is trying to hack apart my friend," said Shiro.

"The filthy Norwegian from the shack on the river?"

"I've got to stop him!" Shiro punched his palm.

"*Bastardo!*" Dr. Caravaca pounded the side of the basket, and the whole balloon shook with her fury. "It's just . . . I'm afraid there's nothing we can do from up here."

"That's not true." Shiro snatched the kendama from her hand and hurled it over the side.

Dr. Caravaca was starting to catch on. "But we're too far away." She watched as the kendama fell short of the clearing, just like the field guide.

"Leave that part to me," said Shiro. "Lower the balloon and hand me that rope!" He tied it to his waist with a figure-eight knot and secured the other end to the bottom of the basket with a double hitch. He picked up the mostly melted carton of prune ice cream, climbed onto the side of the basket, and looked down.

"Wait, what are you going to do?" Dr. Caravaca reached out to stop him.

"I'm going to save my friend's butt!" Shiro leapt out of the balloon.

He dove through the air, high above the jungle. The rope snapped taut and stopped his fall. He nearly dropped the carton. Fifty feet up, the basket jostled, sending the birders tumbling all over themselves again. Dr. Caravaca peered over the side. The view made her dizzy.

"Please don't die!" She chewed her braids.

Shiro hung from a thin, fraying rope, twisting in the wind. He clutched the soggy ice cream carton to his chest.

As the balloon sank, he started swinging back and forth. He pumped his feet to gain momentum, arcing wider and wider. He imagined himself like a wooden ball on a string.

In Shiro's mind, the jungle below disappeared. The birds

went silent. All he could see was Kelly sprawled on the ground. All he could hear was the beating of his own heart.

"Just like kendama . . ."

At the height of his swing, at the perfect moment, he flung the carton forward with every ounce of strength he had.

The birders watched the ice cream fly through the air and pick up speed as it hurtled toward the earth.

Shiro clung to the rope and crossed his fingers.

DOWN BELOW, SVENSEN had surrounded the robot with sticks of dynamite. He figured if the hull was indestructible, the explosion would at least shake an arm or two loose from the ground. He backed away from Kelly and lit a match.

A gust of wind blew it out.

"*Uff da,*" muttered Svensen. He lit another match and shielded it from the wind with his cupped hands. "Happy birthdays for me," he sang and leaned over to ignite the fuse.

The greedy poacher was so distracted by visions of future riches that he failed to notice the first wave of tiny prune-flavored droplets that were raining down from above. But as the barrage grew stronger and the purple projectiles grew bigger, he turned around and looked up to see what in the heck was going on.

SHMAPAP!

The carton of ice cream blasted Svensen right between the eyes. His head snapped back, his body slumped forward, and the match went out as he hit the ground.

The poacher was knocked out cold.

"YOU DID IT!" announced Dr. Caravaca, peering through her binoculars. The birders cheered.

Shiro almost fainted with relief. He uncrossed his fingers and started climbing the rope.

With the birders holding her legs, Dr. Caravaca leaned over the side of the basket and held out her hand. Shiro reached up for it but accidentally grabbed ahold of one of her pigtails instead. When he pulled, the long gray braid came loose. It was a clip-on.

Dr. Caravaca's eyes went wide. Shiro quickly handed back the braid, grabbed her hand, and clambered aboard. The doctor fumbled to reattach her hair. Lucky for her, the birders were too busy congratulating Shiro to notice.

"Can I see?" He borrowed a pair of jumbo binoculars, pressed them to his face, and twisted the knobs to focus. What he saw made his heart drop into his stomach. Svensen was knocked unconscious and splattered with purple ice cream. But Kelly was also unconscious, and there wasn't a drop on her.

"You don't understand," Shiro huffed as he slunk to the floor of the basket. "I was aiming for Kelly."

"What?" asked Dr. Caravaca, still adjusting her hair. "Why?"

"It's . . . Never mind." Shiro clutched his knees to his chest.

"Look"—the doctor scanned the horizon—"once we find a suitable landing site, Luis can drive us into town. We'll call your mom, and she'll fix everything!"

Shiro groaned. "I was just trying to take care of myself for once."

A CURIOUS MONKEY tiptoed out into the clearing. He eyed the fallen poacher and the sleeping robot suspiciously. He made a small whoop, but the poacher didn't move at all. Neither did the robot.

The monkey crept closer, toward the mysterious purple slush that had rained down from the sky. He grabbed a handful. It was cold! The monkey turned up his nose. He held it closer to his face and touched it with his tongue. It was too tart! The monkey puckered his lips.

No longer interested, he tossed the ice cream over his shoulder.

The purple glob wobbled through the humid air, shedding droplets as it flew. It landed with a tiny splat right on Kelly's face.

A small blue light flickered to life in the corner of Kelly's display visor. One of her arms began to tremble. It pulled out from the ground and flopped onto her body. Her claw twitched and scraped the ice cream into her intake hole. Her power meter blinked back on, deep red.

Kelly's display visor lit up. She scanned the clearing and gingerly rose from the ground. She ingested every speck of cold, sugary ice cream from the branches, leaves, and dirt. Then she stood over the poacher and vacuumed the purple slush from his face. Svensen remained unconscious.

Kelly's power meter blinked from red to orange.

Up in the balloon, Shiro was feeling very sorry for himself. And even more sorry for Kelly. "I hope she'll be okay down there," he muttered.

He worried about what might happen when Svensen came to. He worried about how long it might take to find a spot to land, locate a satellite phone, and admit to his mom that he had screwed up—again. Shiro imagined her making waffles at that exact moment and wondering where he was.

He buried his head in his arms and felt a terrible wave of despair wash over him. But just as the first bitter tear dripped off the tip of his nose, he was surprised by a familiar voice.

"You better hurry or we'll be late for breakfast . . ."

Shiro looked up to find Kelly hovering beside the basket of the balloon.

"What?!"

"You saved my butt," said Kelly. "Thank you. That must have been a heck of a throw."

"I thought I missed!" Shiro was flabbergasted.

"Well, I guess you were close enough." Kelly laughed.

Shiro turned around to face the birders. "We did it!" They made birdcalls in celebration.

Kelly put an arm on the side of the basket. "Dr. Daniela D'Lima Caravaca. I'd recognize those braids anywhere."

Dr. Caravaca giggled uncomfortably. She leaned down and whispered into Shiro's ear. "The ice cream . . . that's her secret fuel source, isn't it?"

Shiro's eyes went wide.

"Don't worry," she continued. "Your secret's safe with me." She stroked her braids. "As long as mine is safe with you."

Shiro hugged Dr. Caravaca and saluted the birders, then leaned against the edge of the basket and gracefully back-flipped over the side.

Kelly was waiting there to catch him.

II

THE ICE CREAM MACHINE

(the one with the ice cream eating contest)

illustrated by

CHARLES SANTOSO

Penelope Perez had been wrestling the antique mower back and forth across Mrs. Mosley's lawn for the better part of an hour. She stopped to retie her long black hair and enjoy a cool gust of wind that carried the smell of the nearby sea.

A rhino in a tank top jogged down the sidewalk and briefly joined in on a game of hopscotch with two young koalas. An ostrich in a sun hat thanked a frog on a bicycle for delivering her newspaper.

Penelope observed the scene and couldn't help thinking what a lovely morning it was in Bayside. She wiped the sweat from her brow and went back to work.

The old mower was push-powered: It looked like a pogo stick on wheels, with rotating blades at the bottom. As an owl, Mrs. Mosley had excellent hearing, and she found the motors on newer mowers too noisy. As a human who wasn't quite fully grown, Penelope found the old mower difficult to maneuver, but this was the third time she'd cut the elderly owl's lawn since moving to town that fall, and she was starting to get the hang of it.

When she finished, the grass looked pristine.

"Thank you, child," Mrs. Mosley said as she handed over a crisp eleven-dollar bill. Penelope struggled to squelch a squeal.

"Mrs. Mosley, this is an *eleven*."

"I know, child." The owl fluffed her feathers. "Call me old-fashioned, but I still believe hard work deserves a fair wage. Why, that reminds me of a time back in twenty aught four. Back in those days, a phone and a camera were two different things . . ."

Penelope nodded politely but stopped listening. She wasn't much interested in history. Plus, on a hot summer day with an eleven-dollar bill in her hand, all she could think about was ice cream. Sweet, cold, delicious ice cream.

Fifteen minutes later, the story wound to a close. "And that's why they don't make movies like they used to."

Penelope thanked the old owl, said goodbye, and dashed out of the yard into the street. She ran straight to the boardwalk: a strip of shops, restaurants, and amusements built on a wooden platform next to the beach on the bay.

The boardwalk was busy that day. Lots of animals were

out enjoying a lovely summer afternoon. Picnicking pandas, sunbathing sheep (freshly shorn), a family of crabs playing volleyball: It was a veritable menagerie of beachside recreation. Not to mention the attractions!

At one end of the boardwalk was a wooden roller coaster, and at the other end, a Ferris wheel. In between, vendors sold yo-yos and boomerangs, buskers twisted brightly colored balloons, and jugglers balanced spinning plates on their noses. There was a hamburger stand, a hot dog hut, a cart for cotton candy, and a video game arcade. Penelope ran past them all without a second glance.

She was headed for Wally's Ice Cream Pot, the most popular attraction on the boardwalk. There was always a line of customers waiting for the friendly penguin to serve up delicious frozen treats.

The ice cream stand had a circular white counter with a tall white menu board against the back. Wally insisted his stand was *not* designed to look like a toilet, but even he had to admit that there was a striking resemblance.

Pretty much every Friday night, teenagers would sneak out onto the boardwalk and paint TY at the end of the sign so that in giant letters above the stand it said WALLY'S ICE CREAM POTTY.

When Penelope finally made it to the front of the line, she propped her elbows on the counter and smacked the eleven-dollar bill down like a cowboy at a saloon.

Wally whistled. "What'll it be, Ms. Moneybags?"

Penelope put her hands behind her back and clicked her heels together. "Two Fudgey Plops, please."

Wally served a dozen different kinds of ice cream at his stand, and Penelope had tried every one of them. Her favorites were Supergloopies, Sugarsloshers, Glow-in-the-Dark Mondo Chompers™, Multi-Flavored Krazy Kones, and, of course, the famous Five-Dollar Fudgey Plops. She'd only had a Fudgey Plop once before. It cost five whole dollars, after all.

Today, she got two. One for herself and one for her little sister, Pam.

Lucky, lucky Pam to have a big sister so generous, thought Penelope.

The second Wally handed the Fudgey Plops over the counter and Penelope got a good grip on them, she headed home. She was in a race against time. Ice cream versus sunshine.

"Thanks, Wally!" she said without breaking her gaze from her hands. "Keep the change!"

"Thanks, P-squared! Enjoy!"

Penelope started speed walking.

The difference between running and speed walking is that when you speed walk, you always have one foot on the ground. When you run, you are sometimes floating, both feet off the ground as you hurl yourself forward at top speed.

It is not advisable to run while holding something as delicate and valuable as a Five-Dollar Fudgey Plop (let alone two of them).

So Penelope speed walked as fast as her skinny legs could carry her. She darted through the crowds on the boardwalk, slid down the railing past the parking garage, and cut through the alley toward Auntie Ellie's apartment. She didn't take a single lick the whole way home.

Penelope tiptoed up the stoop of the building and pressed the buzzer for 8C with her nose. Instantly, her little sister, Pam, popped her head out of a window above. Pam's hair was pulled back in a ponytail, and she wore one of Penelope's old sweatshirts, which was still a size too big to fit.

Penelope tried to hide the Fudgey Plops from her little sister, but it was too late.

Pam gasped and disappeared back into the apartment. Penelope heard the pounding of footsteps down eight flights of stairs, and then—*BANG!*—Pam burst through the front door of the building, already talking.

"Fudgey Plop! Fudgey Plop! You got two! I can't believe it, Penelope! Two Fudgey Plops—five dollars each, and you got two! You're the greatest big sister in the whole wide world, and I'll never forget it as long as I live!"

Pamela Perez never said two words when she had enough air in her lungs for twenty.

"One for me, and one for you." Penelope nodded. "Mrs. Mosley was feeling generous today."

"I love you, Mrs. Mosley!" shouted Pam.

"I love you too, child," replied Mrs. Mosley from a few blocks away.

Pam began to tear the wrapper from her Fudgey Plop.

"Let's go sit in the shade," said Penelope, "so they don't melt so fast."

The sisters hurried under a cherry tree to properly enjoy their famous Five-Dollar Fudgey Plops.

Ah, the Fudgey Plop: part ice cream, part whipped cream, all fudge. Perhaps the messiest yet most delicious treat on the boardwalk. A Fudgey Plop comes wrapped in a tube on a stick. As you press the stick up the tube, the fudge "plops" out the top. A Fudgey Plop fresh from the freezer is one thing, but a Fudgey Plop that has been out for ten blocks on a bright, sunny day? That's a very tricky snack to eat without smudging a fudgy mess all over your face.

Penelope delicately pushed the stick through the tube and carefully balanced the fudge atop the pop. She licked her lips and looked over at her sister.

Pam was already covered in fudge. Her Fudgey Plop tube had been torn in half, and the contents had been vacuumed into her mouth and smeared across her face. She licked the remaining fudge from her fingertips with great satisfaction.

Penelope sighed. "Some people just don't understand the proper way to enjoy a delicacy." She cradled the pop with both hands, closed her eyes, and leaned in to take her first bite.

"Hey! I'm walking here," barked Ian Rodgers. He purposely bumped Penelope's back with his leg as he passed by. The Fudgey Plop went flying from her hands and splattered in the grass.

Ian Rodgers was a rat and the biggest kid on the block. The other kids all tried to avoid him. He had a nasty reputation as a cruel dude.

Penelope stared at the fallen ice cream with her mouth open, and angry tears stung the corners of her eyes. Her hands, still clutched in expectation of that delicious first bite of fudge, began to tremble.

"Sorry." Ian laughed. "I didn't even see you there, PEE-nul-ohp." He mispronounced her name on purpose and winked at his snickering weasel friends, Gin and Sim.

"What's wrong, PEE-nul-ohp?" the weasels said, giggling.

Penelope was trying so hard not to cry that she heard a ringing in her ears.

Pam snarled with her fudge-covered hands on her hips. "For your information, it's pronounced puh-NEL-o-pee."

"Shut up, Pam," growled Penelope, still staring at her fallen Fudgey Plop. She was embarrassed enough without her sticky little sister standing up for her.

Pam was confused. She was only trying to help. Why would Penelope tell her to shut up? They were on the same team! She began to cry.

"You shut up!" Pam shouted, wishing she had thought of something more clever to say. She ran inside.

"Awww, you made your wittle sister sad, PEE-nul-ohp," mocked Ian. He turned to the weasels. "Check it out, guys— free Fudgey Plop."

Gin and Sim looked at each other, shrugged, and began to scoop the fudge off the grass into their weaselly little mouths.

"Gross!" Ian laughed. "I can't believe you did it!" The weasels looked back at each other, shrugged again, and began to laugh too.

"Let's go throw rocks at cars," said Ian, and the three delinquents slunk down the block, leaving Penelope alone.

She cleaned all the Fudgey Plop trash from the grass and stormed upstairs to wash her hands. By the time she walked through the door of the apartment, her face was purple with rage.

"I hate that stupid rat more than I hate history homework!" she huffed.

"Now, now," said her Auntie Ellie, a meerkat. "Don't cry. Come here." Auntie Ellie had been looking after the girls for almost a year. She wore bifocals and soft sweaters. Her apartment was buried in secondhand books. Auntie Ellie loved the girls as if they were her own children. She knew it wasn't easy being the only two humans in town.

Pam was nuzzled in Auntie Ellie's soft, fuzzy lap. She had already explained what happened with Ian. Penelope joined them on the couch, laying her head down and throwing her arm around her sister with an apologetic hug. Auntie Ellie gently scratched the girls' backs with her paws. She sang a funny little love song from the 1980s.

> *"Home is where I want to be*
> *"But I guess I'm already there . . ."*

When she got to the instrumental parts, she did all the synthesizer sounds with her mouth. The girls giggled.

Auntie Ellie always knew how to make them feel better.

IN THE MORNING, Penelope and Pam went out to search for coins under the boardwalk. The walkway was built from thick planks of wood and elevated six feet above the beach. Sometimes people would accidentally drop their change through the slats and the coins would fall into the shady sand below.

Mr. Frankenson was already there, sniffing around with his metal detector. He was a hound with long floppy ears, who always wore oversize headphones and sunglasses.

"Good morning, Mr. Frankenson," chirped the girls in unison, but the dog couldn't hear them above the Talking Heads lyrics blasting through his headphones at full volume.

Sunshine sparkled against the crashing waves behind them as Pam and Penelope squinted to see in the shadows. Each held a poking stick for prodding the piles of random stuff that had fallen from the boardwalk above.

"Look what I found!" said Pam. "It's a wig." She picked up a pile of hair from the ground and put it on her head.

"Gross," said Penelope. "Stop messing around. We need to find five dollars so we can get another Fudgey Plop. Unlike some people, I didn't get to have any."

"It was so good." Pam licked her lips. "So fantastically fudgy. The fudgiest thing I've ever tasted. I can see why it's famous."

Penelope scowled at her sister.

"Sorry!" Pam blushed and tried to be helpful. "What about a Cruncheroo? It's only two dollars."

"I don't want a Cruncheroo," muttered Penelope as she poked through the sand in search of something shiny.

An hour later, they had collected three quarters, two pennies, and a miniature sewing kit.

"Okay, worst-case scenario, we split a Cruncheroo," Penelope grumbled.

"Hey, look at this!" Pam shoved a blue flyer under Penelope's nose.

Penelope read the flyer: 347TH ANNUAL ICE CREAM EATING CONTEST. Below the text was a picture of an ice cream cone on fire. "What's this all about?"

"Don't ask me." Pam shrugged. "I've never even been in a contest in my whole life! I just found the paper. I like the blue color and the picture of the ice cream cone. It reminds me of the Cruncheroo we could get if we could find one more dollar and twenty-three cents. We have seventy-seven cents now, and two dollars minus seventy-seven cents is—"

"Wally will know about this," Penelope said. She scrambled out from under the boardwalk, and Pam went clambering after her, still chattering away.

The girls raced to Wally's toilet-shaped Ice Cream Pot, where a long line of animals were waiting to order. A giraffe on a skateboard, a gorilla with a rugby ball, two llamas in love. Wally was very busy.

"Hi, Wally," said Penelope as she snuck around the back of the stand.

"Hey, P-squared. I'm kind of busy right now." Wally slid a freezer door closed with one flipper and popped open the cash drawer with the other. "That'll be twelve dollars and fifty cents, please."

"Thank you, sweetie," said a fat rabbit as she hopped off with a tray full of treats.

"Hi, Wally!" Pam stood on her tippy-toes to see over the counter.

"Hi, Mini P-squared."

"What the heck is this all about?" Penelope smacked the contest flyer down for Wally to see.

"That is a blank piece of paper," said Wally as he turned to his next customer, an iguana in a Hawaiian shirt.

Penelope groaned and flipped the paper over.

"This!" She pointed at the text. "What the heck is this?"

"It's the three hundred forty-seventh annual ice cream eating contest," said the iguana, trying to be helpful.

Pam rolled her eyes. "We can read, you know."

"Well, excuse me," said the iguana.

"Sorry, ladies," said Wally. "The ice cream contest is for adults only."

"An ice cream contest for *adults*?" Pam slapped her palm against her forehead. "That's the stupidest thing I've ever heard."

"What's so hard about eating ice cream?" asked Penelope. "Everyone likes ice cream."

"Sure, sure," Wally said, "but if you eat too much ice cream too fast, you get . . . *brain freeze*."

The iguana sucked air through the back of his teeth, and the whole boardwalk seemed to go quiet.

"Brain freeze," someone whispered.

The llamas winced. "Brain freeze," they said, fluttering their eyelashes.

"It's okay, folks. Don't worry," Wally announced over the

sudden silence. "No one's got brain freeze." The animals breathed a collective sigh of relief and resumed chatting happily.

Wally leaned over the counter to Penelope. "Frankly, the contest isn't even fun anymore." He crumpled up the flyer. "It used to be great, and good promotion for the stand, but now the same pig wins every year. The other competitors don't even come close. They all wind up rolling around on the floor, clutching their brains, frozen with agony. The pig just sits there and eats and eats and laughs and laughs." Wally frowned. "He's immune to brain freeze. No one can stop him."

"He sounds like an ice cream eating machine," said Penelope.

"That's what they call him," Wally whispered. "The Machine."

THE MACHINE WORKED at the impound lot down by the pier, in a tiny little booth made of unbreakable glass. His real name was Herman. He preferred The Machine.

If anyone parked in the wrong place at the wrong time, their vehicle got towed to the impound lot. They might tow your car, your bicycle, even your scooter. If you wanted it back, you had to deal with The Machine.

The first thing you'd notice as you approached his booth was that he seemed too big to fit through the door.

Somebody started a rumor that he lived in there, and the only time he ever came out was once a year, to win the ice cream eating contest.

On the wall of the booth was a calendar marked with the day of the event. On the front of the booth was a hand-made sign that read THE MACHINE: FOUR-TIME ICE CREAM EATING CHAMPION. Squeezed inside, next to the pig, was his ice cream eating trophy, which took up nearly as much room as he did.

The Machine spent most of the day polishing his trophy and watching the history channel on his portable TV. He liked to memorize facts and figures from the past. Though he never shared this information with anyone.

The pig always wished he were friendlier, but he was scared of saying the wrong thing. Being mean was much easier for him. So he generally avoided the company of others and always got grumpy when a customer showed up.

"Excuse me, sir, I believe you have my vehicle," said a turtle with a tie. "I had only stepped into the store for one minute, but when I came out, the car was gone."

The Machine didn't raise his eyes from the TV. He was watching a documentary about World War II.

"I'm quite sure there's been a mistake," explained the turtle. "Isn't there anything you can do?"

"Read the sign," grunted The Machine. He pointed to the list of fees that was posted on the window.

"But, sir," the turtle pleaded.

"*Read the sign!*" The Machine pounded on the glass so hard, the whole booth shook. The turtle fell backward and retreated into his shell.

The Machine turned up the volume on the TV so he wouldn't have to listen to the sound of the shell rocking back and forth on the pavement outside.

The pig sighed and drew an X through the date on the calendar.

Only four days left until the contest.

ALL THE TALK about brain freeze had piqued Penelope's curiosity. She decided to conduct an experiment. After another hour of searching for coins under the boardwalk, the Perez sisters managed to scrounge up enough change to buy a Cruncheroo. They sat on the swings and split the frozen treat down the middle.

Pam took her half of the ice cream and furrowed her brow.

"Are you sure you're ready?" Penelope narrowed her eyes.

Pam nodded.

"One, two, three!" The girls shoved the ice cream into their mouths and swallowed as quickly as possible.

For a moment, they stood there blinking at each other, confused.

Then Pam started shrieking.

"Aiiieeeeeec—my brain!" She clutched her head with her hands. "It's frozen!" She started hissing hot breaths, trying to get the pain to stop. She fell backward off the swing and curled into a ball, moaning.

Penelope waited. She
felt her forehead. She poked
at her temples. She looked
around. She felt no brain freeze.
She felt fine.
"Weird," she said.

THE NEXT DAY, Penelope skipped breakfast and hurried over to Wally's Ice Cream Pot to beat the morning rush. The penguin was up on a ladder, scrubbing away the TY that had been painted on his sign the night before.

"I'm immune to brain freeze," announced Penelope, "and I want to sign up for the ice cream eating contest." She crossed her arms and tried to look as grown-up as possible.

"Don't be ridiculous," said Wally as he climbed down from the ladder.

There was no door to the Ice Cream Pot, which meant Wally had to belly up and tumble over the counter each time he wanted to get in or out. Not an easy task for a penguin. He flopped onto the counter headfirst, wiggled and rocked around to rotate, then slid back onto his feet inside the stand.

"Kids aren't allowed in the contest. If they were, every kid in town would enter! They'd all line up down the block for the free ice cream, and I'd be put out of business." He shook his head. "Besides, it's too dangerous. You could freeze your brain permanently."

"Permanent brain freeze?" Penelope considered this.

"I've seen it happen." Wally lowered his voice. "George, the goose who works at the sunglass shack, entered the ice cream eating contest a few years back, and he hasn't been the same since."

Wally looked up and waved at George, but George didn't

move a muscle. He just stared, cross-eyed, into the distance, at nothing in particular.

"That's the thing." Penelope smiled. "I don't get brain freeze."

Wally looked skeptical. "Don't get brain freeze, huh?"

"Nope." Penelope sniffed. "I don't even know what it feels like. I'm gonna enter the contest and beat The Machine." She nodded at her own idea. It was a good one.

"Look, P-squared, I like you a lot. You're a nice kid, but I gotta show you something," Wally warned. "It's for your own good."

He opened the top of the freezer, reached in, and shuffled the frozen treats around until he found what he was looking for.

"There it is." Wally grabbed ahold of something and began to pull, but it was stuck in place. "Hang on a sec." He leaned down, and his head disappeared inside the freezer. His little penguin feet lifted off the ground. He kicked, grunted, and pulled until—

THWUCK!

Wally tumbled backward out of the freezer.

"Are you okay?" asked Penelope, peering over the counter.

Wally hopped to his feet and held up the oldest Supergloopie that Penelope had ever seen. It was frozen solid and covered in ice. The packaging was a hideous combination of green, red, yellow, and orange. The design looked like an explosion of confetti, and the only thing that Penelope could read through the frost was ZESTY!

"What is that?" Penelope frowned.

"It's been sitting down there for two and a half years. Experimental nacho flavor. No one would buy it. I kind of forgot about it, and now it's got freezer burn. I'm afraid it won't taste very good, but it will teach you a valuable lesson."

"Yuck. Nacho ice cream?"

"That's right." Wally handed the nacho pop to Penelope. "If you can eat this iced monstrosity without freezing your brain, I'll sign you up for the contest myself."

The skin on Penelope's fingertips stuck to the frosted wrapper as she peeled the paper away bit by bit.

"But don't say I didn't warn you."

Penelope banged the orange slab against the counter. It was as hard as a rock.

"You'll sign me up for the contest?" She looked at Wally.

He raised a flipper. "I swear."

Penelope wedged the Supergloopie into the corner of her mouth and started to gnaw at it with her back teeth. She ground and huffed and slowly wobbled the stick back and forth until she started to make a dent. Finally, a chunk popped off, into her mouth. It immediately stuck to her tongue.

"*BLAAAAAAH.*"

She stuck out her tongue with the frozen chunk waggling, and gagged.

Wally winced. He sucked air through the back of his teeth.

"I can't watch." He turned away.

Penelope pulled her tongue back into her mouth. She chomped the cheesy ice chunk in half and swallowed hard.

Wally gasped.

She took another big bite, threw her head back, and gulped it down.

Wally wrung his hat. "No way!"

Penelope had a wild look in her eyes. She gnawed and tore at the nacho pop until there was nothing left but a clean wooden Popsicle stick. She dropped it on the counter like a microphone.

Wally's mouth fell open.

"We better go sign up before more customers arrive," said Penelope.

The penguin hesitated. "Okay—a deal is a deal."

THE ICE CREAM eating contest sign-up sheet was posted at the lifeguard stand.

"Meet me behind the ring-toss booth in five minutes," Wally whispered to Penelope as he flopped over the counter and waddled to the beach.

Brock the tiger was perched atop the lifeguard stand, keeping watch over the swimmers while spinning his whistle around by the string. He wore a visor, a cutoff tank top, and very short shorts. The tips of his hair were dyed blond.

"Hey, Wally, waaassuuup?" Brock said from above.

"Hi, Brock," said Wally.

"No, man." Brock bristled. "I say, 'Waaassuuup' and then you say, 'Waaassuuup.'" He leaned back in his chair. "Waaassuuup?"

"Waaassuuup," Wally said.

"Nice!" purred Brock.

"I'm, uh, here to sign up for the ice cream eating contest," Wally stammered.

"Really?" Brock looked confused. "But don't you, like, sell ice cream? What are you gonna do with a year's worth of free ice cream? Sell it? That's weird, Wally."

"No, no." Wally shifted his weight from one foot to the other. "I'm actually signing up a friend."

"Oh, nice." Brock smiled. "Who?"

"Oh." Wally rubbed his flippers together and tried to think quickly. "You don't know them. They live in Canada."

"Okay . . . Whatever, dude." Brock pointed to the clipboard hanging under his chair next to the life preserver. "There should be a pen down there somewhere." He went back to twirling his whistle.

Wally tried to act casual as he scribbled on the sign-up sheet. But his flippers were shaking, and he fumbled with the pen.

"Okay, all set. Ha ha. Thanks, Brock." Wally waddled off as quickly as a penguin can travel on sand, looked over his shoulder to make sure Brock wasn't watching, then ducked behind the ring-toss booth to meet Penelope.

"How did it go?" she asked.

Wally was sweating. "I didn't want to use your real name,

since kids aren't allowed in the contest, but I had already written the 'P,' so I had to make something up on the spot." Wally lowered his head. "I panicked."

"What the heck did you write?" asked Penelope.

"You're gonna need to wear a disguise," said Wally.

"Professor Freeze?" said Brock, lowering his sunglasses as he examined the sign-up sheet. "Cool name."

PENELOPE WENT BACK home to dig through Auntie Ellie's closet. She found a leather jacket, a motorcycle helmet, and some sparkly red high heels. She put them on and checked her outfit in the mirror.

She looked like a munchkin biker who had stolen Dorothy's shoes.

No good.

She rummaged around in some dusty boxes and found a frilly pink dress, a fuzzy winter hat, and a feather boa. She put them on and checked the mirror again.

She looked like a ballerina from Antarctica.

Still not right.

Finally, she pulled out an old trench coat, a lucha libre mask, and a cowboy hat.

"What are you doing?" asked Pam from the doorway of her aunt's bedroom.

"Shhh! Nothing!" Penelope shoved the costume pieces back in their boxes.

"Can I play?" Pam walked into the closet.

"No," Penelope blurted. Pam frowned. Then Penelope had an idea. "Wait." She climbed on Pam's shoulders.

"Ouch!" said Pam.

"Hold still!" Penelope draped the trench coat over the both of them.

They stumbled over to the mirror to take a look.

"I am Professor Freeze," said Penelope in her deepest voice.

"Who?" Pam was confused.

"I am Professor Freeze," Penelope tried again in a different voice.

"Is that what professors sound like?" Pam asked.

"I am Provessor Vreeze," said Penelope with a thick Russian accent.

Pam giggled beneath the coat.

"Shhh!" said Penelope. "Legs don't talk."

When Auntie Ellie left for work the next day, Penelope and Pam practiced walking around in the costume. After bumping into a few walls, they worked out a system.

Penelope would squeeze Pam with her legs to signal when to stop and go. She would tilt her feet up and down to signal a turn. The system wasn't perfect, but it worked well enough, and luckily they didn't have to run an obstacle course to enter the ice cream eating contest.

"My shoulders hurt," complained Pam. "You're bigger. You should be the one on the bottom. I'll go on the top and wear the mask. You be the legs. I've been the legs the whole time! How come I'm always the legs?"

"Okay, geez! Fine. I'll be the legs." Penelope climbed down. "As long as you're not worried about getting brain freeze again."

"Oh, right." Pam sucked her teeth. "Actually, you can be on top and eat the ice cream. I just need to take a little break. That's all."

The day of the ice cream eating contest arrived, and the weather was perfect. Warm and sunny, with a gentle breeze. One of those days when you could wear shorts or jeans with a T-shirt and be comfortable either way.

The contest began at sunset. Penelope and Pam had perfected their disguise. Penelope wore gloves and Pam wore boots, and the costume seemed pretty convincing—in the mirror, at least.

They decided to test it on Mrs. Mosley, who was sitting on her porch, folding origami, as usual.

"Good evening, madame," bellowed Professor Freeze as he walked by.

"Well, hello there, handsome," cooed Mrs. Mosley.

"It worked!" blurted Pam.

"Pam?" said Mrs. Mosley, looking around the street, but the girls quickened their pace and headed toward the boardwalk.

Everyone was taking their seats in the stands of the outdoor pavilion to watch the big event. Professor Freeze got some strange looks from the animals waiting in line to check in for the contest.

"Next, please," announced Wally as he finished helping a hungry hippo.

"I am Provessor Vreeze. Pleeezed do meechu!"

Wally dropped his pen. He didn't know what to say.

"Vish me lock in zee condest!" Professor Freeze saluted Wally and wobbled away.

"This is gonna be very interesting," the penguin muttered to himself.

A refrigerated truck backed toward the stage with a loud beeping noise. A badger opened the cargo doors, and a gopher wheeled a handcart up the ramp. He emerged pushing ten giant drums of chocolate ice cream. Mist rose off the frost-covered barrels in the warm summer night.

As the sun disappeared below the horizon, the lights above the stage came on and exciting music began to play over the loudspeakers.

An orangutan took the stage, wearing a top hat and a sash that said MAYOR. He had made the sash himself. "Welcome to the three hundred forty-seventh annual Bayside board-walk ice cream eating contest!"

The crowd cheered, whooped, and whistled.

"Remember, the winner of this contest receives a year of free ice cream and the coveted championship trophy." The mayor attempted to lift the giant trophy with his free hand, but it was too heavy. "This year's ice cream eating contest is sponsored by our local chamber of commerce and, of course, Wally's Ice Cream Pot."

"Potty!" yelled Ian Rodgers from the back of the audience.

The mayor tried not to giggle. "Let's meet the contestants."

An exotic menagerie of misfits paraded across the stage: a poodle wearing ski goggles, a pelican in a cape, and a hedgehog covered in glitter, among others. The contestants waved to the crowd and began warming up.

Penelope clutched the railing as Pam struggled to climb the stairs to the stage. They hadn't practiced stairs. When they finally did make it onstage, they nearly toppled over the table before slip-slumping into a chair. They hadn't practiced sitting either.

The rest of the contestants found their places. In front of each one was a full gallon tub of chocolate ice cream and a large wooden spoon.

"Hang on," said the mayor as he noticed an empty spot at the end of the long table. "We seem to be missing someone. Where's Herm . . . I mean, The Machine?"

The stage suddenly went dark, and rock music wailed over the loudspeakers. A single spotlight shone down into the audience and onto the enormous pig. He bounded onstage, effortlessly lifted the giant trophy, and held it as if it were a guitar. He mimed a solo to match the music that was playing much too loud.

The crowd booed.

"Shut up!" belched The Machine. He laughed and rubbed his butt on the trophy.

"Booo!" yelled Brock and Wally. "Booo!"

The Machine plucked the top hat from the mayor's head and put it on his own before taking his seat. The mayor laughed nervously and covered his bald spot with his hand as he scurried offstage.

"All right, here we go," announced the mayor over the loudspeakers. "On your marks, get set, dig in!"

The crowd cheered as the contestants peeled the lids off their tubs and scarfed their first spoonful.

Each competitor had a slightly different technique. Some licked the ice cream from their spoons, others took bites. The armadillo used two spoons. The anteater just used her tongue.

The pace was fast and furious, and the crowd was going wild. There were groups of supporters with matching signs and shirts to show their allegiance. Competing chants filled the pavilion as the fans cheered for their favorite ice cream eater.

Three minutes in, the poodle had already given up. He was draped over the table, squeezing his temples.

"Brain freeze!" he groaned.

Everyone in the audience sucked air through the back of their teeth.

The pelican moaned and fell backward out of her chair. The hedgehog dropped his spoon and started to cry.

The Machine hadn't even started eating yet. He just laughed and pointed at the hippo, who was lying on the stage, wincing with pain. "Awww, poor baby!" taunted the pig.

"What's happening?" whispered Pam from beneath the table.

Penelope, whose mouth was too full to talk, grunted sternly to silence her sister. She scooped another giant wad of ice cream out of the tub and swallowed.

"We're in the lead!" she squealed quietly.

Finally, The Machine peeled the top off his tub and flung it into the crowd like a Frisbee. The audience ducked out of the way to avoid the spinning disc.

FWAP!

It knocked the camera right out of a mouse's hands.

The Machine laughed, bit his spoon in half, and shoved his face into the tub. He started to scarf and snort and swallow at an incredible rate.

The audience booed again.

"People sure do hate that pig," said Ian Rodgers.

"Of course they do, little dude," said Brock. "No one likes a bully."

Gin and Sim laughed, but Ian was silent.

Soon there were only four contestants left. The Machine, a polar bear in a tutu, a mama raccoon, and Professor Freeze.

The mayor climbed back onstage. "How about a hand for our finalists, folks? I don't know how many of you have ever tried this, but—"

The Machine swatted the mayor away without lifting his head from his tub. He was more than halfway done.

"I give up," said the raccoon. She grabbed her tub and walked offstage. "Come on, kids." Four overexcited little raccoons began to happily devour the remainder of the ice cream, but soon they were running around squeezing their skulls.

"Brain freeze!" they cried in little raccoon voices.

Not long after that, the polar bear set down his spoon and stepped away from the table. He took a deep breath, then vomited all the ice cream he had eaten back into his tub. He gently dabbed his mouth with a napkin and lay down under the table to take a nap.

There were only two contestants left: The Machine and Professor Freeze.

The pig looked up and stared at Penelope. Even with her mask on, she felt like he could see right through her. She quickly pulled her hat over her eyes.

"That professor sure can eat ice cream," said Ian Rodgers with awe. The weasels snickered mindlessly.

Penelope was starting to feel sick. She didn't have brain freeze, but she wasn't sure she could fit the rest of the ice cream into her stomach. Her belly was only so big. Suddenly, her vision went blurry, and she heard a loud hiss. She set her spoon on the table and clutched her stomach.

"Are you okay?" Pam was worried. She couldn't see what was going on.

"I . . . I don't think . . ." The room started to spin, and Penelope prepared to pass out.

"*BUUUUUURRRRPP!*" She belched so hard, her chair slid back.

The crowd went silent.

"Awesome!" shouted Ian. The rest of the crowd agreed.

"Freeze! Freeze! Freeze!" they chanted.

Much to her surprise, Penelope instantly felt better. She retrieved her spoon and shoveled another wad of ice cream into her mouth. She was nearly finished.

"Boy, am I glad that didn't come out the other end," whispered Pam from below the table.

The Machine looked up from his tub, ice cream dripping from his chin and eyebrows.

"Hey, Professor, here's a lesson for ya!" He lifted his carton, tipped back his head, and let the ice cream pour down his throat without even swallowing. It was like dumping sludge into a garbage chute. The pig shook loose the remaining globules from the bottom of the container and slurped them away and licked his lips. He tossed the empty carton aside and stood, ready to bask in his victory.

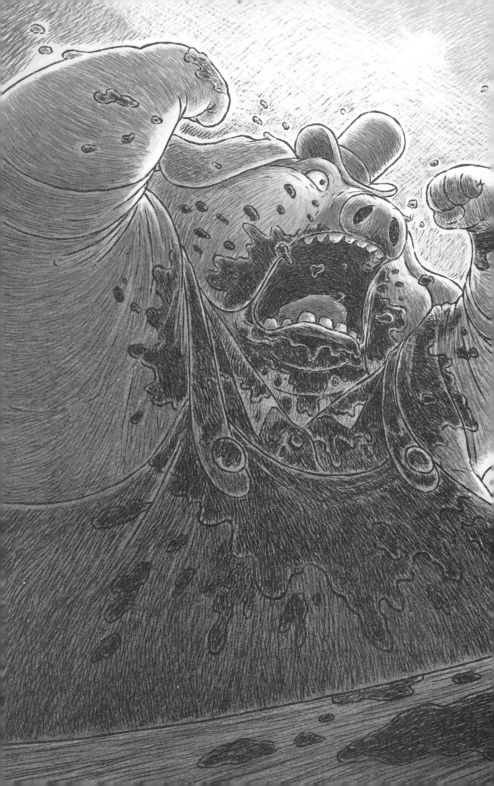

That was the moment he saw the mayor raising Professor Freeze's arm and declaring a new ice cream eating champion.

"Freeze! Freeze! Freeze!" chanted the audience.

PENELOPE WAS STUNNED. Pam was screaming with joy from underneath the trench coat, but the crowd was too loud for anyone to hear her.

"Your new champion!" exclaimed the mayor. He plucked his top hat from The Machine's head and put it back where it belonged. The crowd was going bonkers. "Would you like to say a few words?" The mayor held the microphone for Professor Freeze.

"Shhh!" yelled Ian Rodgers, and the crowd hushed.

"Go on, Professor," whispered the mayor. "Say something."

"Uhhh," stammered Penelope. The microphone screeched with feedback. "I . . ."

"Yes?" The mayor nodded.

"I . . . need to go to ze batroom!"

The audience roared.

"Dude," marveled Brock, "he's so real."

"Oh," said the mayor, blushing. "Of course! But come right back. We need to present you with your trophy!"

"Let's go!" hissed Penelope. She kicked Pam with her heels beneath the coat, and they spun around to face the stairs. Pam slipped on a puddle of melted ice cream as they toddled offstage, but Penelope caught the railing before they toppled. The audience simply assumed Professor Freeze was having tummy troubles. He had just eaten an entire gallon of ice cream, after all.

The girls ran from the pavilion into an alley, out of sight

of the crowd. Penelope slid down from Pam's shoulders and stripped off her hat and trench coat.

"Quick, shove everything in here!" She lifted the lid off a trash can and helped Pam stuff the costume inside.

"You did it!" Pam hugged her sister. They laughed and danced and hugged again. Then they ran back over to the pavilion to see what was going on.

"Wait!" Pam yanked the mask from Penelope's head and stuffed it in her pants.

Just as they entered the crowd, a foot stretched out and tripped Penelope. She landed on her chin.

"Sorry," sneered Gin.

Sim laughed. "Didn't see you there!" he added.

The weasels looked to Ian Rodgers for approval. But the rat was staring at the pig sitting all alone onstage. Some people in the crowd were still booing him.

Ian turned to face the girls. "You missed the whole contest."

Penelope felt a trickle of blood drip from her lip.

"You bully!" screamed Pam. She jumped onto Ian's back and grabbed his ears. The greasy weasels scraped her off and tossed her on top of her sister.

"I didn't do anything!" growled Ian as he rubbed his ears.

Just then, Wally waddled over and ushered the girls outside.

"You ladies better be getting home," he said quickly. "It's getting late."

"But Wally!" protested Pam.

"Shhh!" Wally covered Pam's mouth with his flipper and leaned down with a nervous look in his eyes. "Not a word."

Reluctantly, the girls slunk off into the night. The sound of the crowd faded in the distance as they headed home.

"Freeze! Freeze! Freeze!"

Little did they know, the chanting continued for a solid twenty minutes before a brave volunteer searched the bathroom only to discover that the mysterious new ice cream eating champion had vanished without a trace.

PAM AND AUNTIE Ellie were already eating breakfast by the time Penelope rolled out of bed the next morning. She had hardly slept at all, thanks to her nocturnal stomach rumblings.

"Good morning, sweetie!" sang Auntie Ellie as she offered Penelope a plate of sweet potato pancakes.

"No, thanks," Penelope groaned, and clutched her belly. It felt like snakes were wrestling in her guts. "I'm not hungry."

"Oh, really?" teased Pam. "Why not?"

Penelope flared her nostrils at her sister, and Pam made a fart sound with her mouth in return.

Auntie Ellie picked up the morning paper to check the weather report. That was when Penelope spotted the photo on the front page. She nearly screamed.

The headline read ICE CREAM MYSTERY, and there she was, wearing Auntie Ellie's trench coat, cowboy hat, and lucha libre mask.

Surely Auntie Ellie would recognize her clothes if she saw them, thought Penelope. She would be angry that the girls had taken them without asking. She would be even angrier that they had thrown almost all of them away in the trash.

Penelope smacked the paper out of Auntie Ellie's hands before she could catch a glimpse of the photo. The pages scattered and fluttered to the floor.

Auntie Ellie gasped. "What in the—"

"Spider!" Penelope shouted. She stood from her chair and tried to look serious. "There's a spider."

Auntie Ellie leaped onto the countertop. She was terrified of spiders. "Where? Get it!" She looked around frantically and grabbed a frying pan for protection.

Pam, who was indifferent to spiders, searched by her feet. "What spider? I don't see any . . . Ouch!" Pam felt Penelope kick her under the table. Then she saw the front page of the paper lying on the kitchen floor. "Oh my gosh!"

"Is it big?" Auntie Ellie shut her eyes and began to tremble. "Don't tell me. It's huge, isn't it?" She pulled her sweater over her head.

Penelope winked at Pam. "I'll get it!" She dove on top of the newspaper and crumpled it into a ball.

"You got it!" Pam said, playing along.

"Better go flush it down the toilet." Penelope said, clutching the wadded paper like it might explode at any second.

"Yes. The toilet." Pam pushed her chair back from the table. "I will help you."

The girls ran down the hall to the bathroom.

"Be careful!" Auntie Ellie called after them.

Penelope locked the bathroom door, then uncrumpled

the newspaper. She quietly read the article to Pam: *"After four years of dominance, Herman 'The Machine' Hanold was beaten by a mysterious stranger in the annual Bayside ice cream eating competition."*

"That's you!" Pam squealed.

"Shhh!" Penelope continued: *"Known only as 'Professor Freeze,' this year's winner disappeared before the presentation of the championship trophy, and their whereabouts remain unknown. If you have any information regarding the identity or location of Professor Freeze, please contact the mayor's office immediately."*

Penelope fell silent.

"Are we in trouble?" Pam asked.

"Not as long you can keep your mouth shut," Penelope warned.

Pam looked at the ground.

"Uh-oh . . ." She frowned.

"Hey, Wally!" Brock sauntered up to the Ice Cream Pot and took off his sunglasses. "Your Canadian friend really knows how to gobble the goop."

Wally swallowed hard and tried to look busy.

"Why did he vamoose before the trophy presentation?" Brock leaned over the counter and lowered his voice. "Icy diarrhea?"

Wally coughed. "Ha! I, uh . . . I don't know. She's not

really a friend—more of a friend of a friend. An acquaintance of an acquaintance, really."

"She?" Brock raised an eyebrow. "Professor Freeze is a lady?"

"Did I say 'she'?" Wally stammered. "I meant, gee . . . he's not really a friend."

"Can I have two Glow-in-the-Dark Mondo Chompers™, please?" a young kangaroo asked from the other side of the counter.

"Oh! A customer!" Wally hurried away from Brock. "Gotta go."

"Did I hear you say that Professor Freeze is a friend of yours?" asked the young kangaroo.

Wally started to sweat. "No, no. No. Who?"

All day long, rumors swirled around the Ice Cream Pot.

"I heard he's not really a professor," said twin turkeys.

"I heard he's a drifter from the South," said a buffalo in a bikini.

"I heard he's a ghost," said a rooster on Rollerblades.

"Gosh, I really don't know," Wally kept repeating.

THE MAYOR WAS starting to lose patience with the giant trophy taking up so much space in his office. Though it had given him great pleasure to confiscate the thing from the pig at the impound lot, now he was almost tempted to throw it away. It was hard to get any work done with the behemoth prize distracting him. He kept thinking about all the people who had come to visit Bayside just to enjoy the ice cream eating contest. He remembered those happy faces fondly.

He stroked his homemade sash and saw visions of smiling animals spinning on their toes, leaping through the air, purchasing quality goods and services from local businesses.

"Hooray," whispered the mayor in a high-pitched baby voice.

"What's that, sir?" Leslie asked from her desk outside the door. The swan gracefully poked her neck around the gleaming metal ice cream trophy, notepad in hand.

"Nothing!" The mayor looked around the room. "Who rang? I said, 'Who rang?'" He wiped the tears of joy from his eyes.

Leslie was confused. "No one rang, sir."

"Very good, then."

They stared at each other for an awkward moment before Leslie returned to her desk.

The mayor sighed and looked at the picture of Professor Freeze he had clipped from last week's newspaper. He removed a large magnifying glass from a drawer and hovered over the photo, searching for clues.

"What kind of a professor wears a wrestling mask?" wondered the mayor out loud.

"I heard he's a scofflaw whose car had been towed by The Machine," offered Leslie as she poked her head in again. "They say he came back for vengeance to teach that awful pig a lesson."

THE PIG HAD learned a lesson, in fact.

Losing the only thing that had brought him happiness made him realize how terribly lonely he was. Everyone in town had rooted against The Machine. They'd booed and hissed.

But the reason they all hated him was because, deep down, he hated himself. As a nerdy little piglet, he'd been so afraid of being teased, he became a bully instead. Herman became The Machine and pushed everyone away so they couldn't get close enough to hurt him.

Staring at the discolored circle of carpet where his trophy used to sit, it dawned on him. This was his chance to start over.

He bought a plant to fill the empty space in his booth. He washed his overalls. He changed the nameplate in the window to HERMAN. He actually said thank you to a customer.

The next day, someone actually said thank you to *him*!

Herman made small talk about historical trivia. He felt himself grow happier. He recognized that his life was changing for the better, and he had only one person to thank for it: Professor Freeze.

WALLY WAS SURPRISED and a bit nervous to see the giant pig lumbering toward his stand on the boardwalk. He looked different. He was wearing bifocals and carrying an almanac.

"Hello, Wallace," said the pig. He sounded almost happy.

"Hello . . . ," said Wally, confused.

"I was wondering if you had any information about your indomitable friend Professor Freeze."

"Why?" Wally took a step back. "Do you want to hurt him?"

Herman laughed so hard, he hiccuped. "Hurt him? No!" He smiled. "I want to thank him, whoever he is."

Just then, Wally saw Penelope and Pam heading toward the Ice Cream Pot. He dropped a tray of Sugarsloshers to the floor.

"Oh—excuse me!" The penguin backed away from the pig to the other side of the stand, spun around, bellied up, and somersaulted over the counter. He tumbled onto the boardwalk, rolled onto his feet, and rushed to intercept Pam and Penelope.

"Hi, Wally," said Pam, "we've come to collect the free ice cream we won in the—"

"Shhh! Go, go, go." Wally hurried them off the board-walk, out of earshot. "No one can know you won the contest! They'll accuse us of cheating." He pleaded with the girls. "They'll think it was rigged—that we're in cahoots! Everyone will be furious!" Wally looked over at the giant pig by his stand. "Especially him."

"We won't say anything. I swear." Penelope put her hand to her heart.

"But what about our free ice cream?" asked Pam.

"You can have your free ice cream," Wally assured them. "We'll figure it out. But not yet. Everyone's still too suspicious."

"Don't worry." Penelope took hold of Wally's flipper. "It's our secret."

"But our ice cream!" whined Pam. "When do we get our free ice cream? It's a perfect day for ice cream eating, and the only thing that—"

"Look," Wally said, "I think it's best if you two don't come around here for a while."

The customers waiting in line were starting to stare.

"What?" Pam balled her hands into fists.

"Why?" asked Penelope.

"Everybody's asking me questions about Professor You-Know-Who, and if you two are here, it's . . ."

Penelope kicked the sand.

"I'm sorry, ladies." Wally put a flipper on each of their shoulders. "Just until the rumors die down."

He waddled back over to his stand and flung himself over the counter into the center of the pot. He climbed to his feet and brushed himself off.

"What can I get you?" he asked a flamingo with a fanny pack.

Penelope lowered her head and sulked away.

Pam tried to comfort her. "Don't be sad, Penelope. You should be proud! You're famous."

"No, I'm not," sniffed Penelope. "Professor Freeze is!"

"I HEARD HE's a cybernetic experiment that escaped from a government laboratory," said a stork pushing a stroller.

"I heard he's a crime fighter from the big city," said a seal with a sunburn.

"I heard he's two little girls stacked on top of each other," said Pam.

Everyone laughed. "How could two little girls eat all that ice cream? It wouldn't even fit in their stomachs."

Pam scrunched her face and turned red. "It would too! My sister could eat that much ice cream all by herself, and she wouldn't even get brain freeze either!"

Everyone laughed again. But harder this time.

The only one who wasn't laughing was Wally, who angrily shooed Pam away from his stand when no one was looking. No one except for Ian Rodgers, who was starting to suspect the penguin knew more than he was letting on.

Ian had been hanging around the Ice Cream Pot a lot lately. He even stuck around at night to chase off the teenagers who liked to spray-paint the sign. The curious rat made Wally nervous, especially because he never ordered any ice cream.

Most folks assume that rats will eat anything, but Ian had a very sensitive stomach. Any food with milk in it made him puke like a fire hose. As a little kid, he was so embarrassed about it that he started making fun of everyone, just to make sure they never had a chance to make fun of him.

But he had never actually recognized himself as a bully until the night of the ice cream eating contest.

When he saw The Machine onstage, with everyone booing, it dawned on him: If he wasn't careful, that could be him someday. In that moment, Ian realized there is no one lonelier than a bully.

The pig seemed to have learned his lesson. Here he was at the Ice Cream Pot, buying a round of Krazy Kones for everyone. Folks were laughing and patting him on the shoulder, reminiscing about past ice cream eating contests.

"Please, call me Herman," said the pig with a smile.

Ian backed away from the stand so he wouldn't have to make up an excuse for not wanting a Krazy Kone. "I don't want to puke like a fire hose" would have been the honest response.

Pam left too. Which Ian found odd, since she hardly ever stopped talking about how much she loved ice cream. Why had Wally shooed her off like that? The penguin seemed nervous.

Ian's suspicion grew.

He reached into his pocket and pulled out the picture of Professor Freeze he had clipped from the newspaper. He studied the people in the crowd cheering. Maybe someone near the front had gotten a better look at the professor. He examined the backs of their heads to see if he recognized anyone. He noticed someone in the photo did not have their back to the camera.

It was hard to tell, but it looked like a little girl, someone he knew . . . It was Pam Perez! But why was she facing the camera, turned away from the stage at the big moment?

"She was *on* the stage!" exclaimed Ian Rodgers. "She was under the coat! Pam was telling the truth! I can't believe it!"

Ian ran over to the Ice Cream Pot and jumped onto the counter. He held up the paper and pointed at the front-page photo.

"It was PEE-nul-ohp!" he exclaimed.

"Who?" asked an octopus wearing swimmies.

"PEE-nul-ohp! I mean, Penelope!" Ian passed the photo around. "Penelope Perez. She's Professor Freeze. She's the ice cream eating champion."

Wally ducked his head.

The crowd murmured.

"A little girl?" Herman laughed. "I was beaten by a little girl? Well, I'll be a monkey's uncle."

A chimpanzee standing next to him cleared his throat.

"No offense," Herman said.

"Look at the little arms," Ian went on. "She must have been sitting on her sister's shoulders."

The crowd was convinced. Word spread quickly through Bayside, and soon the mayor came running out of his office, carrying the enormous ice cream eating trophy with Leslie's help.

"Young rat," announced the mayor, "you must take us to the little girl so that we can award her the championship trophy!"

Everyone cheered.

Wally abandoned his stand and waddled off to warn the girls, but by the time he arrived, there was already a huge crowd gathered outside of their apartment building. It seemed the whole town was there.

"What's all this commotion?" asked Mrs. Mosley.

"We're here for Professor Freeze!" explained Herman. "The greatest ice cream eater in town!"

The crowd began chanting, "Freeze! Freeze! Freeze!"

"Yes, yes. Settle down." The mayor straightened his sash as he made his way to the front of the crowd. "What's her real name again?"

"Penelope Perez," shouted Ian Rodgers.

The mayor tried to open the front door of the building, but it was locked.

A deer with groceries approached and took out her keys. She eyed the mob suspiciously. "Who are you here to see?" she asked.

"Penelope!" responded the crowd in unison.

"Which apartment does she live in?"

The crowd muttered and stammered with a confused burbling sound.

The deer shook her head and opened the door just enough to squeeze herself inside. "I can't let you in. Sorry." She locked the door behind her.

"Jangus!" spat the mayor.

Upstairs, Penelope was suffering through a summer homework assignment for her least favorite subject—history. She could never keep the dates straight. Was it 1876 or 1768? She couldn't see the point in learning about things that happened so long ago. She dropped her head onto the open book.

Auntie Ellie knocked on the door. "Penelope? You have some visitors."

"Who?" Penelope lifted her head from the page.

"Well . . . everyone," said Auntie Ellie.

She led Penelope into the kitchen. Pam had her head out the window and was shouting to someone down below. "And now, I proudly present, your reigning ice cream eating champion, Professor Freeze!"

Penelope leaned out the window. She couldn't believe her eyes. There was a crowd of hundreds of animals gathered outside.

Suddenly, she felt a pressure on her head and her vision went black.

Pam had pulled the lucha libre mask over her sister's face.

The crowd below went wild.

THAT WEEKEND, THERE was an official ceremony to award the trophy to Penelope and take her picture with the mayor.

Herman was there to gracefully pass on the championship title. And after hearing the girls complain about homework, he volunteered to help with tutoring. They would sit in the park while the pig regaled them with thrilling stories of past battles and events, acting out the parts and even doing different accents. Auntie Ellie came to watch too.

Ian Rodgers apologized to all the kids he used to bully, including Penelope and Pam. He revealed his secret tummy trouble and admitted how afraid he was of being teased for it. He wanted to be an ice cream eating champion too, but he couldn't even take a whiff of the stuff without feeling queasy.

When Wally found out about the rat's dairy sensitivity, he made a slushie special just for Ian. It was icy and delicious but didn't contain a single molecule of milk.

Unfortunately, slushies can cause even worse brain freeze than ice cream.

Ian took one overly enthusiastic slurp and immediately doubled over in pain. He started making crazy snorting sounds to try and get the brain freeze to stop. Penelope and Pam tried their best not to giggle. The weasels, however, couldn't help themselves.

The best part of the whole thing was the free ice cream. Auntie Ellie wouldn't let them go every day, but at least once a week, Pam and Penelope would skip to the boardwalk, hand in hand, and pull up two stools to the counter of Wally's Ice Cream Pot. Penelope would sign autographs, and Pam would tell the story of their glorious championship, which got more and more dramatic with each retelling.

Even during the off-season in the winter, after the weather had turned crisp and the crowds had gone home, Pam, Penelope, and Wally would enjoy a round of Fudgey Plops together every Saturday afternoon. No rush, no racing, just a nice, relaxing treat. They each ate as slowly as possible and savored every single bite.

III

THE ICE CREAM MACHINE

(the one with the genius inventor)

illustrated by

LINIERS

Rhonda Helmie snored softly in bed as a small circle of light slid slowly across the floor of her room. The beam was reflected through the window by a series of mirrors that had been carefully calibrated and precisely positioned by Rhonda, with the help of a very tall ladder and some complex astronomical diagrams. She called her invention the Shine & Rise. Even though her bedroom window faced west, away from the sunrise, thanks to her solar-powered reflector system, she woke up every morning in the most peaceful and natural way possible—bathed in the warmth of the dawn.

The spot of light crept up the side of Rhonda's pillow, illuminating the wild almond-colored curls that framed her round face. When it reached her eyes, she blinked awake, yawned, tousled her hair with both hands, and plucked a dog-eared notebook from the nightstand. She clicked her pen.

"June twenty-fourth. Time?" She checked the clock. "Six fifty-four a.m. Energy level? Six out of ten. Morning breath?" She held her hand to her mouth, exhaled sharply, and took a whiff. "Yeesh, nine out of ten." Rhonda recorded the data in her notebook with tight, precise strokes.

"Note to self: adjust angle of mirror zero point two five degrees north, and don't forget to brush your teeth before bed."

A poster of the periodic table of elements hung above Rhonda's dresser. Her shelves were stuffed with books about rockets and bridges. On her desk was a formidable model airplane collection and above that, a vanity mirror, though it had been papered over long ago with sheaves of colored-pencil schematics.

Rhonda threw back the covers, swung her legs over the side of the bed, and lowered her feet into a custom-designed machine she called the Spring-Loaded Dress-A-Ma-Jiggy.

SNAP! WHAP! FLAP!

As Rhonda's heels hit the floor, they triggered a switch, which released a spring, which activated a pulley, which tugged her blue jeans onto her legs. She raised her arms, and a gray wool sweater dropped over her head from a

clamp mechanism she had installed on the ceiling. Dressed in under five seconds.

Rhonda grudgingly bent down to pull on her boots manually. She hadn't invented a machine for that part yet.

OUT IN THE yard behind the farmhouse, Rhonda's father was chopping wood. He had already been up for hours (morning chores start well before sunrise when you work on a farm). He was a tall and spindly man, with strong, calloused hands; a large, onion-shaped head; and long, delicate eyelashes. His real name was Reginald, but everyone called him Swirly on account of his unusual sense of equilibrium.

Swirly had been hit by lightning when he was a kid, and the shock left him with an inner ear condition that affected his balance. It caused him to "swirl."

It was almost as if gravity worked completely differently for Swirly. Sometimes it pointed down, sometimes it pointed diagonally, and sometimes it spun around, like water flushing down the toilet bowl. If you didn't know any better, you might assume he had just stepped off a particularly violent roller coaster. The condition didn't hamper his farmwork too much, but, sadly, he'd had to give up on his dream of learning to juggle.

Though Swirly looked more like a scarecrow than a lumberjack, he was able to split eight logs at once, thanks to Rhonda's Octo-Chopper machine.

The Octo-Chopper was fashioned from eight bars of bamboo attached to a circular base. It almost looked like a cylindrical cage, but at the top of each vertical bar was a razor-sharp axe-head.

Swirly placed a log onto each of the eight stands that surrounded the machine. The pieces of wood were spaced out evenly in a circle, like the numbers on a clock.

As he walked, he teetered back and forth and twirled like a wobbly top. A gaggle of happy chickens followed his every step, clucking and pecking through the grass for worms. Swirly climbed inside the cage of the Octo-Chopper, and the chickens gathered at his feet.

"Stay close now," he warned.

Swirly yanked a rope above his head, and the eight bamboo bars fell outward, like the arms of an octopus, swinging their axe blades down hard on top of the logs.

CH-CH-CH-CH-CH-CH-CH-CHOP!

Each log split in two and fell to the ground. The startled chickens scattered. Swirly climbed out of the contraption to collect the firewood and reset the axes to their vertical positions for another round of chopping.

AFTER BRUSHING HER teeth as quietly as possible, Rhonda lifted the handle of the bathroom door and pulled it open silently. She crept down the hallway of the creaky old farmhouse to her parents' bedroom, carefully avoiding the knots in the floorboards that groaned underfoot. She steadied herself against the wall and peeked through the half-open door. Her mother was still in bed, sound asleep.

In fact, Rhonda had never seen her mother out of bed. Not once in her whole life. She had seen her open her eyes a few times, heard her mumble in her sleep on several occasions, but never heard her speak.

Karen Helmie had fallen into a sort of coma the night that Rhonda was born. The birth had been unusually complicated, and the people at the hospital suspected that the coma might have been caused by brain trauma. They worried that Karen might never wake up.

Swirly refused to believe them. He insisted his wife might snap out of it at any moment. He'd read articles about patients who had awoken from yearslong comas thanks to a loud noise or a random, unrelated medication.

When the people at the hospital lost hope, he brought Karen home to the farm and resolved to take care of her himself. He spoke to his sleeping wife as if she could hear every word. He brushed her curly hair and changed her IV and did her physical therapy every night when he was done with his farmwork.

"When your mother wakes up, she's gonna be so proud to see what a bright young lady you've become," Swirly would say to Rhonda.

But Rhonda felt terribly guilty. She couldn't help thinking it was all her fault even though her father had promised her a thousand times that it wasn't. Even worse, she was afraid of the silent sleeping woman—afraid of her own mom. She worried that if Karen did wake up someday, she would be disappointed in her. Disappointed that her daughter was so *different*.

Rhonda didn't have any friends. She found the other kids her age confusing and preferred the company of farm animals to people. Even her father didn't make much sense to her sometimes. For Rhonda, emotions were too loose and fuzzy. People rarely said how they really felt out loud. They hid clues in their eyes, expecting her to read their lips, to know what they were thinking by the way they held their head. It was very frustrating for Rhonda. No matter how she tried, she couldn't quite understand her fellow human beings. But science was just the opposite. Even the most complicated equations made perfect sense to her. Everything was right there on the page, clear and concise. No snickering, no sarcasm, no jokes she might have missed. People made her nervous, but science gave her comfort.

"GOOD MORNING, LADIES," said Swirly as he opened the door to the barn. Bubbles, Blossom, and Buttercup picked up their heads to greet the farmer.

"Moo!" said Bubbles. She was the happy one.

"Moooooo," said Blossom. She was the dramatic one.

"Mrrr," said Buttercup. She was the one with a slight speech impediment.

Swirly walked at a forty-five-degree angle to the ground.

He wobbled around in circles as he slid a metal bucket beneath each cow's udder. The chickens clucked at his feet, searching for bugs in the hay on the floor of the barn and scattering to avoid his unpredictable steps. Swirly reached for the handle of the Synchro Milker and lowered it into position.

Another one of Rhonda's ingenious inventions, the machine looked like a sideways ladder that had sprouted six arms. At the end of each arm was a gloved hand.

Swirly sat on a stool and slipped his own two hands into one of the pairs of gloves. He clapped. The other two pairs of hands clapped too. He reached beneath Bubbles, and the other two pairs of hands reached beneath Blossom and Buttercup.

As Swirly squeezed the udder of one cow, torrents of milk sprayed into the metal buckets below all three.

BRRRAP! BRRRAP! BRRRAP!

"Karen was talkin' in her sleep last night," Swirly whispered to the cows. "Couldn't quite make out what she was sayin', but it sure is nice to hear her voice once in a while."

"Moooooo," said Blossom, intrigued.

"Moo!" said Bubbles, delighted.

"Meow," said Buttercup, trying her best.

"The habanero peppers I planted are ready to pick. I'm gonna give her a tiny little nibble. I bet that'll wake her up!"

Soon, all of the buckets were full of hot, fresh milk. (City folk might not realize this, but fresh-squeezed milk comes out of cows at body temperature.)

Swirly heard Rhonda ring the meal bell on the back porch of the house.

"Yum, breakfast," he said. "I'm so hungry, I could eat a whole cow."

"Moo!" snorted Blossom.

"Oh, relax." Swirly rolled his eyes. "It's just an expression."

He put out the salt lick (a tasty way for cows to get their minerals), patted Blossom on the head, and wobbled out of the barn, back to the house.

"Morning, Pa," Rhonda called from the porch. She was holding a tape measure and trying to determine the exact height of the meal bell. "I'd like to rig up the bell to ring automatically as soon as your coffee is finished percolating."

She slipped a notebook from her back pocket and clicked her pen. "The weight of the water as it drips into the coffee pot could trigger a counterbalance that acts as a fulcrum for—"

"G'mornin', kiddo." Swirly swooped down to kiss his daughter on the top of her head. "No science talk till after breakfast, okay?"

Swirly stepped into the house, over the tiny fence that Rhonda had installed in the doorway to prevent the chickens from following him inside.

"Stay," pleaded Rhonda as the birds pecked at the fence, but chickens are not very good at obeying commands.

On the table was a basket of hard-boiled eggs, a bowl of pickled beets, and a plate of sourdough toast slathered with dandelion jelly. Some of the family's recipes had been passed down for generations, and Rhonda followed them precisely. She especially enjoyed baking and pickling, since they felt like science experiments.

Most of the food they ate was grown right there on the farm. Fresh fruits and vegetables, plenty of milk and eggs. Swirly traded the extra crops for supplies at the general store in town.

The kitchen table had been carved from a cherry tree that had fallen in a storm. It was long—intended for a large family—but since her grandparents had passed away when she was little and her mother never left the bed, Rhonda only ever set two places at mealtime.

The neighboring farms all had six or seven farmhands

each, but Swirly was basically working the Helmies' farm by himself. His daughter's inventions were a big help, but running a farm, even a small one, requires a tremendous amount of manual labor. Rhonda pitched in with some of the chores, but Swirly insisted she spend most of her time on her studies.

He had enrolled her in correspondence courses designed for students twice her age. The local elementary school had kicked her out when she started dismantling the furniture to build catapults. The principal called her "a distraction to the other students," but Swirly suspected the teachers simply found it too exhausting to keep up with a kid who learned so quickly.

Rhonda was a mechanical prodigy. She had started taking things apart when she was three. She had built her first machine by the time she was four. When she was six, she learned how to use an acetylene torch. With Swirly's supervision, of course.

The farmer was incredibly proud of his daughter's engineering genius. He had never received a formal education himself, so he was doubly determined to make sure Rhonda had plenty of time to nurture her intellect.

Swirly washed the dirt from his hands in the kitchen sink.

"What do you think of the soap?" Rhonda asked as she poured hot coffee into his mug. "I tried a new formula."

Swirly smelled his fingers. "It's nice. Do I detect a hint of rhubarb?"

Rhonda nodded.

"This all looks delicious, kiddo. Thank you." He sat at the table and took a big swig from his mug. Though Swirly wobbled and swayed even while seated, he never spilled his coffee.

"I brought the mail in," Rhonda said. She carefully spread a dollop of fresh-churned butter on the crust of her toast. "Nothing good. I was hoping my new soldering iron would arrive, but it was just another bill from the hospital. Why do they send you so many bills anyway? Ma's not even there anymore."

"Ah." He cleared his throat. "Well, even when the well's run out of water, some folks still want a glass of dirt. Know what I mean?"

Rhonda stared at him blankly.

Before Swirly could explain, the power in the house shut off.

"Speak of the devil," he muttered.

"I'll check the circuit breaker." Rhonda hopped up from her chair. "Dang, this would be the perfect project for my new soldering iron."

"I don't think it's the old wires this time, sweetie." Swirly sighed. "But maybe we don't need electricity anyhow. Your great-grandpappy ran this farm before they had electricity. What do we need it for?"

Rhonda scrunched her face. "Well, the lights for one, and the water heater."

"We'll use candles. And what's more refreshing than a nice cold shower?"

"What about the fridge? Won't all the food spoil?"

"Ah, heck." Swirly pursed his lips. "I forgot about the fridge."

Rhonda and Swirly unpacked the refrigerator and brought the perishable food to the old icebox in the cellar. (Iceboxes were what folks used to store food in back before they had electricity.) It was a big insulated metal chest filled with giant blocks of solid ice. Rhonda hoisted the heavy lid and peered inside.

There were deep-frozen meatballs, soups, beans, butter, and bread, each bag carefully labeled by Rhonda with dates, ingredients, and weight in grams. But as she was shifting things around to make extra space for the food from the fridge, she noticed a frosty pink carton hiding in the corner.

She reached over for the mysterious container, leaning in so far that only her legs were sticking out. She clawed and tugged with all her might, but the carton was frozen in place.

"What are you doing?" asked Swirly as he came down the stairs carrying extra bags of ice.

Rhonda didn't answer. She was busy using her fingernails to scrape away the frost that had cemented the carton in place. She whacked it a few times with a frozen fish. She grabbed a turkey leg to use as a mallet for her fish chisel.

THWUCK!

The carton came loose, and Rhonda went tumbling out of the icebox into her father's arms.

"Oh, wow," said Swirly when he saw what Rhonda had found.

"What is it?" she asked, wiping the frost from the label.

"I'm sure it's gone bad. Must be ten years old at least."

It was a carton of ice cream, frozen solid. The label said KAREN's and showed a picture of a smiling woman with curly almond-colored hair.

"Is that Ma?"

"Sure is." Swirly smiled. "She used to make the tastiest ice cream in the whole state. Won a blue ribbon at the fair

five years in a row." Swirly picked up the carton and stared at the label with hearts in his eyes. "Your ma had a little stand down by the end of the road there. Everyone in town used to come by."

"What?" Rhonda cocked her head. "How come I never knew this?"

"Gosh, that was a long time ago, before you were born."

Rhonda studied her father's face. It had an expression that was unfamiliar to her. She wasn't sure if he was feeling a positive emotion or a negative one.

"I want to learn to make ice cream. How do you do it?"

Swirly chuckled. "With an ice cream machine, of course. I put it away up in the attic somewhere after . . . well, you know, a few years back." He returned his attention to the carton and managed to pry off the lid. The ice cream inside had decayed into a million tiny ice crystals. It looked like a geode. "Wanna try a spoonful and see if it makes us sick?"

Swirly looked up, but his daughter was nowhere to be found.

RHONDA SPRINTED UP the cellar stairs, through the kitchen, and up to her room. She rummaged around in her closet, pulled out an old football helmet, and plonked it on top of her head. She put on a thick canvas jacket and a pair of snow pants.

"Helmet: check. Pants: check. Jacket: check. Gloves?" She slipped on her work gloves. "Check." Fully armored, she knelt and pulled out a box from under her bed. "Time to test my secret weapon."

She flipped open her notebook and clicked her pen. *"Wind-Up Attacker Whacker, experiment one."*

The device was constructed from an umbrella, a bungee cord, and six rolled-up newspapers. Rhonda wound the top of the device until the bungee cord was twisted tight.

She grinned. "Those darn squirrels won't know what hit 'em."

Most squirrels are very friendly, adorable even, but not the family of squirrels that lived in the attic of the Helmies' farmhouse. As far as those squirrels were concerned, the attic was their private property and anyone else who went up there was trespassing.

Swirly hadn't been in the attic for years (he didn't like being attacked by bushy-tailed rodents), and he'd warned his daughter to stay out of there as well. But once or twice, Rhonda had let her curiosity get the better of her. She couldn't help it. There was all sorts of fabulous junk up there: boxes of old gadgets and gizmos from as far back as when her great-grandparents had built the house. Every time Rhonda had ventured into the attic, the squirrels had chased her off before she could get a good look around.

But this time, she was coming prepared.

Rhonda tiptoed up the attic stairs, Attacker Whacker at the ready. She opened the door slowly, lifting the handle to prevent the rusty hinges from squeaking, then paused to listen for squirrel sounds.

Even though it was midday, it was dark in that dusty old attic. Looming towers of cardboard boxes were stacked all the way to the wooden beams in the ceiling. They blocked the daylight from the one tiny window at the back of the room.

Rhonda reached into her pocket, pulled out a flashlight glued to a suction cup, and slapped it onto the side of her helmet.

She stepped over piles and ducked under cobwebs, scanning the labels scrawled across the sides of the boxes: *Blankets, Trophies, Photos*. Some seemed to be written in gibberish: *Bric-a-Brac, Ham Radio, VHS*.

Rhonda heard something flutter behind her. She spun around, finger on the trigger of the Attacker Whacker. The beam of her headlamp darted across the room as she searched for squirrels. The light revealed nothing but a labyrinth of dusty cardboard.

Maybe they would leave her alone if she stayed quiet and left quickly. Rhonda calmed herself with the thought. She stepped forward with renewed confidence and walked face-first into a cobweb.

"Bleh!" blurted Rhonda. She stumbled backward and knocked over a box of percussion instruments. Bells, tambourines, and cymbals went jangling to the ground.

So much for keeping quiet.

"Jangus!" she muttered under her breath.

Rustling sounds stirred from all sides. A bead of sweat dripped into Rhonda's eye. She squeezed the Attacker

Whacker tightly and scanned her path for surly squirrels. As she crept forward, an old pair of snow skis bonked against her helmet, knocking the suction-cupped flashlight to the ground and out of sight.

Rhonda dropped to the floor and scrambled after the flashlight, crawling on her hands and knees. The rustling grew closer. The squirrels had her surrounded.

A scraggly one-eyed squirrel led the attack. He leapt onto Rhonda's back, scratching and nibbling at her jacket.

She quickly activated the whacking device to defend herself from the furious fuzzballs.

WHAP! WHAP! WHAP!

The spinning newspapers smacked the squirrels out of the air and sent them flying in various directions across the room. Still, one managed to get a foothold on Rhonda's helmet, and her vision was suddenly blocked by a swishing squirrel tail.

"Ahhh! Get off me!" She panicked and ran, crashing straight into a tower of cardboard.

Twenty-two boxes and a gang of angry squirrels landed in a heap on top of Rhonda Helmie. Luckily, she was wearing protective gear. Her whacker got snapped in half, but she checked all her limbs and they were still intact.

From under the pile of boxes, Rhonda heard the squirrels complaining. She climbed to her feet and found the one-eyed leader perched atop a yellow box, surveying the mess. He was hopping mad.

"Screep! Screep!" the angry squirrel screeped at Rhonda.

"I live here too, you know!" she shouted as she dusted herself off. "Hey, wait a second . . ."

Rhonda brandished the broken whacker to shoo the squirrel from the yellow box and immediately recognized Swirly's crazy, slanted handwriting: *Ice Cream Machine.*

She dropped the whacker, grabbed the box, and ran for the door.

Swirly was outside pulling weeds in the vegetable garden, bent over backward, nearly parallel to the ground. The chickens were hunting for beetles in the soil between his feet.

"Pa!" Rhonda ran over, panting. "Look what I found." She held a wooden bucket with a metal crank attached.

Swirly stood up, straight as a plumb bob. "Would you

look at that?" He ran his fingers over the wooden exterior. "I haven't seen this old gizmo in a long time."

"How does it work?" Rhonda asked.

Swirly didn't answer. He just stared at the bucket with his eyes glazed over.

"Pa?"

"Huh?" Swirly snapped out of it. "What?"

"How does it work, Pa?"

"Oh, well, uh, I never made any ice cream, kiddo. I only ever ate it." Swirly stretched his suspenders. "I got a feeling you'll figure it out just fine, though. What with your mind for doohickeys and thingamabobbers and whatnot. You just let me know when it's ready."

Rhonda trudged off to the barn with the mysterious machine. She set it on her workbench and disassembled all the pieces for closer examination. Inside the wooden bucket was a metal canister that connected to the crank mechanism. Turning the handle caused the mixer inside the canister to rotate.

Rhonda determined that the ice cream ingredients should go into the metal canister while the rest of the bucket was packed with ice. Turning the crank was crucial, because it stirred the ingredients inside the canister. Otherwise, only the outer crust of the mixture would freeze, since that part was touching the cold metal, which was chilled by the surrounding ice.

Rhonda decided to conduct an experiment. She took

out her notebook and clicked her pen. *"Ice cream machine, experiment one."*

She poured milk into the canister and turned the crank, and the mixer inside stirred the liquid.

"Now for the ice," she said to the curious cows, who were watching over her shoulder.

Rhonda went back to the cellar and retrieved a bag of ice, which had been in the freezer upstairs before the power went out.

The ice cubes went into the bucket, and she started cranking the handle. Around and around and around . . .

"How's it going, kiddo?" Swirly poked his head in sideways through the open door and climbed into the barn. The chickens followed after him.

"This is hard!" huffed Rhonda.

"Never stopped ya before." He winked. "Tell ya what, I'll heat up some lunch while you work on dessert."

"My arms are too tired to crank anymore." She flopped them to her sides like wet noodles.

"Well, don't use your arms, then."

Rhonda sat up. "What do you mean, 'Don't use—'" She stopped mid-sentence as she noticed the bicycle hanging on the wall of the barn.

She took down the bike and started working in a frenzy, setting the frame on some wooden blocks and attaching the back wheel to the crank handle with a length of rope.

Rhonda mounted the bicycle and began to pedal. As the wheel turned, so did the crank on the ice cream machine.

A few minutes later, Swirly came back with two steaming bowls of sweet potato soup. It was actually kind of amazing to watch the man wobble around like a bowling pin without spilling. The chickens at his feet waited for a drop, just in case.

"Lunchtime!" said Swirly as he pulled two spoons out of his back pocket.

Rhonda checked the ice cream mixture inside the machine, but it hadn't frozen yet. "Hmm." She checked the temperature with a thermometer. "It's not cold enough." She clicked her pen. *"Ice cream machine, experiment one: FAIL."*

"Think while you eat," said Swirly. He handed her a bowl.

Just then, they were startled by a loud crash. The chickens scattered and ruffled their feathers. Swirly and Rhonda dashed out of the barn and discovered that a large hole had appeared in the roof over the attic.

Swirly hurried across the lawn and went upstairs to check on Karen. Rhonda went to the attic to investigate.

When she opened the door, a cloud of dust poured out. She coughed and pulled the neck of her shirt over her nose. She didn't need a flashlight to see anymore; the sun shone bright overhead. A section of the ceiling had caved in—for so many years, a stack of old boxes had been just barely holding it in place.

The squirrels were furious.

"CHEEEP, CHEEEP, CHEEEEEEEEP!" they screeched, which is squirrel for some very foul language.

Swirly walked in and waved his handkerchief in front of his face. He looked up at the hole in the roof. He looked down at the pile of boxes that Rhonda had crashed into earlier that day.

Swirly put his hands in his pockets and frowned. He was experiencing an emotion, his body language and facial expressions making his feelings clear, but Rhonda couldn't read the clues. Her powerful mind could unlock complicated mechanisms, but for some reason, emotions were indecipherable.

"Are you mad?" she asked her father.

"No, I'm not mad," he snuffled. "It's not your fault. It's an old roof."

Swirly didn't have enough money to repair the roof. He didn't even have enough money to pay the electric bill. He knew it was only a matter of time until the man from the bank showed up.

But Rhonda didn't know about any of that. Nor did she have much interest. The only thing she wanted to know was how to get the old ice cream machine working again.

THAT EVENING, RHONDA ate her supper in the barn, staring at the wooden bucket by candlelight. After she finished her meatloaf, she munched on super-sour garlic-pickled cucumbers (her favorite).

"What if the bucket were bigger?" she wondered aloud.

Rhonda pulled out her notebook and clicked her pen. She started sketching new ideas. "But then I'd need more ice!" She crossed out her sketch and turned the page. She chewed her pen, deep in thought. "I could chop up the big chunks from the bottom of the icebox. There must be ten kilos in there."

She thought harder and chewed on her pen harder until her teeth bit straight through the plastic and broke the pen in half.

She spat blue ink from her lips.

It was not the first time she had accidentally gnawed through a writing utensil while thinking too hard.

Rhonda examined the broken pen: a long barrel of plastic with a thin tube of ink inside. It had two layers: interior and exterior, just like the ice cream machine. Rhonda felt as if the pen were trying to tell her something. Long and thin with two layers. One tube inside of another. She was on to something, but she wasn't sure what.

"Moo," said Bubbles.

"That's it!" Rhonda threw down the pen pieces and ran out of the barn.

"Moo?" said Blossom.

Rhonda sprinted into the house.

"Where are you going?" asked Swirly as he looked up from a pile of bills he had spread across the kitchen table. He held a calculator at arm's length, as if it were a poisonous snake.

"Need some stuff from the attic," she called without pausing.

She bounded up the stairs two at a time.

"Truce, truce, truce!" Rhonda pleaded with the squirrels as she burst into the attic, waving her flashlight. She could see a sliver of moon in the sky through the hole in the roof. She tore through the boxes like a tornado until she found a bicycle pump, a garden hose, and a big coil of flexible aluminum tubing.

"Thank you, squirrels!" she yelled as she dragged her supplies down the stairs.

"*Screeep?*" said one squirrel to another.

RHONDA DISMANTLED THE back wheel of the bicycle and replaced it with the blade from the lawn mower. She set a big hunk of ice into a tub under the blade and pedaled furiously to chop it into smaller pieces.

Next, she threaded the garden hose through the middle of the aluminum tubing, which she then filled with the shaved ice. She carefully funneled the milk from the canister into the hose and screwed the ends together. Most of the hose was hidden inside the giant loop of tubing. It looked like a big silver doughnut.

Finally, Rhonda jabbed the needle of the bicycle pump into the small exposed section of garden hose between the two ends of the tube. Her plan was to use pressurized air to mix the liquid inside.

"Mrrr?" asked Buttercup inquisitively as she lapped at the salt lick.

"More surface area," explained Rhonda. She started pumping. "More contact between the liquid and the ice. Now it should get cold enough to freeze!"

Twenty minutes later, Rhonda stopped pumping. She unscrewed the hose and held a cup underneath.

Liquidy slush pooted out.

"Chicken plucker!" Rhonda threw the cup to the ground. "It's still not cold enough!" she cried. "It's not *ice* cream. It's just chilly cream."

Begrudgingly, she clicked her pen. *"Ice cream machine, experiment two: FAIL."*

LATER THAT NIGHT, after he had finished tucking the chickens into their coop and singing them a lullaby, Swirly tiptoed into the barn with a lantern.

The candles had burned out, and Rhonda was asleep atop the bicycle in the dark. The cows had sandwiched her on either side to make sure she didn't fall.

"We'll give it another go tomorrow, eh, kiddo?" Swirly lifted his daughter over his shoulder. "Any of you ladies know how to make proper ice cream?"

"Moo," said Blossom.

"Yeah, that's what I figured."

Swirly carried his sleeping daughter up the stairs, swaying and bobbing this way and that. He laid her down, pulled off her boots, and tucked her in. Swirly sat on the side of the bed and brushed an auburn curl from Rhonda's forehead.

"You look so much like your mother," he whispered. "You've got her smarts too." He felt his eyes getting wet. "I just wish you could have gotten to know her. I wish *she* could have gotten to know *you*."

Swirly stood, wobbled out of the room, and shut the door behind him. He lowered his head and shuffled down the hall to where his wife slept a slumber so deep that he could not wake her, no matter what he tried.

He took off his shoes and settled into the chair beside the bed.

"Hey there, sweetie. Sure could use your advice right about now." Swirly stared out the window at the stars, because he knew if he looked at his wife's face, he would cry. "The bank is gonna take the house. They've been real understanding of our situation and all, but bills are bills. I know that. Comes a time you've got to pay what's owed."

Swirly crossed his arms. "I just want what's best for our girl. I know you would too."

He started to cry even though he hadn't let himself look at Karen, and since he was already crying, he figured it couldn't hurt to lean over and give her a little kiss on the cheek. So he did. He whispered good night and fell asleep in the chair beside the bed, just like he had for as many nights as he could remember.

IN HER ROOM down the hall, Rhonda was having a very strange dream. Maybe it was because it had been such an emotional day. Maybe it was because she had an unfinished project on her mind. Maybe it was because she ate too many sour pickles before bed. Whatever the reason, she was dreaming of dancing cows.

Harps strummed as Rhonda skipped through a meadow, arm in arm with her three bovine buddies.

Blossom jumped and twirled.

Bubbles cartwheeled.

Buttercup did back handsprings.

Suddenly, they were riding on a rainbow, laughing and singing and eating perfect ice cream cones.

"Ice cream!" Rhonda exclaimed, but no sound came out. Instead, the words appeared written in the sky.

Then *POOF!* Her ice cream cone was gone.

"Why?" Rhonda asked, and she saw the word float out of her mouth.

Blossom held up a salt lick.

"This ain't no party," mooed Blossom. She took a lick and passed it to Bubbles.

"This ain't no disco," mooed Bubbles. She took a lick and passed it to Buttercup.

"This ain't no fooling arooooooound!" sang Buttercup as she slurped the salt.

Rhonda took the salt lick and held it to her lips.

"Moo!" said Rhonda. "Moooooo!"

Rhonda awoke with her feet on the pillow and her head under the covers. She sat up and pulled the blanket off her head.

"Moo!" she said. "I mean, salt! That's it!"

She could picture the *solution* so clearly in her mind. The problem was that ice alone wasn't cold enough to make ice cream.

Once an ice cube leaves the freezer, all it wants to do is melt. Well, ice made from plain water melts at zero degrees Celsius (thirty-two degrees Fahrenheit, for any non-scientists). Once ice starts melting, it just stays at zero degrees for a while, absorbing heat from the air in order to change from a solid (ice) into a liquid (water). Zero degrees is pretty cold, but it's not cold enough to make ice cream.

However, Rhonda remembered that when you add salt to ice, everything changes. Salt water is much harder to freeze than plain water—it can get down to minus twenty degrees Celsius before freezing solid. So when you sprinkle salt over ice, some of the ice melts and turns into salt water. That's the key: The leftover ice cools the salt water instead of melting into regular water. Which means the salt water becomes *colder than ice*.

Rhonda snuck out of bed and slid down the banister to the kitchen (much quieter than taking the creaky old stairs). She rummaged through the moonlit pantry, looking for table salt until she remembered the big bag of rock salt her father kept in the garage.

During the winter, he would sprinkle salt on the walkway to make the pavement less slippery. Mostly for Rhonda's benefit; Swirly never slipped on ice. His legs would flail out in four directions at once, but his top half stayed perfectly steady.

Rhonda dragged the twenty-pound bag of salt to the barn and stuck a thermometer in a cup of ice. When she sprinkled some salt on top, the temperature went down.

She cracked her knuckles and got to work.

SWIRLY AWOKE THE next day at 3:47 a.m. It was still dark outside, and he was surprised to find Rhonda awake, waiting for him at the kitchen table with a fresh-brewed cup of coffee.

"What are you doing up?" he asked, wiping the sleep from his eyes.

"I was conducting an experiment concerning ionic solutions and freezing-point depression."

Swirly took a sip of coffee. "I don't know what any of those words mean."

"Come to the barn, and I'll show you."

When Swirly saw Rhonda's new and improved ice cream machine, he almost spilled his coffee.

The first thing he noticed was the big vertical loop of silver tubing that stood six feet tall in the center of the barn. At the bottom of the loop sat the bicycle, which was now rigged up to the pump.

Rhonda poured a pitcher of milk, sugar, and vanilla extract into the funnel end of the garden hose, which poked out the side of the machine. Then she mounted the bicycle and began to pedal.

"The missing ingredient was salt," explained Rhonda. The pump moved up and down as the gears on the bicycle turned.

"Salty ice cream?" Swirly was skeptical.

"No, no." Rhonda shook her head. "The salt gets mixed with the ice in the outer tube, while the ingredients circulate through the hose in the middle. The lower temperature and increased surface area make the freezing process extremely efficient."

She hopped off the bicycle and held a bowl under the nozzle. A stream of perfect vanilla ice cream poured out.

Rhonda pulled a spoon from her back pocket and handed it to Swirly. "I'm still tinkering with the recipe, but give it a try."

He scooped up a dollop and shoved it in his mouth. He smiled and stood stone still without wobbling. For a moment, he couldn't move at all.

Fifteen seconds later, Swirly blinked and gasped for air.

"Great googly-moogly!" He dug his spoon in for another bite. "You did it, kiddo." He tousled her mop of curly hair. "I'm so proud of you!"

"Thanks, Pa." Rhonda blushed and looked at the ground. "Is it as good as Ma used to make?"

"Absolutely!" exclaimed Swirly. "I mean, your Ma never served it straight from the machine; she used to make it in batches." He examined the aluminum tubing and the pump attached to the bicycle. "Just look at this contraption. You're serving the ice cream the moment it's frozen." Swirly patted the machine with approval. "You couldn't possibly get any fresher!"

"Huh . . ." Rhonda paused with her mouth open. She had an idea.

Sometimes ideas come in little bits, and it takes hard work to organize the pieces, to figure out how they fit together. But every so often, an idea comes all at once, and when it's a really big idea, it takes up so much space in your mind that your eyes bug out of your head a little bit to make room.

When Rhonda turned to face her father, her eyes were bugged out of her head.

"Cow to Cone!" Rhonda smacked her forehead.

"What?" Swirly was confused.

Rhonda turned to face the cows. "I need to build a ramp."

Swirly helped Rhonda collect some planks from behind the barn. They constructed a long ramp that started outside, stretched through the doors, and gradually led to the lofted platform at the back of the barn. Swirly bobbled up the ramp and cleared some room in the loft.

"All set," he called to Rhonda. "You really think this is gonna work?"

"Well," said Rhonda, "you said the ice cream couldn't get any fresher." She turned to Blossom and offered her the salt lick. "Let's find out."

"Moo," snorted Blossom as she turned her head away from the treat.

Rhonda tried the next cow. "Come here, Bubbles."

Bubbles pretended to find something interesting on the ground at the other side of the barn.

"Fine. Be that way!" Rhonda stamped her foot. "Buttercup, I'm not gonna hurt you. Don't you want some delicious salt?" Buttercup sniffed it and took a lick.

"Mrrr!" The cow purred with delight.

"That's right. Come on." Rhonda slowly backed up the ramp. "Just follow me if you want some more."

The ramp creaked and swayed, but it held strong as Buttercup stepped onto the lofted platform. Swirly soothed the cow while Rhonda scooted down the ladder back to the ground.

She hopped on the bicycle and pedaled furiously to chop a bucket of fresh ice with the lawn-mower blade attachment. She dumped the ice into the aluminum tubing, along with a few cups of rock salt. She poured a sugary vanilla mixture in through the funnel, then handed the hose up to Swirly so he could position it under the cow's udder.

"Okay," Rhonda called to Swirly, "Cow to Cone ice cream machine, experiment one."

Swirly began tugging at Buttercup's udder. Milk sprayed through the funnel into the garden hose, which threaded through the ice-packed coil of tubing, which cooled the milk as it mixed with the sugar and vanilla already in the hose. Rhonda pedaled, which moved the pump, which circulated the mixture. After a few minutes, she signaled for her father to stop milking.

"Was that enough time?" Swirly licked his lips as he climbed down from the loft.

Rhonda opened the nozzle over a bowl. "You tell me."

Swirly scraped a tiny sliver of ice cream onto his spoon. It was as white as snow. He placed the spoon in his mouth and let the ice cream melt over his tongue slowly.

He closed his eyes.

The taste triggered a tiny little explosion somewhere deep within the squishy folds of Swirly's brain. The barn and the cows and the hay beneath his feet flew away and disappeared. When he opened his eyes, he found himself standing in a memory from many years before, reliving the moment as if it were somehow happening again. Swirly could smell the aroma of fresh-picked gardenias. He could hear familiar laughter like a secret in his ear. He felt the warm touch of his wife's hand upon his face. He could even see her smile, as clear as day, right in front of his nose. It all felt incredibly real.

"Pa, are you okay?"

Swirly blinked and looked around the barn.

"Do you like it?" Rhonda studied her father's face, looking for a clue.

"Do I like it?" Swirly scooped up another spoonful and gazed at it lovingly. "This ice cream is so good, I think it broke my brain."

He took another bite and closed his eyes again. Once more, he was transported. He savored the strange sensation for as long as possible this time, standing still, grinning ear to ear, spoon still hanging out of his mouth.

When he opened his eyes, Rhonda was gone.

Rhonda stood outside her mother's room, trying to build up the courage to go in. Her hands were shaking so badly that she nearly dropped the bowl of ice cream she'd brought from the barn.

"Ma?" Rhonda tried to sound calm as she opened the door. "I have something for you."

She sat on the edge of the bed. Her mother was sleeping, like always. Rhonda carefully scooped a small bit of ice cream onto the spoon and gently placed it between her mother's lips. She tucked the spoon against her top lip and slid it out of her mouth. The same way you feed a baby.

Karen swallowed, and Rhonda held her breath. She watched her mother's chest move up and down slowly. Rhonda studied her face and waited with great anticipation, but nothing happened.

After a while, Rhonda lowered her head. She wasn't sure what she was expecting exactly, but nonetheless she felt terribly disappointed. She stared at the ice cream until a tear dripped from her cheek into the bowl.

Rhonda wiped her eyes and got up to leave. But when she glanced back over her shoulder from the doorway, she noticed that her mother's eyes were open.

"Ma?" Rhonda whispered.

Karen blinked.

Rhonda rushed to the bed and fed her mother another tiny sliver of ice cream.

Karen swallowed, and her eyes turned wild, darting from side to side until they settled on her daughter's face with a steady gaze.

"Ma?" Rhonda's voice trembled.

Karen parted her lips slowly. She tried to say a word, but no sound came out. Rhonda leaned in closer.

Karen burped and threw up a little onto her nightgown.

"Oh gosh!" Rhonda put down the bowl and cradled her mother's face in her hands.

Karen struggled to speak.

"It's okay." Rhonda brushed the curly almond-colored hair from her mother's face and wiped her chin with a napkin. "It's okay." She kissed her forehead.

That was when Rhonda heard her mother speak for the very first time in her whole life. It was only a faint whisper, but the words rang clear in Rhonda's ears.

"You're so big."

Swirly came sprinting up the stairs, bouncing off the banister and knocking pictures off the walls in the hall. He stopped cold in the doorway of the bedroom when he saw his wife and daughter hugging, crying, and laughing together.

"Karen," Swirly gasped.

She smiled, her face covered in tears.

"Swirly." Her voice was weak and hoarse. "The ice cream . . . It's delicious."

Swirly shed happy tears and collapsed into the bed with his family. He wrapped his arms around them and laid his head on top of theirs. He thought he might be perfectly content to stay there forever.

Unfortunately, just then, there was a loud knock at the door.

"I'LL GET IT," chirped Rhonda. She bounced out of the bed, scooted down the hall, and slid down the banister.

There was a man in a gray three-piece suit waiting

outside. He was punching numbers into something that looked like a calculator.

"Hello," said Rhonda as she opened the door.

The man pressed ENTER on his machine, and a long strip of paper printed out.

"Your doorbell seems to be broken," he said as he checked his calculations.

"Our power is out," replied Rhonda, examining the leather briefcase at his feet.

"Ah, yes." He looked up. "About that . . . Is your father home?" The man took off his hat and smiled warmly.

"Who are you?" Rhonda asked, though she was more curious about his adding machine.

"I'm from the bank. My name is Hank."

Rhonda took out her book, clicked her pen, and made a note.

"Pa!" she shouted as she walked away. "Hank from the bank is here!"

Swirly stumbled downstairs in a daze.

"Good morning, Swirly," said Hank from the bank. "I'm sorry to drop by unannounced, but I tried calling and there was no answer."

"She's awake," muttered Swirly. A huge grin spread across his face.

"Who? Karen? Really?" Hank set down his calculator. "That's incredible news, Swirly! What happened?"

"She's awake," Swirly said again, shaking his head with disbelief.

"That's fantastic, Swirly. I'm so happy for you." Hank extended his arm to shake Swirly's hand. "What happened?"

Swirly shook Hank's hand slowly at first, then faster and faster. "She's awake! She's awake! She's awake!" he shouted with excitement.

"Hooray!" said Hank, though he was a bit confused.

"Swirly?" called Karen faintly from the bedroom. Before she had even pronounced the -ly, he was racing upstairs, the rug shooting out from under his feet.

Rhonda returned to the front door, carrying a bowl and a spoon.

"What happened?" Hank asked her.

"This," she said, handing him the bowl.

"Oh!" He looked excited. "Did your mother make this?"

"Actually, I did," said Rhonda proudly.

Hank from the bank paused. He seemed to be doing mathematical calculations in his head. He scooped up a spoonful and examined it. The color and texture reminded him of a fluffy cloud.

"You know"—he gestured with his spoon—"I used to visit your mother's ice cream stand every Friday after school." He took a bite and stopped talking.

He closed his eyes.

The crush of numbers vanished from Hank's mind. The constant calculations of compound interest, addition, subtraction—gone. Instead, he was transported to a moment thirty years prior. He was sitting on the floor of his childhood bedroom, holding a hammer over a piggy bank.

He smashed the porcelain pig, and shiny coins spilled out in all directions. He giggled.

Rhonda grew curious. "Do you—"

"Shhh," said Hank from the bank.

He leaned against the doorjamb and smiled. He took another bite and slowly slid down the doorframe into a sitting position. He took a third bite and started humming to himself. He was lost in bliss.

Rhonda cleared her throat to remind him she was still there.

Hank opened his eyes and came back to his senses. He stood and straightened his tie.

"I'm sorry," he said. "It's just . . . this is the most perfect thing I've ever eaten. It tastes like happiness itself." He held out the bowl. "Can I have some more?"

"Well, I'm still experimenting with the recipe," admitted Rhonda, "and I've got some improvements planned for my machine."

"Your *machine*?" Hank raised an eyebrow.

"Yeah," said Rhonda. "Come on. I'll show you."

Hank from the bank wiped his shoes on the mat and followed Rhonda through the house and out the back door to the barn.

"This is incredible!" he said as he marveled at the shiny loop of aluminum tubing. He furiously punched numbers into his calculator, and a ribbon of complex figures printed out. "You built all this yourself?" he asked in disbelief.

Rhonda blushed.

Swirly burst into the barn, with the chickens following close behind. A flurry of feathers filled the air.

"Karen says hi, Hank." Swirly was weeping with joy. "She says hi!"

Hank walked over and put his hand on Swirly's shoulder.

"She woke up!" whispered Swirly.

"You always said she would."

Swirly hugged the man from the bank.

"I'm sorry," sputtered Hank. He took a step back. "It's just that . . . I'm here because, well, the bank wants to take your house. The whole farm, actually. I feel horrible, but you've been behind for years, and it just didn't seem like you'd ever be able to pay all the bills. I've been trying to think of a way around it. I really have."

Swirly's shoulders slumped.

"The thing is . . . there may be a better solution now." Hank ripped the long printout from his calculator and snapped it like a whip.

Rhonda started to leave so the grown-ups could talk about boring business stuff. "Hang on there, Rhonda," said Hank from the bank. "This concerns you too."

"Huh?" Rhonda was confused. She had never been to the bank.

"I believe that this ice cream machine is a work of staggering genius. The ice cream it makes is so fresh, so delectable—it must be shared with the world." Hank spread his arms wide and shook his head with admiration. "I don't know much about ice cream, but I do know a good investment when I see one." He turned to Rhonda. "And what I see in this barn is unlimited potential."

Hank opened his briefcase and pulled out some documents. "These papers say that you owe too much money to pay your bills, and therefore, the bank now owns this farm."

Swirly swallowed hard and lowered his head. He felt ashamed. He felt defeated. Until he heard the sound of ripping paper.

"I've got a different idea." Hank let the torn pages fall to the floor of the barn. "We go into business together. Swirly grows the ingredients, Rhonda designs the machinery, and I'll handle the rest." He ran his hands over the machine and looked back at Rhonda. "But you're the boss, Rhonda. You're in charge; it's your machine, after all. We can call it something like Rhonda's Fresh-Made Ice Cream."

Rhonda looked over at Swirly. He shrugged with a grin.

"Cow to Cone," Rhonda suggested.

"Cow to Cone. I love it," said Hank from the bank. "We can start up the stand again, right down at the end of the road. Just like the good old days." He put one arm around Swirly and waved the other through the air, envisioning the whole thing. "I'll rent a billboard off the highway to drum up some publicity. Then who knows? Maybe we start selling cartons at the general store. Maybe we go national." He took a breath. "But I'm getting ahead of myself."

Hank knelt beside Rhonda. "First things first. You said you wanted to make some improvements to your machine." He plucked a leather-bound notepad and a fancy pen from his jacket. "What exactly do you need, boss?"

THAT SUMMER, PEOPLE drove from miles away just to get a taste of "the freshest ice cream in the world" (that's what it said on the billboard, under the picture of three dancing cows).

The Cow to Cone machine had become a sensation, but the final version bore little resemblance to the jury-rigged prototype that Rhonda had constructed in the barn that spring. Thanks to the support of Hank from the bank, she had upgraded the equipment considerably.

Blossom, Bubbles, and Buttercup stood perched atop a twenty-foot tower of glass. Gleaming crystal-clear tubes spiraled down from the cows like the tracks of a death-defying roller coaster. At the bottom of the tower was the ice cream stand.

After they placed their orders, customers could watch from the counter as robotic auto-milkers worked the udders of the cows above. The milk sprayed into the glass tubes, swirling around and around, getting colder and colder, thanks to a supercooled gas called liquid nitrogen.

Halfway down the tower, the chilled milk mixed with farm-fresh flavors: blueberry for Bubbles, peach for Blossom, and strawberry for Buttercup. Then the three different colors whooshed through the twisting tubes toward the ground.

By the time the mixtures reached the brass serving nozzles at the bottom of the tower, the liquid had been transformed into perfectly frozen ice cream, just moments after being squeezed from the udders above.

Cow to Cone was so good, people would show up hours before opening time just to secure their place in line. There

was a one-bowl limit per customer, and the stand sold out every single day. Hank from the bank was quite pleased. Swirly was overjoyed.

Word of the ingenious young inventor had spread far and wide, so some people were surprised to find a curly-haired older woman working behind the counter. That's because it wasn't Rhonda, but her mother, Karen, who ran the ice cream stand. Just like the good old days.

The customers loved Karen. She called everyone "hon" and gave kids free triple-swirl cones on their birthdays. She loved to show off the special wheelchair that Rhonda had designed to help her get around.

But the young inventor rarely visited the ice cream stand at the end of the road. It was too crowded for her liking. Too many people. She preferred to spend her days alone, tinkering in her workshop, pondering her next project.

Well, not exactly alone. She had made peace with the squirrels from the attic (a little acorn-flavored ice cream goes a long way). The fuzzy rascals became curious about her other experiments and often hung around the workshop to lend a hand.

At night, after the farmwork was done and the ice cream stand was closed, Swirly and Rhonda and Karen would gather around the long cherrywood table for dinner. They had moved it outside to the yard so the animals could join them. Bubbles, Blossom, Buttercup, the chickens, and the squirrels all had a place at the table. It was a big, happy family.

One night that fall, as the ice cream season was winding down, they invited Hank from the bank to join them for dinner. He was flattered. He proposed a toast to the wild success of the ingenious young inventor, he gushed over Karen's meatloaf, and he laughed so hard at Swirly's jokes that milk shot out his nose. But just when he thought the evening couldn't get any better, Rhonda stood from the table and asked him to follow her into the barn.

Hank from the bank nearly squealed. Swirly giggled. Karen winked.

They gathered in the barn with breathless anticipation. In the center of the room, a large machine was covered with a sheet. For the first time, Rhonda felt confident she could recognize the looks on everyone's faces as she whipped away the cloth and revealed her latest invention.

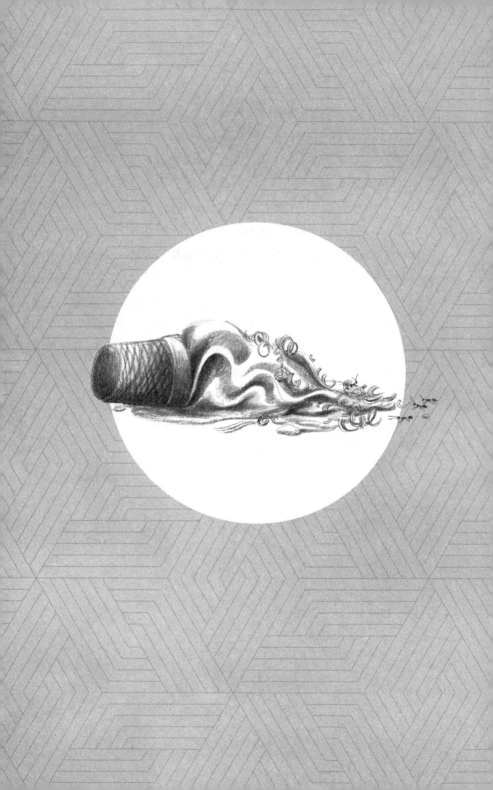

IV

THE ICE CREAM MACHINE

(the one with the evil ice cream man)

illustrated by
EMILY HUGHES

Cromulous Blotch was the worst ice cream man the world had ever seen. He was mean, he was filthy, and, worst of all, he hated ice cream. He drove his grimy truck at top speed around the neighborhood, hardly ever stopping for kids to get frozen treats. Instead, he shouted insults at them as they dove out of the way to avoid getting run over.

"Hey, four-eyes, go fall down a hole!"

"Yo, ugly! Your face makes me barf!"

"Attention, tiny loser: you stink!"

Occasionally, he did actually give a kid an ice cream cone, but not before dipping it in coffee grounds or chalk or sand. His favorite trick was "accidentally" dropping the ice cream to the ground just as a kid reached up to grab it.

"Watch it, dummy!" he would say as he wagged a bony finger. "Stupid is contagious, you know." Then he would cackle like a maniac and speed away with "Pop Goes the Weasel" blaring at full volume from the rusty speakers mounted on top of his truck.

Usually, an ice cream song is the most exciting thing a person can hear. A single note can stir a frenzy of joy and inspire urgent giggle sprints. But that summer—the summer Cromulous Blotch became the ice cream man in the Dells—the kids learned to *fear* the twinkly sound of the ice cream truck approaching . . .

THE DELLS WAS a sprawling residential neighborhood nestled between Old City and Other City, off a twisty little road that had once been considered a highway. There were 347 houses arranged in rings of branching cul-de-sacs (which is a fancy French word for dead-end streets shaped like circles).

Way back when, before they'd built any of the houses, the neighborhood had been farmland owned by Thaddeus Vandersnoot, the railroad tycoon. Well, the aforementioned Cromulous Blotch was a direct descendant of Vandersnoot, and as such, he had inherited the big dusty mansion at the top of the mountain overlooking the neighborhood.

Peering down from above, with his pointy nose pressed against the window, Cromulous always thought the Dells resembled a snowflake—an intricate pattern of circles surrounding circles, connecting with other circles. The faintly fractal form reminded him how much he missed winter.

Even in the summertime, Cromulous insisted on wearing black: black pants, black shirt, black boots, a black floppy hat, and even a long black cape.

A pear-shaped, stick-legged dollop of a man, Cromulous seemed much older than he really was. It hadn't been long since he'd left school, but his eyes looked tired and his pale skin had begun to wrinkle from frowning all the time.

He'd been slightly happier in his youth, though no one around him had had very much fun. The boy was downright nasty. He seemed to take pleasure in other people's pain. No one could reason with him, not even his own parents. So when he turned eighteen, they packed their belongings and moved to Fiji without him.

It wasn't long before all the folks who worked in the mansion quit and left too. Cromulous wound up alone in that big old house, and since he was too spoiled and lazy to bother cleaning, the place quickly fell into disrepair. The garden was overgrown, muddy boot prints stained the carpets, and the kitchen smelled like dirty socks.

No one had visited the Vandersnoot mansion in months. The sanitation trucks stopped collecting the garbage, the pizza guy refused to make deliveries, and the postal workers started leaving the mail at the bottom of the driveway. They had learned their lessons the hard way.

Without anyone around to tease or torment, Cromulous had grown even crankier. His tantrums became violent. He felt frustrated and angry, like he'd somehow lost his purpose in life.

But one afternoon, while staring gloomily out the window, he'd noticed a boxy white truck with a big plastic ice cream cone on top, puttering around the looping streets of the neighborhood below.

Wherever the truck went, crowds of kids came running. They stopped their games, burst out of their houses, jumped off swings, and raced toward the truck screaming, *"Ice creeeam!"*

Cromulous himself couldn't stand the taste of sweet frozen cream, but the neighborhood children seemed almost hypnotized, drawn to the truck like moths to a flame.

In that moment, Cromulous Blotch hatched a devious scheme. A wicked smile slid across his lips, like a snake slithering over a hot rock. The very next day, he bought that truck outright and made it his personal mission to ruin ice cream for every single kid who lived in the Dells.

TIFFANY BABISH WAS playing fetch with her dog, Fomo, in the front yard. She wore speckled leggings and a bright-colored T-shirt. She had bangs that hung down over her eyes. Fomo was a Rottweiler/terrier mix of some sort, who had one tooth that didn't quite fit in his mouth. He also had bangs that hung down over his eyes.

Tiffany launched a ball into the air, and Fomo scampered after it. They were training to someday compete on their favorite game show, *K9 Commando*. Tiffany was a bit younger than the trainers on the show, and Fomo was a bit smaller than their dogs, but as she watched the plump little mutt sail through the air to catch the ball, she imagined them both as future champions.

She felt happy and began singing to herself. Loudly.

> "The world was moving, she was right there with it, and she was.

> "The world was moving, she was floating above it, and she wa-a-as."

Tiffany had a voice that was bigger than her body. Whenever she spoke, it bordered on a holler, like someone trying to talk in a helicopter. She was not a gifted singer, but what she lacked in talent she made up for in volume.

Unfortunately, by the time Tiffany heard the tinkling ice cream truck song over the sound of her own booming voice, it was too late to hide. The truck was already in sight.

Tiffany stopped singing. Fomo whimpered.

She had heard that the new ice cream man was a terror. But she had also heard that he gave away his ice cream for *free*. As scared as she was, as desperately as she wanted to flee, the promise of a free ice cream cone was just too good to turn down.

The truck screeched to a halt in front of her, and Tiffany held her breath.

A pale, sweaty man-child in a floppy black hat stuck his head out the window. "You sound worse than a pig in a blender!" he said. "I could hear that racket from ten blocks away!"

Tiffany frowned. Fomo growled.

"Beat it, you mongrel." Cromulous chucked a soggy towel from the window of the truck, and Fomo went dashing after it.

Tiffany tried to be brave. *Ice cream*, she reminded herself. *Free ice cream.*

"I've heard rusty hinges sing better than that!" Cromulous snickered.

Tiffany's lip began to tremble.

Cromulous climbed out of the truck and crept onto the grass. "Are you practicing to audition for *America's NOT*

Talent?" He leaned over and whispered, "If I had a voice as horrible as yours, I'd glue rocks in my ears and never speak again!"

Tears welled up in Tiffany's eyes.

"There you go," Cromulous purred as he removed a glass tube from his pocket. "You really should cry about it."

Tiffany began to wail like an ambulance siren. Cromulous pressed the vial to her cheek, and tears dripped into the tube.

The wailing turned to words. "Yoooooou are the mean-est person in the world!"

Cromulous winced. "Enough! That noise is even worse than your singing." He plugged the vial with a cork and admired the liquid inside with a greedy smile. He turned his attention to Tiffany and sneered. "If you shut up, I'll give you a free ice cream cone."

Tiffany sniffled and went quiet.

Cromulous marched back to his truck, reached in through the window, and pulled out a crooked, half-cracked vanilla ice cream cone. He offered it to Tiffany, but just as she reached to take the treat, he let it go splat on the grass.

Tiffany howled as Cromulous drove away, laughing. Fomo howled too.

When the truck was out of sight, she picked the ice cream cone up from the ground and flicked off the blades of grass and clumps of dirt. She took a tiny bite from the cleaner side of the cone and immediately felt better. Free ice cream. It was almost good enough to put up with that sinister scoundrel Cromulous Blotch.

But not quite.

When Tiffany asked her next-door neighbor Barney Fantasmanoodle to get an ice cream cone for her the next day, he bravely agreed even though he was just as scared of the evil new ice cream man as all the other kids in the neighborhood.

Barney looked younger than Tiffany, but they were the same age. He hadn't hit his growth spurt yet, and he was very sensitive about his height. He wore high-top sneakers and trucker caps to seem taller.

Some people got annoyed by Tiffany's loud voice, but Barney actually admired it. He had a stutter, which meant he sometimes struggled to get the words that formed in his brain to come out of his mouth. Because of this, he often kept his thoughts to himself. Tiffany, on the other hand, said whatever she was thinking at the top of her lungs. Barney respected her for that.

They had been friends since the second grade, and she had never teased him about his stuttering. Not even once. She just waited until he was able to pronounce whatever words he was trying to say. It was usually something about remote-controlled cars.

Barney loved his cars almost as much as Tiffany loved Fomo. He had learned how to customize the springs and gears that came with the kits, to make the vehicles go faster, turn quicker, and jump higher. He had built a whole fleet and raced the cars around the cul-de-sac, with Fomo chasing after them.

Rumor had it that Cromulous Blotch would gleefully run over any toys left in the street. So when Barney heard the ice cream song in the distance, he quickly stashed away his cars and waited empty-handed by the curb to get a free ice cream cone for himself and his friend Tiffany, who was hiding in the garage, trying as hard as she could to keep quiet.

"Nice hat, baldy," scoffed Cromulous as his truck ground to a halt with an ear-piercing squeal.

"Thank you?" Barney was confused.

"What's that, baldy?" Cromulous leaned out the window. "Everyone knows you're bald; you don't have to wear a hat to hide it."

"I-I'm not bald," Barney said, putting his hand to his head to assure himself.

"Yeah, right," said Cromulous. "Prove it."

Barney lifted his hat to show his hair. Cromulous snatched the hat away with rodent-like speed. Then he held it under the soft-serve machine and filled it with a mountainous swirl of chocolate ice cream.

"Bwah-ha-ha-ha-haha!" Cromulous laughed so hard, he snorted.

Barney felt tears sting the corners of his eyes. His favorite hat was ruined.

Cromulous offered it back, and for a moment Barney felt better; he was about to get a hatful of free ice cream. But as soon as he stepped forward to retrieve it, Cromulous plopped the chocolate-filled cap onto Barney's head.

Ice cream melted into his hair and dripped down the back of his neck. Barney tore the hat from his head and threw it to the ground.

Cromulous sensed an opportunity. He scrambled from

his truck and whipped out his tear vial, careful not to spill any of the previously collected droplets inside.

"I'm sorry," said Cromulous in a mocking voice. "Did I make the baby sad? Little baby gonna cry? It's okay, baby."

Barney hated being called a baby. Hot tears streamed down his face and into the vial until the glass tube was nearly full.

"I love this job!" Cromulous cackled.

BARNEY WAS WEARING his second-favorite hat when he and Tiffany asked their neighbor Ping Zamfrax if she would be brave enough to face Cromulous for a chance at free ice cream.

Ping was big into computers. She had coded her own website and was working on programming a video game. She brought her laptop with her everywhere she went: in the bathtub, on the seesaw, everywhere. Well, she didn't bring it with her when she went to get ice cream from Cromulous Blotch. She knew he would smash it if he got the chance.

Barney and Tiffany waited inside, peeking through the blinds. Ping paced nervously on the sidewalk, picking at her sparkly nail polish as the ice cream truck approached.

"Look at this little nerd!" shouted Cromulous to no one in particular as the ice cream jingle jangled from his truck.

Ping touched her short hair and tugged at her blue jump-suit self-consciously. "Hang on," said Cromulous, scratch-ing his hairless chin. "Are you a nerd, or are you a dork? Let me get a better look."

Ping crossed her arms and stared at the ground. "Three choco-vanilla swirl cones, please, Mr. Blotch."

"Mr. Blotch!" Cromulous adjusted his big floppy hat. "So polite. Oh my. Well, what do you know? We have a special offer today just for polite little dork-nerds like you." He smiled a wicked, rotten-toothed grin. "Free topping."

Cromulous filled three cones with choco-vanilla swirl, then plunged each one into a bowl of what looked like cookie crumbs. "Here you go, nerd—I mean, dork."

Ping grabbed the cones before he had a chance to drop them.

"What's with the haircut?" Cromulous teased. "Did you get your head stuck in a lawn mower?"

Ping felt tears welling up in her eyes. She quickly turned and ran so as not to give him the satisfaction of seeing her cry.

When the truck drove away, Tiffany and Barney came outside. They all sat on the curb and prepared to enjoy their cones.

"He's meaner than I thought," Ping said. "But hey"—she brightened—"free ice cream!" She took a lick and paused.

Tiffany already had her mouth full and a befuddled look on her face.

Barney spit his ice cream into the gutter. "Blahhh!" He retched. "It's covered in sawdust!"

Ping scraped her tongue with her fingers. Tiffany swallowed and immediately regretted it. They each tried to wipe as much of the sawdust from the ice cream as they could.

"It is still free ice cream," sighed Tiffany as she gave Fomo a taste from the vanilla side of the cone. The dog wagged his tail so hard, his hind legs lifted off the ground.

"Wh-wh-what's up that guy's butt anyway?" asked Barney.

"He's just a sad old bully," growled Tiffany. "Someone ought to put him out of business."

"How?" asked Ping. "He's the only ice cream man in the neighborhood."

Tiffany's eyes twinkled. "What if he wasn't?"

"No one can compete with him," Ping explained. "He gives the ice cream away for free. He's so rich, he doesn't need the money."

"I heard his butler made a hundred thousand dollars a year"—Tiffany wiped her hands on the grass—"and he quit anyway, because Cromulous is too horrible to be around."

"I heard the p-p-post office leaves p-packages at the bottom of his driveway just to avoid looking at his f-f-face." Barney popped the last bit of cone into his mouth.

Ping and Tiffany laughed.

But they stopped laughing when they spotted little Yolanda Sinclair sulking down the street. Her face was red and streaked with tears.

"What happened, Yolanda?" asked Tiffany.

"Mean old Cromulous Blotch." Yolanda sniffled. Her shorts were filled with ice cream. "Caught me playing soccer in front of Nolan's house."

"It's okay, Yolo," Barney said. "W-w-we can get your ice cream from now on."

Yolanda pouted. "I don't even like ice cream anymore."

Ping and Barney gasped. Yolanda lowered her head and slowly walked away.

"This has gone too far!" shouted Tiffany, so loud that Ping's earrings jangled. "We've got to do something!"

CROMULOUS HAD ALREADY collected a full vial of tears, so he decided to head home early. His truck herked and jerked up the steep driveway that led to the top of the mountain. When he got out, he slammed the door, which fell off its hinges and clanged to the pavement.

The truck was in bad shape. Cromulous hadn't washed it once since he'd bought it. *That's what rain is for,* he figured. He hadn't serviced the engine. *It's supposed to smoke like that,* he told himself. Worst of all, he hadn't cleaned out the sludge-covered ice cream machine. Not even once.

Cromulous trudged into the garage and carried two large

cartons of ice cream mix out to the truck. He dumped the powder into the machine and carelessly tossed the empty boxes to the ground atop a pile of wet and rotting cardboard covered with ants. He smacked a switch on the side of the machine, and the mixers started to chugalug. Cromulous left the thing going overnight, knowing that the next day there would be ice cream inside.

He never ate any ice cream himself. He preferred sweet potatoes. That was all he ate, in fact. He had once read about a guy in Papua New Guinea who survived on nothing but sweet potatoes, and he decided he would do the same.

Cromulous flung his sweaty hat across the room and shoved a sweet potato in the microwave. Then he flopped onto the couch with his dirty boots still on.

"All in a day's work." He smirked as he pulled out the glass vial and marveled at the clear liquid inside. He popped the cork and inhaled deeply, wafting the salty aroma toward his nostrils with his free hand. He puckered his lips and took a tiny sip, letting the droplets swish around in his mouth.

All his problems seemed to melt away. He felt powerful. He felt proud of himself. He felt he had found his purpose in life. Even though the kids hated him with a passion, they were too weak to resist the sweet frozen treats that he dangled under their noses. He had concocted the perfect scheme.

DING!

The sweet potato was done cooking. Cromulous grabbed it from the microwave, tossing it from hand to hand so

as not to burn his bony fingers. He ripped the potato in half and carefully poured the contents of his vial over the steaming orange vegetable. He licked his lips. For Cromulous, children's tears were the perfect seasoning.

AFTER DINNER, TIFFANY, Ping, Barney, and Fomo met in the middle of the cul-de-sac. Fireflies blinked in the warm summer night. Barney raced his remote-controlled car around the circle, and Ping pecked away at her laptop. Tiffany plucked a stick from the grass and hurled it into the air for Fomo.

"What if we got our own ice cream truck?" Tiffany proposed, her voice booming.

"Shhh!" shouted a neighbor. Tiffany blushed.

Barney rolled his eyes. "We're not old enough to . . . to . . .

We're not old enough to drive." He shook his head. "B-b-believe me, I've tried to convince my dad to let me try a thousand times."

"We'd be a million times better than Blotch," said Tiffany as quietly as possible (which was still pretty loud).

"Nicer, certainly," added Ping without looking up from her screen.

Barney swirled the joystick on his controller. His car popped up on two wheels and spun like a ballerina. Fomo barked with approval.

Ping stopped typing. "What about a remote-controlled ice cream truck?" She opened a new program on her computer and made a quick 3D sketch. It looked like a washing machine on a roller skate. She turned to Barney and showed him the drawing. "We could mount an ice cream machine on top of your car."

"Wh-wh-wh . . ." Frustrated with his stutter, Barney adjusted his hat and tried again. "Where are we going to get an ice cream machine?"

Tiffany smiled like a cat who had caught a bird. "I think I might have an idea . . ."

THE NEXT MORNING, Tiffany led Ping and Barney to a trail at the edge of the neighborhood. She whistled, and Fomo jumped into the basket of her scooter. Barney didn't have his own scooter, so he carefully balanced on the back of Ping's. He had to hug her waist to hold on, which made him blush.

Down the trail they went. It was a bumpy ride—Barney fell off twice. They crossed through the woods that separated the Dells from Old Route 304 and headed down the hill that led to the local junkyard, where Gorby the Fletch lived.

Gorby the Fletch was a cannonball of a man, whose limbs were just a bit too short to be useful. His neck was so squat, he had to turn his whole body to look around a room. He had strong hands, wild gray sideburns, and tiny, little eyes. He wore coveralls patched with colorful cloth at the elbows and knees. All his clothes had been found in the dump, yet somehow he always smelled clean and fresh, like pine cones.

Ever since he was a kid, Gorby the Fletch had loved garbage. Some people say that one man's trash is another man's treasure. Well, Gorby was that other man. When the dump trucks showed up each day to drop off their loads, he strapped on his galoshes and his goggles and went traipsing through the piles with a pitchfork. He felt like he was hunting for treasure.

Gorby had built a little house from discarded scrap metal and leftover lumber supplies. The chimney was crooked and the roof tiles didn't match, but even though it had been cobbled together from old junk, the house was remarkably charming.

The yard was carpeted with the old Astroturf from the high school football field. His barbecue had once been an oil drum. Gorby had even built himself a pool from a broken-down water tower. He was very handy with an arc welder (a blowtorch so hot, it can glue different pieces of metal together).

Sometimes a motorist would stop by the junkyard looking for a specific car part. Gorby would lead them right to it. He always knew if he had it or not. He had a map in his mind of every object in the dump.

Tiffany had met Gorby the Fletch a few years earlier, on a field trip with her science class. The students were studying buoyancy. The assignment was to search through the junkyard to find heavy things that might float. At the end of the day, they pushed a refrigerator into the pond in the middle of the dump, and everyone cheered as it bobbed back to the surface. Tiffany still considered it the greatest field trip of her life.

The kids scooted over to the little house. Tiffany knocked on the door.

"Who is it?" sang Gorby. The kids weren't sure how to answer.

"Excuse me, Mr. . . . the Fletch?" shouted Tiffany. "We're looking for an ice cream machine."

The door creaked open a crack.

"Who sent you?" whispered Gorby. He poked his head out and looked around.

"N-n-no one sent us," explained Barney. "We just want to make some ice cream."

"Quite a lot of ice cream, actually," added Ping.

"Does this have anything to do with"—Gorby swallowed hard—"Cromulous Blotch?"

"Well, yes," admitted Tiffany. "We want to get rid of him. He's ruining ice cream for all the kids in the neighborhood. Some kids don't even like it anymore!"

"It's true," said Ping, who was taller than Gorby.

"Cromulous Blotch"—Gorby's eyes narrowed—"is a rotten fink."

"W-w-we know." Barney sighed.

"He used to come around here with stuff from the old Vandersnoot mansion," Gorby recalled fondly. "Incredible treasures—some from the 1920s!" Then Gorby's face fell, and he looked at the ground. "But he never left any of it. He'd just tease me and call me Trash Man, give me noogies, and drive away laughing." Gorby went silent and shuffled his feet.

"Someone's got to teach that brat a lesson!" growled Tiffany.

"Shhh." Gorby looked nervous. "Come. Come inside. But, please, take off your shoes. I like to keep a tidy home."

The inside of the house was immaculately clean. Gorby washed his hands in the kitchen sink while the kids made themselves comfortable in the living room, on a couch with five different-colored cushions.

The shelves were lined with knickknacks and doodads of all shapes and sizes. The walls were covered with a wide variety of paintings: antique, abstract, modern. Everything in the little house was a hodgepodge, a mix of styles that shouldn't fit together, and yet somehow they made a cozy combination.

As the kids admired the unusual decorations, Gorby poured cups of cocoa from a pot on the stove and brought them over on a tray.

"Cromulous Blotch." Gorby shook his head. "He's so angry about what he doesn't have that he's blind to what he's got." Ping raised an eyebrow as Gorby continued. "Most people are guilty of the same thing. Though they aren't nearly as horrible about it.

"Look around." Gorby spread his arms wide. "Everything in this house . . . these clothes, that couch you're sitting on . . . heck, even the mugs you're drinking from—someone just threw it all away."

Barney made a face and quietly spit the cocoa back into his cup.

Gorby pointed out the window at the junkyard. "Endless treasures. Anything you could want is out there somewhere. You could choose to look at it as 'garbage,' or you could choose to see the beauty in it." He sat in a rocking chair that had been fixed up with duct tape and old skis.

"You know what would be beautiful?" asked Tiffany. "Getting rid of Cromulous Blotch."

Gorby chuckled. "And how do you plan to do that? Cromulous won't go away so easily." He patted his knee, and Fomo jumped onto his lap.

"We're going to start our own ice cream delivery service," explained Ping.

"All the kids in the neighborhood will get their ice cream from us instead," Barney added. "We'll be a million times better than B-b-b . . ." Barney banged his fist on the table. "A million times better than Blotch."

"I like the sound of that," said Gorby.

"But we can't do anything unless we have a way to make our own ice cream," Tiffany trumpeted. She noticed that Gorby seemed nervous, so she lowered her voice and whispered. "That's why we came to you."

Gorby scratched his ear. "Well, I might have just the thing."

He pulled on his galoshes and led the kids out into the junkyard, past a broken-down school bus that was missing its roof and some sort of satellite with Chinese characters on the side.

The round little man climbed into a crane mounted on tank treads and started the engine. "Hop in."

Everyone climbed aboard, and Gorby cruised across the junkyard. He stopped in front of a metal heap and activated the crane, which swung around and dropped a large metal claw from a thick cable.

Gorby expertly operated the levers and switches to pluck out the object he was searching for. When the claw emerged from the junk pile, a big metal box was held delicately in its prongs.

"It's missing the nozzles and the handles," explained Gorby, "but this baby served up ice cream down in Cucamonga County for twenty years. Two flavor chambers, and it even does the swirl."

"Wow!" said all the kids in unison.

"And if you promise to use it to teach Cromulous Blotch a lesson, you can take it for free."

"Are you sure?" asked Ping. "According to my research, a machine like this costs hundreds of dollars."

Gorby chuckled. "I don't need the money." He gestured around at the piles of "treasure." "I'm already rich!"

The kids laughed.

Gorby's eyes darted toward the top of the mountain, and he suddenly grew serious. "Just don't tell Cromulous you got it from me."

A flatbed truck filled with junk pulled up to the dump and honked its horn for Gorby to open the gate.

"More treasure." He rubbed his hands together. "You kids sure you can get that machine back home on your own?"

It was dark outside by the time they finally wrestled the big metal box into Barney's garage. They had wrapped the machine in a tarp and pushed it through the woods, with the help of some broken skateboards wedged underneath.

Things had gone smoothly until they stopped to rest after climbing a steep hill. The machine had rolled down the other side without them, and they had only barely managed to prevent the runaway contraption from crashing into a cherry tree.

Fortunately no one got seriously hurt, but they were all pretty scratched up. And to add insult to injury, Barney had lost his second-favorite hat.

They cleared a space in the middle of the garage, between some winter sports equipment and the folding chairs Barney's family used for Thanksgiving. The back wall had a workbench area that Barney used for building his remote-controlled cars.

As they unwrapped the machine, Ping glanced over at Barney's collection of vehicles. The ice cream machine was twenty times bigger than any of them. "Do you think one of those battery-powered engines will be strong enough to carry this thing?"

"N-n-no." Barney crossed his arms. "No, I do not."

"That's okay." Tiffany found an outlet and plugged in the machine with an extension cord. "We'll make the ice cream here and use the cars to deliver it, one cone at a time." Fomo grabbed a mouthful of tarp and thrashed it back and forth.

Ping opened her laptop and did a quick search. "Ice cream supplies are surprisingly cheap in bulk."

They ordered a ten-pound box of powdered mix and

144 cones—it was called a *gross* (which doesn't make any sense, because ice cream cones are delicious). They agreed to use their allowance money and split the cost.

By the time the package arrived three days later, they had cleaned out the machine and found suitable replacements for the missing parts.

Tiffany stirred some powder and water together, poured the liquid into the top of the machine, and turned it on. The mixers inside rumbled to life. She blew her bangs out of her eyes. "I sure hope this works."

"How will we know when it's done?" Barney poked at the control panel.

"When the light turns green, it's ready." Ping pointed to a small red indicator light.

"How long is that gonna take?" Barney slumped in his chair.

It took two hours and fifteen minutes (but it felt like forever).

Scientifically speaking, no one knows exactly how much ice cream a human being can eat before getting sick, but that afternoon, Ping, Tiffany, and Barney ate way too much. They filled bowl after bowl. They held their mouths open directly under the nozzles.

Eventually, they all collapsed onto the ground, clutching their stomachs while their guts made gurgling noises. Even Fomo ate enough to get a bellyache.

"I'll never eat ice cream again." Tiffany burped.

"We wasted half the powder," moaned Ping.

Barney raised his arm. "Maybe I'll just have one more spoonful," he said, but he couldn't get up from the floor.

CROMULOUS HAD DECIDED to take the day off from delivering ice cream in order to sleep in. He sometimes slept twenty hours a day.

When he woke up that evening, he microwaved himself a sweet potato, dipped it in a bowl full of tears, and put on an abstract jazz record.

Cromulous hated music, but he loved abstract jazz. It had no melody you could hum along to, no rhythm you could tap your foot to. One track sounded like a goose in a washing machine; another sounded like a robot falling down a staircase.

For most people, abstract jazz sounded like noises that had been made by accident. But that's why Cromulous enjoyed it so very much. It made him feel sophisticated, unlike that juvenile tune that jangled incessantly from his truck. He hated that stupid weasel song, but he had to admit—it drove the children wild with desire for ice cream.

After Cromulous had eaten and enjoyed a nonmusical interlude, he thought about new and exciting ways to make ice cream as unpleasant as possible.

He had recently abandoned a chili-pepper dip after accidentally getting some of the spicy powder in his eyes. He opened a beat-up notebook and made a sketch of a firecracker tucked inside an ice cream cone. He drew a diagram of a boxing glove that would shoot out and punch his customers right in the belly.

Something about children made him furious. Even more irritated and depressed than usual. Somehow, their suffering brought him relief.

A trained psychologist might suggest that Cromulous recognized his own crippling fears of powerlessness in the most helpless members of society and thus sought to mask his insecurities by intimidating children.

An untrained psychologist would simply label him a villainous wretch.

DOWN IN THE Dells the following afternoon, Ping was showing Barney the souped-up radio controller that would allow him to drive his car around the whole neighborhood. His old controller had a range of only fifty feet, but Ping had added a huge antenna to the car and boosted the radio signal enough to reach half a mile away. She had also outfitted the car with a tiny camera. It's amazing what you can learn on the internet.

Barney adjusted his third-favorite hat and slipped on a pair of VR goggles. "I can't see anything!"

"You've got to turn them on first." Ping flipped a switch, and the video screen in the goggles blinked on. It was a live video feed from the front of the car.

Barney tentatively pressed the control toggle and

watched the car move forward, as if he were sitting in the driver's seat. "Whoa."

Tiffany brushed her bangs from her eyes and pressed the button on the garage door opener. "Give it a whirl around the block," she suggested loudly.

Barney carefully maneuvered the car out of the garage and into the street. He quickly familiarized himself with the controls. Then he set the engine to full throttle, and the car peeled out down the road.

Asphalt and bushes whizzed by in the video feed. He did a 720-degree spin and made himself dizzy. The little car zoomed across the neighborhood, through the streets, and onto sidewalks, hopping over storm drains and weaving through hedgerows. Barney was sweating with excitement by the time he pulled the car back into the garage, and it skidded to a stop at his feet.

He lifted the goggles and smiled at Ping. "Th-th-that was awesome!"

Ping blushed.

"Let's deliver some ice cream!" roared Tiffany. Fomo jumped into her arms, barking and licking her face. They all agreed that their very first delivery should go to Yolanda Sinclair. It was important to restore the little girl's faith in ice cream.

Tiffany loaded a cone and nestled it into the passenger seat of the remote-controlled car. "Drive carefully," she said to Barney. "It's not super secure."

Barney directed the car out of the garage and down the
street, with the ice cream cone wobbling. Ping tracked the
location on her computer. It was tricky for Barney to keep
directions straight as he drove through the circular streets
of the neighborhood, so Ping acted as a navigator.

"Make a left," she said. The car turned. "No, your other left." The car swerved back around, nearly toppling the ice cream cone.

"Careful!" shouted Tiffany as she watched the video feed on Ping's laptop.

"S-s-sorry," muttered Barney.

Yolanda Sinclair was juggling a soccer ball in her living room when she noticed something strange moving in circles at the bottom of her driveway. She peeked out the door to get a better look. It was a little car with huge antennas and an ice cream sitting shotgun.

At first, she worried it was a trick. She could still feel the cold squish of ice cream in her shorts. She poked her head out, looked around, and decided to investigate.

"Here she comes!" said Barney.

Tiffany and Ping smiled and high-fived as they watched the video feed.

But suddenly, Yolanda's expression changed from curiosity to fear. She spun around, sprinted up the stairs, and slammed the door shut behind her.

"What happened?" wondered Tiffany.

Then they heard it. The ice cream truck song jingling in the distance. Cromulous was approaching, and Yolanda had been spooked.

When Barney turned the car around to retreat, the ice cream cone fell out and went splat in the street.

"We've got to figure out a more efficient delivery method," noted Ping.

Fomo barked and picked up what looked like a giant plastic ice cream scoop on a lacrosse stick.

"Not now," scolded Tiffany.

Fomo whined insistently.

"What is that thing anyway?" asked Ping.

"It's a ball launcher. I use it to help Fomo train for *K9 Commando*. It's our favorite TV show, and we're gonna win it someday."

Fomo wagged his tail. Tiffany loaded the launcher with a ball, and the little dog dashed out of the garage just as the remote-controlled car pulled in.

"Actually, this might be exactly what we need. Watch." Tiffany followed Fomo outside, reared back, and flung the stick forward as hard as she could. The ball soared high into the air. Barney squinted as it disappeared into the light of the sun and went hurtling to the earth at the far end of the street, in the exact spot where Fomo was waiting to catch it.

CHOMP.

The dog raced back to Tiffany, dropped the ball at her feet, then dashed back down the block again, barking his little head off and wagging his tail.

"He's got a lot of energy." Tiffany launched the ball again.

"I don't get it." Barney scratched his head. "What does this have to do w-w-with ice cream?"

"It's a catapult!" Ping exclaimed.

"A Cone-A-Pult," Tiffany said.

"ARE YOU SURE about this?" Barney stood in the driveway and tried not to move, his head in the center of a target drawn in chalk on the garage door.

Across the street, Tiffany fiddled with the angle of the Cone-A-Pult. Ping had rigged up Fomo's ball launcher to a remote-controlled launching mechanism. Tiffany closed one eye and gingerly positioned an ice cream cone into the scoop.

"Ready?" asked Ping.

"I think so," said Tiffany.

"Ready?" called Ping to Barney.

"N-n-not really."

She pressed the release button.

WHOOSH!

The arm of the Cone-A-Pult flung forward. The ice cream soared into the sky. Barney watched the creamy glob flying toward his face and closed his eyes.

WHAM!

Barney's head snapped back and hit the garage door. His whole face was covered with ice cream. The cone smashed on his forehead and stuck there like the horn of a unicorn. He groaned.

Tiffany observed the scene from across the street. "Maybe a little less force?"

Ping hit some buttons on the computer, which adjusted

the tension of the bungee cords that powered the Cone-A-Pult.

Tiffany reloaded the launcher and crossed her fingers. Barney blew bits of sugar cone from his nostrils.

"Try to catch it with your hands this time," suggested Tiffany.

Ping triggered the release and sent another cone flying.

Barney scrambled to the left, scrambled to the right, and held out his hands to catch the ice cream, but it slipped through his fingers and dropped to the pavement with a *SPLAT*.

After several more attempts, the driveway was littered with shattered ice cream cones.

"We're wasting perfectly good ice cream here!" squawked Tiffany. "Maybe the Cone-A-Pult was a bad idea."

"Hang on," said Ping. "Maybe not." She ran to her house and came back with a pile of napkins and a spool of string.

"What's all that for?" asked Tiffany.

Ping folded a napkin into triangles and threaded the string through the corners of the packet. Then she tied the string around an ice cream cone and loaded it into the launcher.

"One more time!" called Ping to Barney.

Barney was letting Fomo lick his face and fingers clean. He stood and reassumed his position in the center of the target.

The girls sent another cone soaring. Barney flinched as the ice cream flew through the air. But this time, when the cone reached the apex of its flight, the napkin packet unfolded into a parachute.

The ice cream wafted gently toward the earth and landed safely in Barney's outstretched hand (instead of hurtling into his face).

"Wow!" said Barney. He took a big bite of ice cream and detached the napkin to wipe his mouth.

Tiffany hugged Ping. "You did it!"

"We did it!" Ping said.

They mounted the Cone-A-Pult to Barney's biggest remote-controlled car and decided to call the vehicle the Zippity-Flipper. Then they drew up advertisements for their new ice cream delivery service, which they called Lickety-Split.

Between Ping's posts online, Barney's flyers, and Tiffany shouting at the top of her lungs, word spread quickly to all the kids in the neighborhood.

THAT NIGHT, CROMULOUS Blotch couldn't sleep, so he decided to go for a midnight drive. He cruised around the Dells, swerving onto the wrong side of the street to avoid getting sprayed by the lawn sprinklers. It was an odd-numbered day, so all the odd-numbered houses were watering their grass that night.

As he aimlessly spiraled through the neighborhood, he began to notice strange little posters tacked to lampposts and telephone poles. He stopped his truck and got out to take a closer look. The posters featured a caricature of a sweaty man in a hat and cape. There was a big red X drawn over him.

When Cromulous realized the drawing was of him, he

was both furious and flattered. He ripped the poster off the pole. It said LICKETY-SPLIT ICE CREAM DELIVERY SERVICE. SPEEDY QUICK! NO GROSS TOPPINGS! ORDER ONLINE!

"They think they can get rid of me so easily!" fumed Cromulous. "Don't they realize"—he paused and glanced around the dark, empty streets—"I have nowhere else to go?"

ON THEIR FIRST day in business, Lickety-Split was flooded with orders. Barney, Ping, and Tiffany quickly made back the money they had spent on supplies. It was hard work, but the plan seemed to be a success.

Their second day in business started out the same as the first.

Inside the garage, Barney controlled the Zippity-Flipper. Ping read the orders from her computer and mapped the routes, while Tiffany prepared the ice cream cones and loaded the Cone-A-Pult. Fomo stood guard in the driveway, keeping an eye out for Cromulous Blotch.

"Order for a chocolate cone at 3 Pecan Valley Drive." Ping sat hunched over her laptop, triangulating coordinates on the map. Her sparkly painted fingernails tap-danced across the keyboard.

"Coming right up!" Tiffany prepared the cone and folded a napkin parachute. Then she knelt and tucked the ice cream into the launcher on top of the radio-controlled car. "Order ready!" She clanged the big bell she kept by the prep table.

Barney covered his ears. "I can hear you loud and clear," he sputtered. "I-I-I don't think we need the bell."

Tiffany lifted the garage door a crack, and the Zippity-Flipper whipped out into the street.

Barney watched the bushes fly by in his video goggles. "One ch-ch-ch . . . One chocolate ice cream cone, coming right up."

"Make a left," advised Ping as she tracked the location beacon blinking on-screen.

Soon the Zippity-Flipper pulled up in front of 3 Pecan Valley Drive, where Fergus Flanagan was waiting on his doorstep.

"Ready for launch," said Barney.

Tiffany checked the video feed. "Fifty degrees up, forty percent power."

Ping input the trajectory into the computer, and the radio-controlled mechanism on the Zippity-Flipper responded. She hit ENTER to release the Cone-A-Pult.

A waffled blur flew past the camera and soared into the air.

Fergus Flanagan lifted his arms above his head, and the ice cream cone parachuted from the sky into his waiting hands. He smiled, did the floss dance, and waved to the camera.

Ping and Tiffany waved too (even though Fergus couldn't see them). Barney turned the car around to head back to the garage.

"Th-th-that's weird," said Barney.

"What's wrong?" asked Tiffany.

"It's not responding." He jiggled the joystick and shook the controller.

Tiffany and Ping yelped as they watched the video feed. The camera swung wildly and lifted into the air. The shot steadied and turned to reveal the sweaty, twisted face of a man grinning like a goat who has eaten too many cans.

Cromulous Blotch had snuck up behind the Zippity-Flipper and snatched it from the ground. The remote-controlled wheels of the vehicle spun helplessly.

Barney ripped off his goggles and let out a yelp.

Tiffany froze.

Ping banged her head on her keyboard.

Outside, Fomo started barking and scratching at the garage door.

"Shhh!" Barney jumped from his chair. "You'll give us away!" He lifted the door just enough for Fomo to wriggle underneath, but the dog wouldn't stop barking.

"Fomo," Ping whispered. "Shut. Up."

Fomo scratched at the door some more, now from inside the garage, and continued barking his little head off.

"T-t-t-tell him to stop." Barney looked worried. "Cromulous will find us!"

"Fomo, be quiet!" Tiffany shouted so loud that it shook the walls of the garage.

The dog stopped barking. Instead, he pawed at the door, whimpering softly.

Ping blinked and stood up. "You know what? Fomo's right."

"Huh?" Barney scrunched his face.

"We've got to go out there," said Ping. "We've got to save the Zippity-Flipper." She hit the garage door opener, and Fomo bolted out into the street.

"Have you gone cuckoo-bananapants?" asked Tiffany.

"We worked too hard to give up this easily." Ping ran outside.

Barney looked at Tiffany with his mouth hanging open.

"I guess we better go get our car back," said Tiffany.

Barney grumbled and tossed his third-favorite hat on the table. "All right, but I'm not losing another hat."

CROMULOUS BLOTCH EXAMINED the Zippity-Flipper with grudging admiration.

As always, "Pop Goes the Weasel" clanged from the speakers on his truck, drilling into his brain. The three-second pause after each repetition was his only relief.

"Hey!" yelled Ping, louder than Tiffany had ever heard her speak before. "That's ours. Give it back!"

Fomo growled.

"Oh my, I didn't realize!" Cromulous feigned dismay. "Why, certainly, you are right. I must have been confused."

He carefully placed the Zippity-Flipper on the pavement, forced a big fake smile, then lifted his pointy boot to stomp it to bits.

Luckily, Barney had brought the controller with him, and he flicked the joystick just in time to scoot the car forward and keep it from getting crushed.

When Cromulous stomped and missed unexpectedly, he stumbled forward like a toppling pile of dishes. He managed to catch himself in an awkward lunge and held the pose dramatically as if that's what he had meant to do all along.

"So you think you can deliver ice cream for yourselves,"

sneered Cromulous. "Is that right, *chil-dren*?" He accentuated each syllable of "children" in that snotty way adults tend to do when they want the word to sound like an insult.

"Right," said Tiffany.

"Right," said Ping.

"R-r-right," said Barney.

"Ha!" Cromulous swooshed his cape. "Your tiny catapult car can't stop me. You'll run out of ice cream! You'll run out of money! You'll get bored and give up, and I'll still be here with a *real* ice cream truck."

Cromulous smacked the side of his truck, and the muffler fell off.

"Why don't you go back to playing your baby games and leave the ice cream delivery to a grown-up?" hissed Cromulous. "Or else."

Barney gulped, and Tiffany squeezed his hand.

Pleased with himself, Cromulous swooshed his cape again, for dramatic effect, and marched toward the kids with his chin tilted up.

"You're just scared," Ping said suddenly, surprising herself.

"Excuse me, piglet?" Cromulous stopped short and glared at Ping.

"You're scared of being outsmarted by a bunch of kids." Ping put her hands on her hips and stood as tall as she could.

"What?!" He clenched his jaw. "Cromulous Blotch is never scared!"

"Race us for it, then," shouted Tiffany.

"Yeah," added Barney, peeking his head out from behind his two taller friends.

"What kind of race?" Cromulous absent-mindedly fondled the tear vial in his pocket.

"An ice cream delivery race," said Ping, catching on.

Tiffany nodded. "If you win, we'll let you smash the Zippity-Flipper, and we'll tell all the kids in the neighborhood they have to get ice cream from you every day. No matter how mean you are."

"I like the sound of that," cooed Cromulous, rubbing his hands together.

Barney stepped out from behind the girls. "But if we win—"

"Which you won't," objected Cromulous.

"*When* we win," Barney continued, "you have to leave us alone and n-n-never set foot in this neighborhood again."

Cromulous let out a gross little giggle that made the hair on the back of Ping's neck stand up. "I accept your silly wager." He smoothed his cape and adjusted his floppy hat. "You *chil-dren* don't stand a chance."

EVERY KID IN the neighborhood came out to watch the race. The adults were at work or on the internet or running errands. The only grown-up in attendance was Old Man Smithereens, who had gone deaf when the dynamite factory exploded. He had agreed to act as an impartial judge.

The looping jangle of the ice cream truck song grew

louder in the distance. The off-key tune was like nails on a chalkboard. Cromulous wore plugs to try and block out the music. The kids in the crowd covered their ears with their hands and cringed. Old Man Smithereens heard nothing at all.

The truck crested the hill on Sycamore Street, stopped, and revved its wheezing engine. The big plastic ice cream cone on top was spattered with dirt and grime. At the wheel, Cromulous hunched forward with a sinister grin. There were orange flecks of sweet potato stuck in his teeth.

The Zippity-Flipper wheeled into position, a choco-vanilla swirl loaded and ready for delivery. It looked like a toy version of the growling truck beside it.

"Okay," said Old Man Smithereens, "first one to deliver ten ice cream cones wins." He glanced over at the open garage where Ping, Barney, and Tiffany waited in position. "Everybody ready?"

The kids in the garage nodded.

The old man turned to Cromulous. "Ready?"

"Shut up and say 'Go,'" Cromulous sneered.

"Set . . ."

"Ugh, sooo dramatic!"

"Go!"

The Zippity-Flipper raced off toward its first scheduled delivery before Cromulous had even had a chance to shift his truck into gear.

He stalled out, restarted the engine, and managed to roll down the hill backward, away from the starting line.

Then he pressed the gas pedal to the floor, and the tires screeched.

"I scream, you scream, we all scream for ice cream!" shouted Cromulous.

The truck rumbled down the street, and the crowd of children scattered. Cromulous skidded to a stop and leapt out to catch Jimmy Fitz before he could flee.

"What kind of ice cream do you want, you little freak?" He dragged the squirming boy by his ear toward the truck.

"I don't want any!" cried Jimmy.

Cromulous twisted his ear and plucked the tear vial from his pocket. "Sure you do, crybaby. Why don't you cry about it?"

He pressed the vial to Jimmy's cheek, and Jimmy proceeded to cry about it.

"Awww . . ." Cromulous dipped two vanilla cones in garlic powder, then turned them sideways and twisted them against Jimmy's head. "That should make you feel better."

The ice cream filled Jimmy's ears, and the cones stuck in place.

"Don't feel bad; you've never looked better." Cromulous stepped back to admire his work. "That's two for me already!" he announced giddily.

But as he strutted back to his truck, the Zippity-Flipper whizzed past and swept his legs out from under him.

GAHHH!

Cromulous landed flat on his back and let out a squeaky fart. His cape fluttered gently over his head. When he heard the kids laughing at him, he struggled to his feet as quickly as he could. He pulled the cape from his face, but the giggling onlookers had already hidden themselves from sight and the Zippity-Flipper was gone.

Cromulous growled, staring at the glass vial that lay shattered on the pavement.

"Jangus!" He checked to see that his backup vial was still safely tucked into his breast pocket. "Stupid *chil-dren*—"

Out of the corner of his eye, Cromulous spotted a chocolate-covered trucker cap poking out from behind a hedge.

Ice cream was still swirling from the nozzle as he snuck out of the truck with a hastily prepared cone. He tiptoed through the grass to ambush his prey.

"Want some ice cream, snot wad?" Cromulous leapt over the hedge. "Here it is!"

That's when the pathetic wretch discovered he'd been tricked. There was no kid—just a hat propped up on a stick.

"Where are all the filthy *chil-dren*? This place is normally crawling with them!"

THE LICKETY-SPLIT GANG was two steps ahead of the crusty old ice cream jerk. They'd set booby traps to distract Cromulous and slow him down. They'd also told all the kids in the neighborhood to hide inside.

Their instructions were simple: submit your order on the website, pay two dollars, wait for a confirmation, and open the door only after the Zippity-Flipper is visible in front of your house.

And that's exactly what Yolanda Sinclair had planned to do.

She crouched by her window, peeking through the curtains, scared out of her jelly shoes that Cromulous might spot her. She waited, silent and still, until she saw the Zippity-Flipper pull up.

"Ice cream! Hooray!" She unlocked the door and skipped outside.

A cone launched high into the air. Yolanda stood at the top of the stairs and watched with awe as the napkin parachute neatly unfurled. The cone gracefully drifted from the sky toward her outstretched arms.

But at the last moment, a sweaty hand swatted the delicious treat to the ground.

WHACK!

"Oops." Cromulous smiled. "Were you looking for one of these?" He reached behind his back and neatly pressed an upside-down ice cream cone on top of Yolanda's head. "What's that? You want some more?" He revealed three more cones and arranged them like a crown on the little girl's noggin.

Ice cream ran down her face. Cromulous's ears flushed red with excitement.

"Are you crying?" He reached for his vial.

"No!" yelled Yolanda, crying.

Cromulous tried to position the tube under her eye, but

her face was covered in ice cream. Yolanda scrunched her nose and snorted, spraying snot into the vial and all over his hand.

"Ew, gross!" he said.

She escaped to the backyard and locked the gate behind her.

"You brat!" Cromulous shook the snot from his hand and threw the sullied vial to the grass. "Doesn't matter," he called after her, wiping his hands on his cape.

"That's six for me!" he shouted at the Zippity-Flipper as it whizzed away. "You hear that?"

Cromulous ran back to his truck, which was parked on the sidewalk.

VROOOM!

The truck barreled through the streets at top speed. Cromulous had given up on searching for customers; he was hunting for the remote-controlled car. When he spotted the Zippity-Flipper making a delivery at the far end of the street, he revved the engine and headed straight for it.

"He found us!" Barney jumped out of his chair and pulled the controller tight to his chest. "Look!" Barney swiveled the car 180 degrees and sped off in reverse so the girls could see Cromulous's truck in the video feed.

"Oh no!" Tiffany huddled over Ping's computer to get a better look.

Barney tried his best to flee, but the truck's churning black wheels got bigger and bigger, closer and closer to the camera mounted on the Zippity-Flipper.

Cromulous's truck had a full-size diesel engine. Even in its neglected state, it was still much faster than a battery-powered toy car.

"Okay." Barney bit his lip. "His truck might be bigger and faster. B-b-but can it do this?"

The video feed went black.

Ping and Tiffany gasped.

Then, somehow, the screen flickered back to life. The street was empty. Cromulous and his truck had disappeared.

"What happened?" Tiffany tapped on the screen and leaned forward, confused.

"He stopped." Ping smiled.

Barney swiveled the joystick. The camera spun to face the other direction.

On-screen, they watched the back of the ice cream truck speeding away. It had passed right over the top of the Zippity-Flipper.

Cromulous turned around and craned his neck to see the wreckage of the meddlesome toy crushed beneath his wheels. But when he spotted the Zippity-Flipper still intact on the street behind him, he realized he'd been tricked. He also realized he should probably watch where he was going . . .

The speeding truck bounced over a curb and onto a lawn. Cromulous stomped on the brakes and jerked the wheel hard to avoid plowing into a house. The truck swerved and tipped sideways onto two tires.

Cromulous clung to the steering wheel, his skinny legs dangling out of the truck where the door was missing. His hands were so sweaty, he almost slipped out onto the pavement. Somehow, he managed to climb back in and regain control. But as the truck slammed down onto four wheels, one of the tires burst. The truck went into a tailspin. Sparks flew from the metal grinding against the pavement. Cromulous shrieked as the truck skidded across the street, straight into a huge cherry tree.

SMASH!

The deep-rooted tree stopped the truck dead in its tracks, and ripe cherries rained onto the roof. Meanwhile, Cromulous went flying face-first through the windshield, shattering the glass with his pointy nose and landing in a heap ten feet away. (He *really* should have been wearing a seat belt.)

The wheels of the truck kept spinning, and black smoke billowed from the engine as Cromulous lay on the ground, discombobulated and groaning.

Old Man Smithereens declared the Lickety-Split team the winners.

"We did it!" bellowed Tiffany. Fomo howled.

Ping kissed Barney on the cheek, and his face turned neon pink.

The other kids cheered and lifted the trio onto their shoulders.

Cromulous Blotch slowly rose to his feet to slink away. Until Yolanda Sinclair sauntered over and kicked him in the shin as hard as she could. He grunted with pain and crumpled to the ground. Yolanda raised her fists above her head and let out a savage battle cry.

THE LICKETY-SPLIT ICE cream delivery service was a runaway success. But that meant Tiffany, Barney, and Ping spent all their time working while the other kids in the neighborhood got to enjoy the summer.

No one had to hide in their houses after Cromulous was defeated. Kids played basketball and hopscotch in the street. They played capture the flag and had water balloon fights.

Tiffany, Barney, and Ping wanted to join in on the fun.

They decided that what the neighborhood really needed was someone nice and kind who was old enough to drive a real truck and wanted to work in the ice cream delivery business.

When they proposed the idea to Gorby the Fletch, he jumped into the air and clicked his heels. "Of course I'll do it!"

The Lickety-Split team gave Gorby all the money they had earned from deliveries, and he used it to fix up an antique van with a sonorous set of sleigh bells. He painted a picture of a smiling ice cream cone on the side for decoration.

Gorby turned out to be the perfect ice cream man. He always kept his truck spick-and-span. He cleaned out the ice cream machine at least once a week. He remembered the name of every kid in the neighborhood and what their favorite flavor was. He even carried special doggy treats for Fomo.

As for Cromulous Blotch, one morning he awoke to find that his beat-up, broken-down ice cream truck had been towed to the top of the mountain and dumped in his drive-way. It was a useless wreck, but the crash had spared the ice cream cone–shaped speakers, and the horrible jingle blared at full volume.

The tune made his blood boil.

Twenty-nine notes looping over and over, on and on and on and on.

He was desperate to stop the music, but when he climbed into the truck, he discovered that the battery was dead. Yet somehow the jingle kept playing.

Cromulous found a ladder and climbed onto the roof of the truck. He bashed the rusted speakers with a wrench, but "Pop Goes the Weasel" *still* kept playing.

He tried to rip the speakers off. Knees bent, back jerking, he tugged and tugged until his hands started to hurt. He ground his teeth. Not only could he hear the jingle, but he could feel it vibrating in his bones. One last yank and—THWUCK!—the speakers tore loose.

Cromulous tumbled backward, somersaulting from the roof of the truck and landing with a crunch on the pavement below. He saw stars and almost passed out, but he roused himself back to anger when he realized the song continued to wail from the speakers in his hands.

He climbed to his feet and screamed. He stomped the speakers with his pointy boots. He smashed and crashed and crushed them into dust under his heels.

But somehow, the jingle jangled on.

He lit the truck on fire.

At first, the dancing flames were a sweet relief—beautiful and hypnotic. But when the gas tank ignited, the explosion knocked Cromulous off his feet and sent him flying into the bushes.

When he woke up, his eyebrows were missing, and the truck had been reduced to a pile of ash. But when the ringing in his ears died down, he realized he could still hear that blasted song.

Every day for the rest of his life, Cromulous heard the same jingle drone on and on and on. He wasn't sure if he was the only one who could hear it, because there was never anyone else around to ask.

V

THE ICE CREAM MACHINE

(the one with the sorcerer's assistant)

illustrated by

NICOLE MILES

The sorcerer's assistant trudged up the steep cobblestone path beside the castle, dragging two buckets heavy with water. His scrawny freckled arms ached. His tattered robe was soggy from accidental sloshing. The daily task of lugging water from the well was Martin's most dreaded chore, and nothing like the kind of work he had imagined when he had first been hired by the legendary sorcerer.

Socor the Sorcerer's knowledge of magic was celebrated far beyond the white marble walls of the hilltop kingdom. He was renowned for his mastery of medicinal herbs, his deep understanding of the cycles of the weather, and, of course, his ability to perform miraculous feats.

Traditionally, a sorcerer's apprentice is trained in the mysterious rites and rituals of sorcery. But Martin was not the sorcerer's *apprentice*; he was the sorcerer's *assistant*, which meant his responsibilities were limited to running errands and taking notes. A sorcerer's *apprentice* is a highly respected position in the community. But a sorcerer's *assistant*? Not so much.

Martin stumbled through the castle square and set down the buckets to rest his weary hands. He had spilled so much water on his walk from the well that the buckets were only half-full.

"Hey, Marty, you learn any magic yet?" the blacksmith called from his stall. He was a square, hairy beast of a man who made his living bending metal into horseshoes and shields. His arms were thicker than Martin's legs.

Martin offered a weak smile, hoisted the buckets with a grunt, and continued on his way up the hill to the sorcerer's tower.

"Sorcerer!" called a little girl holding a kitten.

"No, no," said the little girl's mother. "That's not the sorcerer; that's his water boy."

"I'm his *assistant*!" Martin called over his shoulder. "I do lots of other things besides fetch water." He stumbled on a cobblestone. Water splashed from the buckets and slapped the ground.

"I should hope so . . ." The woman scoffed.

Martin frowned and quickened his pace. Everyone poked fun at the sorcerer's assistant. Even if their own job was far worse than his.

"Oy! Cast me a spell to clean this mess!" a washwoman

snickered as Martin approached the tower. She was busy scrubbing poo stains from chamber pots.

The washwoman laughed. The seven children gathered at her feet laughed too. Even Martin pretended to laugh along as he collected the sack of mail from the sorcerer's doorstep and stepped inside the tower.

But when the heavy wooden door slammed shut behind him, he stopped laughing and whimpered instead.

SOCOR'S TOWER WAS the tallest building in the kingdom. There were 347 steps from the bottom to the top. A long journey, especially when hoisting a sack stuffed with scrolls and two buckets of water (even if they're only half-full).

Martin spiraled up the narrow stairway. Around and around. He climbed slowly and focused on his footing, trying not to spill another drop.

After two hundred steps, he took a break to admire the view. It was autumn, and the forests surrounding the kingdom were rich with orange, red, and yellow leaves. Busy farmers tended the fields beyond the castle walls. Merchants gathered in the bustling market square.

Martin took out his sketchbook and began to doodle. At first, he simply sketched the scene below. But as always, his drawings soon drifted to famous escapades from Socor's illustrious past.

He drew a picture of the sorcerer defeating the dreaded Feltuvian sky pirates. He drew another of Socor banishing

the ravenous gobblemonsters. He drew an uncanny like-ness of Ximena, the legendary enchantress and Socor's long-lost love. In the drawings, Martin was right there by Socor's side, assisting him. But in reality, the adventures that had earned the sorcerer his renown had happened long before Martin was ever born.

The sorcerer! Martin had lost track of time again. He closed the book and tucked it away in his robe. Socor would be waiting for him upstairs.

Martin hurried to the top of the tower, leaving a trail of puddles dripping down the steps behind him.

By the time he reached the door of the sorcerer's chambers, his neck was wet with sweat. One might think that lugging heavy buckets up 347 steps every day would make the sorcerer's assistant hearty and strong, but somehow the task never seemed to get any easier for poor Martin. He only hoped that Socor wouldn't ask him to fetch any herbs from the garden, moss from the forest, or mushrooms from the bog that day, which would mean additional trips up and down the stairs.

Martin knocked on the gnarled mahogany door and admired the intricate designs carved in the wood.

There was no answer, which was odd. The sorcerer's chambers were not large, and Socor always answered right away. "Enter, my boy! Good morning!" he would say. He was remarkably chipper for such an old man.

Socor had protected the hilltop kingdom since before the great white castle was built. He had counseled five kings and six queens and seen the passing of the red comet four times. It seemed unlikely he would ever die.

But it suddenly dawned on Martin that the sorcerer would have to die someday, just like anyone, and that when he did, it would likely be his loyal assistant who discovered the rotting, dead body. Martin gagged.

"Socor!" he shouted. "Do you need help?" There was no answer.

Martin shivered with fear.

What would the hilltop kingdom do without a sorcerer? Martin often dreamed of filling the position himself, but unfortunately, he simply didn't have "it": that elusive quality that makes some people magic. "It" is exceedingly rare. Socor had been searching for someone with "it" for a very long time. It was important that he train a successor and pass down his knowledge to the next generation. But a worthy apprentice must have "it," and Martin most certainly did not. He wasn't even really sure what "it" was. He had once tried a little too hard to find "it" and had pulled a groin muscle in the process.

Everyone in the village was understandably surprised when Socor hired the boy to work as his assistant. Most of all, Martin himself. But the sorcerer recognized the boy's skill with a quill and his kind heart. Plus, he needed a helping hand in his old age.

So Martin scrunched his eyes shut—ready to help, though a bit reluctant—turned the knob of the door, and pushed it open.

"Socor?" Martin opened one eye and glanced around the room.

The sorcerer's study looked the same as it always did. Scrolls and folios were spilled over every surface. There was a comfy leather chair by the fireplace, a small wooden desk with a stool, a big black trunk, an enormous griffin-skin rug, an iron chandelier, and shelves full of jars containing

rare natural specimens. But the sorcerer himself was nowhere to be found.

MARTIN HAD NEVER been in the study alone before. It was eerily quiet and surprisingly cold. He had never seen the hearth without a fire. The old man kept a small blaze lit at all times, yet he never asked Martin to fetch any firewood.

"Huh," Martin said aloud, his hands on his hips. He spun slowly, examining the room, then stopped when he noticed something hanging from the door, which had swung closed behind him. It was a piece of parchment.

MARTIN, it said in the sorcerer's nearly illegible scrawl.

Penmanship was not Socor's strong suit, and Martin was one of the few people who could decipher his handwriting. He plucked the parchment from the door and read the letter on the other side. It was not a long one.

Gone to Kookarakala.
Hope to return before harvest celebration.
Water in the cauldron if you're hungry.
Excelsior!

— S the S

Martin sat on the stool by the desk, folded the letter, and set it aside.

At least he's not dead, he thought as he opened the logbook to record the measurements of the day.

This was one of Martin's main responsibilities as the sorcerer's assistant, and easily his favorite. It didn't require any strenuous physical activity. Unlike collecting falcon eggs or catching toads.

He withdrew the quill from the inkwell and wrote the day's date with elegant, looping strokes. Martin had excellent penmanship. No matter how clumsy or daft or lazy the other villagers might have considered him, no one could argue: The boy had beautiful handwriting. Even Socor said so.

Martin took a moment to admire his own script before turning to a collection of technical instruments that hung in one of the three windows. The devices had been designed and built by the sorcerer himself: a thermoscope (to measure temperature), a barometer (to measure atmospheric pressure), a wind wheel (to measure wind direction and speed), and a moisture gauge (to measure the humidity of the air). Socor had taught Martin how to operate them all.

But just as Martin was about to record the first measurement in the logbook, something about Socor's letter struck him as odd.

"Water in the cauldron if you're hungry?"

He put down his quill and unfolded the letter to read it again. "Is that some kind of joke?"

He stood and crossed the room to the fireplace to peek inside the cauldron. It was bone dry. Normally, it was full of delicious stew.

Though now that Martin thought about it, he wasn't sure where the meat or greens or onions or potatoes in the stew came from . . . He was never asked to fetch any of those ingredients. Only water. Socor would instruct him to add a few splashes throughout the day to keep the stew from getting too thick as the broth boiled. At least that's what Martin had always assumed.

A cold gust blew in through the window and fluttered Martin's robe. It was chilly in the study without a fire going. He decided to light one. He just needed to find the flint and tinder and maybe some small twigs to get it started . . . Yet, come to think of it, Martin had never seen Socor tend to his fire even though it burned constantly.

He inspected the fireplace. Maybe there was a secret stash of fire-making supplies in there somewhere. He snooped through the hearth and perused the mantel for clues.

Martin examined the ladle in the pot and gave it a sniff. It smelled like metal. He gave it a lick. It tasted like metal too. Not a good taste. He took a long sip from one of the water buckets and gargled heartily to wash the metal flavor from his mouth.

Then he turned back to consider the cauldron. He peered inside. A drop of water dribbled from his chin and landed in the bottom of the pot.

The water droplet sizzled and evaporated as if the cauldron were blazing hot.

Martin was perplexed.

He reached his hand into the pot, and the bottom felt warm. As a test, he scooped a ladleful of water from the bucket and poured it into the cauldron.

Smoke rose beneath the pot, and suddenly, flames burst forth as the fireplace roared to life.

Martin dropped the ladle and backed away until he bumped against the door.

Sorcery. He had done sorcery. He gasped.

Inside the cauldron, the small scoop of water boiled and churned. The color deepened, and a savory aroma filled the room. Martin's stomach growled.

He picked up the bucket and emptied it into the copper cauldron. The water hissed and threw off a thick column of white smoke. When Martin waved his hands to clear the air, he couldn't believe his eyes. The cauldron was filled with a roiling broth of chunky vegetables and hearty meats.

Martin clapped his hands. "Sorcery!" he cried.

He knelt in front of the hearth and warmed himself by the fire. He scooted a bit closer, leaned over, and held his head directly over the cauldron. He closed his eyes, inhaled deeply, and let out a long, satisfied sigh. The fire was so relaxing, a delightful comfort on a crisp autumn day. The stew smelled more delicious than ever—savory, sweet, and also a little bit like burning cloth.

Martin opened his eyes.

His robe had caught fire.

He frantically smacked at the flames. He hopped on one foot and tried to blow them out. Thinking better of it, he picked up the second bucket of water and poured it over his head.

The robe was no longer on fire. Instead, it was sopping wet. Considerably charred as well.

"Jangus," muttered Martin as he rubbed the singed edges

of the fabric. No matter. He wouldn't let a small mishap distract him from the fact that he had performed an act of sorcery. Finally!

"I am a sorcerer," he announced in his deepest voice.

Martin grabbed a bowl from the shelf and served himself some stew. He sat on his little stool and took a big slurp. Perhaps it was because he had made it himself for the very first time, but the stew tasted better than it ever had before.

Martin filled his belly with three bowls. He hung his robe to dry, then waddled over to the sorcerer's leather chair, figuring it was all right to make himself comfortable since Socor wasn't around. He curled up his legs, pulled the woolen blanket over his lap, and began doodling.

Not long after, his eyelids grew heavy and his sketchbook fell to the floor.

MARTIN HAD MEANT to close his eyes for only a minute, but he slept better than he had in months. The leather chair was far more comfortable than the floor of the barn, where he normally slept. Plus, it didn't reek of goat urine. Martin dozed soundly for hours.

When he blinked his eyes open, he noticed that the sun had already set. Then he noticed the open logbook on the desk.

"Oh no," Martin yelped. "The measurements!" He sprang from the chair and hunched over the logbook, staring at the empty boxes labeled with that day's date.

Temperature, pressure, wind speed, humidity . . . he hadn't recorded any of them. And now it was too late. The day was already over.

Martin flipped back through the gigantic tome, hundreds and hundreds of pages dutifully marked with measurements. Now, for the first time in who knows how long, a day had gone by without record.

He grabbed two fistfuls of his wild hair and paced around the room in his underpants until he had what felt like a brilliant idea: He would simply take the readings tomorrow, then split the difference with yesterday to fill in the blanks for today.

"Genius!" exclaimed Martin with his fist in the air. He sat at the desk, filled with determination.

He was too distracted to notice the large black bird approaching the window at top speed. So when the raven swooped into the room, it startled Martin so badly, he fell off his stool, banged his leg on the desk, and sent ink splattering across the pages of the logbook.

The raven flapped its wings and settled onto a perch that Socor had built for him next to the comfy leather chair by the fireplace.

"Why do you always have to sneak up on me like that?" scolded Martin as he blotted the spilled ink with his still-soggy robe.

"I come bearing a message from His Royal Highness," said the raven.

The bird's name was Lewis. He was King Gary's royal

messenger. Socor was quite friendly with the bird, his only regular visitor aside from Martin. The sorcerer would feed Lewis biscuit crumbs, and the bird would tell dirty jokes.

The royal raven made Martin nervous. He was never sure if Lewis simply repeated memorized phrases or if maybe he could actually speak. Nonetheless, Martin stepped forward to retrieve the scroll tied to the bird's foot.

Lewis stepped back. "Where's Socor?" he asked.

Martin paused.

The raven whistled.

"Can you talk?" asked Martin.

"Can *you* talk?" Lewis parroted back sarcastically.

Martin was determined not to let himself be outwitted by a literal birdbrain. He put on his burnt, ink-stained robe and puffed out his chest, trying to look official.

"The sorcerer has gone." He gestured around the empty room as proof.

The raven cocked its head to the side in the same way that humans sometimes do when someone says something incredibly stupid.

"The sorcerer . . . has gone," Lewis repeated.

For some reason, when the bird said it, Martin felt scared. Who would brew remedies for the sick? Who would advise the ministers of trade? Who would protect the kingdom from supernatural evil?

Martin clarified: "Not *gone* gone. Gone *out*. The sorcerer has gone out. He's gone to . . ." Martin shuffled the mountain of papers on his desk, looking for the letter that Socor had left him. A pile of documents cascaded to the floor, and the raven whistled again.

Martin frowned, dropped to his knees, and continued searching.

"Kooka...Krooka...Kockarookala!" He misremembered.

Martin looked up expectantly, but the raven had already flown away.

THE NEXT MORNING, Martin awoke feeling rested and relaxed. He had decided to spend the night in the tower. He didn't miss sleeping in the barn with the goats at all. The goats, for their part, didn't miss him either.

Martin yawned and admired the view of the sun peeking over the horizon. With such an early start, he would have plenty of time to fix his mistake from the day before. He reached up and retrieved the thermoscope from its hook outside the window.

Holding the glass cylinder in his arms, he examined the contents and counted which of the colorful liquid-filled orbs had floated to the top. Somehow, this indicated the correct temperature outside.

Martin took a moment to marvel at the genius of the sorcerer's invention. He stroked the delicate glass of the beautiful instrument. Then he shrieked and tossed it over his shoulder in a spasm of fright.

A terrifying black blur burst through the window and flew straight at his face. By the time he realized it was Lewis, it was too late. The thermoscope had shattered to the floor, and the colorful liquids spilled out. The escaping fumes from the alchemical elixirs made Martin feel woozy. He wobbled and steadied himself on the desk as the room began to spin.

The raven chirped and cawed, snooping about the room, fluttering from one place to the next.

"You again!" grumbled Martin. "What do you want now?"

"King Gary requests your presence in the royal hall," said Lewis.

Martin looked confused. "Me?"

The raven whistled.

Martin had only ever been in the presence of the king during the annual autumn harvest festival. It was one of the very few occasions when Socor descended from his tower, and it was Martin's job to help the old man down the 347 steps, and to carry his supplies, which required several trips.

It was an exhausting ordeal for Martin, but for everyone else in the hilltop kingdom, it was the most exciting event of the year. The day was filled with pumpkin heaving, corn juggling, hog races, and the king's royal tournament. The king loved his royal tournament: jousting, sword fighting, Greco-Roman wrestling . . . It was all a bit too sporty for Martin. He preferred the events of the evening.

Once the sun went down, Socor would summon the auroras: neon flashes that undulated overhead, almost like clouds of smoke made of laser light. Long streaks of glistening green, pulsing swirls of electric blue, and sparkles of violet shimmered in the sky. It was as if the heavens above were putting on a fireworks show. And that wasn't even the best part.

The best part of the harvest celebration, nearly everyone agreed, was the icy cream.

After Socor finished conducting the magnificent light show, Martin would lug a wooden tub with a metal lid out to the center of the square.

The sorcerer would invite all the children to gather around, and as he opened the spigot on the machine, strawberry icy cream would swirl from the spout. The children would giggle and fill their bowls. Then the grown-ups would line up to fill their mugs. The knights filled their gauntlets. Even the horses got a taste. And the raven.

The raven!

Martin waved the intoxicating fumes from his face and came back to his senses. Lewis was perched in the window. The chemicals from the broken thermoscope were bubbling and steaming on the floor.

"King Gary requests your presence in the royal hall," the raven repeated.

Martin examined himself in the looking glass on the mantel. "I know, I know. I heard you the first time, bird." He licked his palm, smeared his cowlick to his forehead, and wiped dried stew from the corner of his mouth. "I'm coming."

The raven flew off, and Martin stepped over the sizzling puddle of goo in the middle of the room.

"Right," Martin said to himself. "I'll clean that up later."

MARTIN WAS EXCITED to see the inside of the white marble castle, but as he approached the entryway to the royal hall, two enormous knights crossed their axes to block his path.

"None shall pass," said the first knight solemnly.

"Unless you have an appointment," added the second knight.

Martin eyed their razor-sharp battle-axes and dented armor. Knights always made him nervous, the way they clanged about and the fact that you couldn't see their eyes. He swallowed and forced a smile.

"I'm Martin."

The knights waited.

"Martin who?" asked the first knight.

"Martin of . . ." added the second knight. "Martin, the . . ."

"Martin, the . . ." Martin thought for a second. He knew the answer to this question. "Martin, the sorcerer's assistant." He smiled for real this time.

"Sorcerer?" the first knight harrumphed.

"Show us a trick, would ya?" The second knight withdrew his axe. "I love magic."

255

KIYAAA!

Without warning, an athletic figure leapt through the air and landed a powerful flying side kick. The second knight went crashing to the ground, his axe sent spinning across the floor.

"You totally let your guard down, bro!" King Gary stood triumphantly atop the knight's back and laughed. He wore a golden crown, battle armor, and a crimson cape.

"Excellent sneak attack, Your Majesty," wheezed the knight from underneath the king's feet.

The king stepped aside and greeted Martin. "You must be Socor's apprentice."

Martin bowed. "Assistant, Your Majesty."

"Awesome." The king swept into the royal hall and drew his sword. "Come on in."

The hall was decorated with rich tapestries and illuminated by huge chandeliers filled with hundreds of candles. An opulent banquet table occupied the center of the room, and a throne sat elevated on a platform beneath extravagant stained-glass windows.

As Martin followed the king inside, a knight emerged from the shadows with his sword drawn. He screamed and launched an attack, but King Gary fended him off with a flurry of thwacks and smacks. Another knight lunged forth, wielding a dagger, but the king rolled across the tabletop and planted a boot in his chest, which sent the would-be assassin reeling backward.

King Gary picked up a shield from the ground and turned just in time to stop a mace from crashing down upon his skull. He shoved the mace-wielding knight and struck the weapon from his hand with a swipe of his gleaming sword.

"Ha ha!" The king threw back his head as he laughed. "You'll have to do better than that!"

Martin was cowering under the table, trembling with fear. "Are we under attack, Your Majesty?" he squeaked.

"No! No, bro." The king sheathed his sword. "They're just keeping me on my toes. Gotta stay sharp. Ready for battle."

The king dropped to the floor and began doing push-ups. He turned his head to face Martin, who was still under the table.

"What happened to Socor?" asked the king mid-push-up.

Martin swallowed hard. "He's gone, sir. Your Majesty, sir. He's gone *out*."

The king stopped doing push-ups and popped back to his feet. He wiped off his hands and bounded up the stairs to the throne.

King Gary spun and launched himself into his seat. Immediately, a cluster of maidens, musicians, and jugglers rushed in and filled the hall with jubilation. One servant poured King Gary a goblet of wine. Another offered him a platter of chocolate and cheese.

Martin clambered out from under the table and awkwardly approached the foot of the stairs.

"Where did he go?" King Gary draped one of his legs over the side of his throne and reclined. "Socor, I mean."

"Kracka-lacka, Your Majesty, sir. Or Kookamonga?

Kocka-lock-ula? Something like that, Your Royal Highness."
Martin bowed again, though he wasn't sure why.

"Hmm. Sounds far away." The king straightened up in his chair and reached for a piece of cheese. "Socor is super old, though. Is he gonna make it back?"

Martin shrugged.

"My father used to say that Socor was already ancient when my *grand*father was born." The king laughed. "Can you imagine?"

Martin opened his mouth but said nothing.

The king examined him, looking a bit disappointed. "So are you, like, the new sorcerer now?"

"Well . . ." Martin tried to casually cover the burn hole and the ink stain on his robe. He crossed his arms over his chest and rocked back on his heels awkwardly. "I have been the sorcerer's assistant for almost seven years, and—"

"Perfect! You'll need a new robe." King Gary stood. "Get this man a new robe!" demanded the king.

A bald tailor came rushing in with an armful of garments sewn from the finest cloth. He stopped in front of Martin, considered the various fabrics, pressed swatches against the boy's face to judge the contrast with his eye color and skin tone, and selected a green one, tossing the others to the floor.

He whipped off Martin's old robe, revealing a pale, scrawny frame in yellowed Underoos. But before Martin could cover himself, the tailor pulled the new robe over his head. The bald man stepped back to admire the change in wardrobe. Then he gathered the other garments from the floor and scurried out.

Martin had never owned a robe so nice in his life. It was soft and warm. It didn't smell like onions. It had a hood. It had pockets! He held out his arms and turned in a circle.

"The harvest festival is in ten days," King Gary said as he descended from the throne to throw an arm around Martin's bony shoulders. "And as I'm sure you know"—he winked—"it is also my birthday." The king drew Martin closer. "Do you know how to conjure the celestial luminescence?"

Martin blinked.

"The dancing neon lights in the sky. The aurora! Did Socor teach you his secret?"

"I love the auroras," exclaimed a large, scary-looking knight. "My favorite is the one that goes *woo, woo, woo.*" He waved his hand through the air to illustrate.

"I like the one that goes *waaaaa, waaaaa, piti-piti-piti-piti,*" said an even bigger knight.

"I like the one that goes *ffffff-oooooooooosh,*" said the biggest knight in the room with childlike excitement on his face.

The king brightened. "And what would the harvest celebration be without icy cream?"

Everyone cheered. The knights stamped their feet with approval.

"Strawberry icy cream," the king sang dreamily. He raised his cup in salute. "Lords and ladies come from miles around just for a taste—a tradition that stretches back to my great-great-grandfather." The king turned to Martin. "And this year, the tradition continues, thanks to our new sorcerer . . ." He paused. "Say, what's your name anyway, kid?"

"Martin."

The king raised his cup again. "To Martin." He thought for a moment. "Martin . . . *the Mage.*"

Martin liked the sound of that.

"To Martin the Mage!" The knights and maidens clinked their goblets.

Martin blushed and bowed.

"Show us a trick!" cooed a maiden with wavy hair down to her ankles.

"Oh, I love magic," cried a tall maiden.

"Me too!" said a maiden with a glass eye.

The jugglers stopped juggling, and the musicians stopped playing their instruments. All eyes (including the glass one) turned to Martin the Mage and his brand-new emerald-colored robe.

Martin felt his ears grow hot.

"I'm afraid . . ." He cleared his throat. "I'm afraid I must be going now." He took a long step backward. "So many preparations to be made for the harvest festival."

"Oh, please?" said the maiden with the very long hair.

"Pretty please?" said the tall maiden.

"I'll let you touch my glass eye," said the maiden with a glass eye.

Martin took another long step backward. "Ha! I really am afraid—"

"One trick," announced the king, "before you go." He sat down and leaned back in his throne. "I insist."

Martin scanned the room, looking for help or, even better, an escape route. The maidens, the servants, and the knights drew closer with anticipation. He was surrounded. He felt a vomit-flavored burp start to bubble up in the back of his throat.

Maybe he could ask them all to follow him to the tower, where he could show them how the cauldron turned water into stew. That was the only sorcery he knew.

Or maybe he could demonstrate his excellent penmanship! Surely someone had a quill and parchment nearby.

He stretched his fingers, grasping for a better idea. He stared at his sweaty hands and suddenly remembered something his weird uncle had shown him as a child.

Martin held up two fingers on his right hand and one finger on his left. His arms were shaking with fear. He sheepishly showed his hands around the room. The audience went silent. He took a deep breath, squeezed his eyes shut, and smacked his hands together. There was now only one finger held up on his right hand and two held up on his left.

He opened one eye. "Ta-da?"

No one said a word. Martin was frozen in place.

It felt like an hour passed before the silence was broken by the king's uproarious laughter.

"Hahaha!" He slapped his knee.

The knights joined in the laughing. The maidens as well. The servants applauded, confused.

"Saving the good stuff for the festival, huh, bro?" King Gary descended from the throne again and smacked Martin so hard on the back, it knocked the wind out of him. "I love it. Now go prepare for the celebration. I can almost taste the icy cream already."

MARTIN'S NEW ROBE was soaked with sweat by the time he reached the top of the tower. He had fled up the steps in a frenzy, and now he was afraid he might puke, so he waited outside the door for the feeling to pass.

Relax, he told himself. *The harvest festival is still ten days away. The sorcerer is sure to be back before then. Socor would never miss the harvest festival. He knows how much it means to the king . . .* Martin's mind started swimming with grim visions of what King Gary might do if he were disappointed.

He shook the violent scenes from his mind and instead thought of stew. Hot, delicious stew. That would help him calm down. He'd eat a nice bowl of stew, curl up in the comfy leather chair by the fireplace, and do some relaxing doodling in his sketchbook.

Martin smiled as he entered the study and walked halfway across the room, then fell through a giant hole in the floor.

His new robe was bunched up to his armpits, and his naked legs dangled over the stone stairwell below. The chemicals from the thermoscope had burned straight through the floorboards. Martin clawed his way out of the hole and collapsed onto the rug.

He was scraped, exhausted, and starving, so when he realized that both of the water buckets were empty, he nearly cried. He shook the buckets over the cauldron, but the few drops left were only enough to coax a weak sizzle from the fireplace, which quickly fizzled.

"Son of a fish licker."

Martin harrumphed out the door with the buckets and stumbled down the 347 stairs. His legs felt like they were made of wet rope.

As he shuffled through the square on his way to the well, the last thing he wanted to hear was the washwoman calling after him.

"Look at you," she cackled, "with your fancy new robe." She set down her scrub brush and began a dainty dance. "Sitting on your bum making little scribbles must pay very well!"

Her seven children stopped playing kick the rock and began to point and laugh at Martin instead. They joined in the dainty dance.

"That boy ain't never done a hard day's work in his life!" shouted the washwoman.

Martin held up his empty buckets in protest. "I fetch water from the well every day!"

"Oh, look at *you*!" The washwoman twinkled her fingers and pranced around on her tiptoes. "Woe is me! I have to fetch water just like every other person in the village does every single day of their entire lives." She stopped dancing. "You go around with that sourpuss face, and you don't even realize how good you've got it." She went back to her scrubbing. "Well, phoocy."

Martin was speechless. The children gathered around him to tug at his robe and sing: "Sourpuss! Sourpuss!"

"Stop it!" demanded Martin. He turned to the washwoman for help, but she wouldn't look up from her work. "I will cast an evil spell on them!" he threatened.

The children stopped singing, and the oldest one giggled. "You don't know any magic."

The kids fell about laughing, and Martin stormed off to the well down the hill.

He tried to ignore them as he passed back through the square with his buckets full. He tried to ignore them as he scaled the tower step by step. He tried to ignore them as he heard their song echo through the windows of the sorcerer's study.

"Marty don't know any maaa-gic. Marty don't know any maaa-gic."

Martin pouted. He did know magic, though. It was easy!

He poured water into the cauldron, and the fire roared to life. The clear water swirled and churned and bubbled into stew: dark, chunky, hearty, delicious. But he was too angry to enjoy his meal, so he slurped through a sneer, stewing both literally and figuratively.

All he wanted was a little respect. Well, he also wanted to keep his head attached to his body, and he was afraid that might be difficult if King Gary was upset with his performance at the harvest festival.

Martin had no idea how to summon the auroras. Socor had studied for ages to master the necessary spells. Even other sorcerers were baffled by his technique. King Gary couldn't possibly expect Martin to manipulate the heavens, could he?

On the other hand, there was the icy cream. Which didn't seem nearly as complicated. The cauldron made stew, and it couldn't be easier. Martin was pretty sure he could figure out how to use the icy cream contraption too.

But first, he had to go get it.

Socor the Sorcerer's study didn't have much room for storage. At least not to the untrained eye.

Next to the comfy leather chair under the east window was an enchanted trunk, which contained the entirety of the sorcerer's archives. The trunk wasn't very large, but it served as a secret passageway to a vast hidden cavern. Martin couldn't figure out where the spooky cavern was actually located. It wasn't underneath the trunk; he knew that much for sure. He had lifted it and examined the bottom to check.

Martin hated going into the archives. It was dark, dank, and absolutely swarming with albino bats. But the icy cream contraption was stored down there somewhere. He had put it away himself the previous year after the festival. If only he could remember exactly where . . .

Socor, of course, knew the location of every item in the archives by heart. But he was too old to make the climb into the cavern, so Martin had to go instead. The sorcerer would shout directions from above while his terrified assistant searched by candlelight for some rare scroll or ancient artifact.

Martin shivered at the thought of going into the archives

without the sorcerer to guide him. He would be totally lost in the darkness. It was too creepy to think about. He shook his head.

There were still ten days left until the harvest festival. Martin decided that Socor would return in time for the celebration, and everything would turn out just fine.

MARTIN WENT BACK to his regular routine. Each morning, he fetched water from the well and collected the sacks of scrolls that arrived for Socor. He recorded measurements from the meteorological instruments and made stew and doodled to pass the time. He moved the griffin-skin rug to cover the hole in the floor and repaired the thermoscope to working condition (more or less). He restocked the supply of spiderwebs, polished the divination orbs, and organized the mountains of mail that had arrived for Socor in his absence.

Nine days passed with no sign from the sorcerer. This made Martin nervous. However, he hadn't heard from King Gary either, so maybe things really would turn out just fine. He figured Socor must have been in touch with the king directly. After all, the harvest festival was the very next day, and surely if Martin was still responsible for the most beloved part of the celebration, someone would have checked in with him about it.

That's when the raven arrived with a message:

Hey, Bro—

Can't wait for icy cream tomorrow.

Bring some by in the morning, first thing, okay?

You're the man, Martin. See you soon.

—His Totally Excellent Royal Highness,

King Gary

Martin read the note and dropped the paper to the floor. Lewis clicked his tongue and flew away.

Martin grumbled as he stared at the trunk and paced around the room. He couldn't put it off any longer. The great sorcerer would *not* be back in time to save the harvest festival. It was all up to his assistant.

He marched over to the trunk and scowled. He lifted the latch and kicked open the lid with his foot.

Silence.

Martin stepped forward and looked into the trunk. There was a long ladder hanging from the side, but the bottom was impossible to see in the darkness below. He swung his leg over and found his footing. It wasn't one of those trusty rigid ladders that rested on the ground and stayed in place as you went. No, it was a creaky old rope ladder that twisted around and swung in circles. Especially difficult to manage while holding a lit candle.

Martin wriggled his way down the ladder into the archives. The last rung hung a foot above the cavern floor. He dropped, and the sound of his shoes hitting stone echoed throughout the darkness. Albino bats fluttered above.

Martin looked up, and all
he could see was a tiny rectangle of light among the inky
blackness—the opening of the trunk
high above in the sorcerer's study.

"Let's get this over with," he said as he looked around
and tried to remember precisely where he had put the icy
cream contraption.

He held the candlestick at arm's length, trying to illumi-
nate his surroundings. Towering shelves stretched in every
direction. Row upon row stuffed to the brim with magical
texts and artifacts.

They all looked the same in the dark.

Martin was pretty sure the contraption was somewhere to the left of the ladder . . . but which left? Facing which direction? He took a guess and began walking slowly, in search of anything familiar.

He poked about in the cavern for hours, until he was completely lost. He had no idea where he was going or where he had already been. Worst of all, he had lost sight of the ladder and the glowing rectangle of light from the open trunk above.

At first, he panicked, imagining that someone had shut the trunk, locked it, and thrown away the key.

But he calmed down when he realized the fire had simply gone out and the sun had set. That was why there was no light. The ladder was still up there somewhere, he assured himself.

Of more immediate concern was the rapidly vanishing candle in his hand. If it ran out of wax before he found the ladder, he would be stuck in the cavern until morning when the sun rose and illuminated his only escape.

Martin quickened his pace. But as he jogged along, the air brushed against the flickering flame, threatening to snuff it out. So he walked as quickly as he could with one hand held in front of the candle to shield the fickle fire from the passing breeze.

Martin slipped, and the candle went tumbling across the floor.

He lay facedown for a while, arms splayed in front of him, before picking himself up and blinking in the darkness. Somehow, the little nub of a candle was still lit. He retrieved it with great relief, careful not to burn his fingers, and in the light of the flame, he noticed that his hands were covered with ash.

Of course!

Martin knew exactly where he was. A few months prior, he had accidentally lit a shelf of scrolls on fire while searching for a compendium the sorcerer had requested. It was only a small fire, but Socor was furious nonetheless. Something about ancient wisdom lost for eternity seemed to upset him.

The good news was that Martin remembered where the fire had happened: just around the corner from the place where he stored the supplies for the harvest festival. He rounded the aisle and held the candle to the shelves—close enough to see the contents, but not so close as to light anything on fire again.

He passed ceramic urns, glass tubes full of powder, some sort of wheeled vehicle, a pile of kites, and stuffed prehistoric animals. Finally, he found it: the icy cream contraption, sitting right where he had left it after last year's celebration.

"Booyah!" Martin shouted with joy.

In that moment, two different things happened at the same time. First, Martin pumped his fist, which put out the candle and plunged the cavern into total darkness. Second, the noise of his shouting startled a thousand albino bats.

The bats swooped down to attack.

"YAAAAAAHHH!" Martin screamed as he waved his hands over his head, unable to see. The darkness didn't bother the bats at all, and while they were each too small to inflict any real damage, they resolved to work collectively to pull out the boy's hair, one strand at a time.

Martin shrieked as the bats plucked at his head. He pulled his hood over his face and groped about on the shelf until he felt the icy cream contraption. He grabbed ahold, but it was stuck.

He tugged with all his might until—

THWUCK!

The contraption suddenly came loose, sending him stumbling backward. He landed hard on his bottom and bit his tongue.

Martin pried off the metal lid and put the wooden tub over his head like a helmet.

THUMP, THUMP, THUMP. The bats ricocheted off the underside of the tub. He waved the lid through the air to disperse the barrage of flapping wings.

Trying his best to retrace his steps, Martin eventually bumped into the end of the ladder dangling from the open trunk above. He grasped onto the first rung and pulled himself up, with the wooden tub still over his head and the lid tucked under his arm.

The ladder swung wildly as he climbed, but eventually he reached the top. He heaved the contraption over the side of the trunk and climbed out after it onto the floor of the study. He closed the lid behind him and shut the latch.

"Whew," Martin sighed, and sat on top of the trunk to catch his breath.

The study was dark, so he scooped a ladleful of water from the bucket and flung it into the cauldron. The fire roared to life.

Martin examined his haul from the cavern. It wasn't that fantastic, to be honest: a wide wooden tub with a metal cover and a spout. It would certainly have been more impressive if pink icy cream were pouring out.

Martin had no idea how to operate the contraption.

He put on the lid and turned the spigot.

Nothing happened.

He tried a couple of magic words: "Alakazam. Hocus-pocus." He tried some German sound poetry: "*Bim blassa galassasa zimbrabim!*"

Nothing happened.

"Please?"

Still nothing.

Martin examined every inch of the thing, inside and out, hoping to find a clue. He poked and prodded, turned and twisted, but nothing seemed to work.

The harvest celebration was only hours away, and if he couldn't make icy cream, the king would be furious. He would have him thrown in the dungeon or beheaded. Martin struggled to decide which would be worse.

"Stupid harvest festival," he said, weeping.

It wasn't fair! Socor had never taught him how to make the icy cream, and he'd left him all alone. What did he expect? He wasn't a sorcerer, he didn't have "it," he wasn't even an apprentice; he was only an assistant. He shouldn't be responsible for anything aside from running errands and taking notes.

Martin was ready to give up and admit to the king that he didn't deserve to be called a mage, he didn't deserve the fancy new robe, he didn't deserve any respect at all.

The fire began to die out, so he poured another ladleful of water into the cauldron. The fire grew stronger.

"Sorcery." Martin smiled weakly.

He tapped the ladle against his hand. Something was itching at the back of his brain.

Did he have to go to the bathroom, maybe? No. Was he hungry? Should he pour a bucketful of water into the cauldron and eat his weight in stew before the king could punish him for ruining the harvest celebration? Martin stopped tapping the spoon.

"Water!"

He looked at the buckets of water he had hauled earlier that day. He looked over at the icy cream contraption. He looked back at the cauldron with the fire burning underneath.

"If it works for stew . . ."

Martin flipped open the lid of the contraption, picked up a bucket, and emptied it into the tub. Then he added the water from the second bucket as well, filling the tub to the brim.

He closed the lid and wished himself luck. When he twisted the knob of the spigot, lo and behold, a thin trickle of pink began to drizzle out.

"Icy cream!" exclaimed Martin. He danced a jig. He grabbed his bowl, flung the stew remnants out the window, and opened the spigot all the way.

Thick, frosty strawberry goodness poured out. Martin scooped a dollop with two fingers and plunged it into his mouth.

"Myum," he said, smacking his lips. "Myum, myum, myum!"

Martin kicked up his heels and pranced around the study. He caressed the bowl of icy cream and admired the lovely pink color. He scooped another mouthful with his fingers and relished the cool, milky texture. He closed his eyes and swallowed.

"Sorcery." He smiled.

Martin rushed to the window and stuck out his head. "Sorcery!" he shouted into the night. He was terribly proud of himself and desperate to share the news of his good fortune.

He didn't notice that the icy cream had continued pouring forth from the spout. Actually, it had begun spraying out faster and faster.

Martin had made a lucky guess. It was true that water

activated the enchanted icy cream contraption, but Socor used only a single drop of water to provide enough icy cream for the entire kingdom.

Martin had used two buckets' worth.

The contraption began to shake violently, and icy cream blasted out with the power of a fire hose. The force of the spray sent the tub sliding and spinning across the room. Martin chased after it, but the floor was slippery with strawberry slush, and he nearly fell through the hole under the rug. By the time he managed to catch the contraption, the whole room was slathered in pink icy cream.

Martin wrestled with the spigot and tried to shut it off. As he struggled, great torrents of icy cream knocked pictures from the mantel and blasted books from the shelves.

Soon, he was pressed against the curved stone wall of the study, along with all the furniture, churning in the current of an icy whirlpool. He dove into it, swam through the frozen cream, and managed to reach the door.

When he twisted the knob, the door burst open and a pink tidal wave carried the sorcerer's assistant down all 347 steps of the tower. He landed in the square, and the icy cream continued to pour out after him. He looked up to see powerful streams of strawberry slush blasting from all three windows at the top of the tower. The icy cream rained down onto the roofs of the village and sloshed into the cobblestone streets.

Martin was powerless to stop the avalanche of pink deliciousness.

THE VILLAGERS IN the hilltop kingdom woke up to quite a surprise.

The white marble castle looked as if it had been hit by a blizzard. Everything was covered with a knee-deep layer of strawberry icy cream.

Martin hadn't slept a wink.

He was at the bottom of the hill, frantically dumping

buckets of icy cream into the well. He knew it would be impossible to clear it all before the harvest festival began, but he was desperate and out of ideas.

He had hardly made a dent in the strawberry snow-drift that covered the well when the king and his knights approached on horseback. A trumpet sounded, and Martin turned to face the consequences of his grave mistake.

"Dude," said the king. His armor was polished to a mirror sheen, ready for battle.

Martin winced, preparing for his head to be separated from his body by the king's broadsword.

The King lifted his arms and spread them wide. "This is . . . awesome!"

Martin opened his eyes and turned to face King Gary, who was smiling from ear to ear. The knights were smiling too.

Martin tried to smile, but he was too nervous. "Merry harvest?" he said softly.

"Merry harvest!" cheered the knights in unison.

The king scooped Martin from the ground and plonked him onto the back of his horse.

"Merry harvest, everyone!" cried the king as he galloped through the village.

"Merry harvest?" the villagers asked as they woke to find their homes buried in strawberry icy cream.

"Enjoy this icy cream surprise, thanks to Martin the Mage!" declared the king.

"Martin the Mage!" cheered the blacksmith as he raised a mug full of icy cream.

"Martin the Mage!" cheered the maidens as they danced through the strawberry snow.

"Martin the Mage!" cheered the washwoman's children as they tossed edible snowballs at each other.

The washwoman sneered, "And just who do you suppose will clean up this mess?"

Which was a very good question, because while the knights were building snowmen to battle and the children were making icy cream angels, the clouds parted and the sun shone brightly in the sky.

Martin knew what was coming. He had learned a thing or two about weather patterns after recording meteorological data every day for almost seven years.

ONCE THE SKY was clear, the temperature rose quickly and the icy cream began to melt. By noon, the crisp pink snow had turned to gloop. Sludge dripped from the roofs of the buildings. The children could no longer form snowballs from the slush. All the king's horses got stuck in the muck. Sugary puddles pocked the roads, and everything in town turned sticky.

Before the end of the day, half of the icy cream had melted completely, and the whole village stank like rotting milk.

Swarms of flies arrived. The villagers ran inside and put clothespins on their noses to deal with the stench. They couldn't walk two feet without spatulas to swat away the buzzing insects.

The harvest celebration was ruined, the entire village was a disgusting mess, and there was only one person to blame.

THE SORCERER'S ASSISTANT had slipped away unnoticed and trudged through the sludge to the top of the tower. He watched nervously from above as the king formed a search party to find him.

"Where is Martin the Mage?" screamed the king furiously.

"He's hiding in his tower," said the washwoman.

"Martin!" shouted the king as he led his knights on horseback up the 347 steps to storm the sorcerer's study and capture the supposed mage who had stained his white marble castle pink.

When he reached the top, the king dismounted and removed his helmet. He shushed the other knights and knocked on the door.

"Martin? Are you in there? It's me, King Gary."

Martin was in there. He was sitting in the comfy leather chair, shivering. The room was filled to the ceiling with strawberry icy cream, but he had cleared out a space for himself, like the inside of an igloo.

"Martin the Mage?" The king examined the heavy door, which he assumed was enchanted. "Open up, please."

Martin stopped feeling sorry for himself and instead felt angry at the wooden tub with the metal spout, which had only just now stopped spewing pink icy cream. He kicked the contraption as hard as he could and stubbed his toe.

"Ouch!"

Martin grabbed his foot with one hand and covered his mouth with the other, but it was too late.

"He's in there, all right," said King Gary.

The knights agreed.

"If you don't open the door, Martin," the king warned, "we'll open it for you."

The knights attempted to dismount from their horses and prepare the battering ram, but it was very tight quarters in the narrow staircase. Especially for horses and large men wearing full armor. One knight lost his footing and fell, clanging halfway down the winding staircase, knocking over several curious villagers who were huffing and puffing their way up the steps to see what was going on.

Martin didn't know what would happen to him if the knights broke through the door, but he knew that he didn't want to find out.

He considered hiding out in the archives for a while. But when he opened the lid of the trunk, a torrent of angry bats came flying out toward his face. He tripped over the stool and crashed into the desk.

When the bats got tired of dive-bombing him, they found their way out the windows.

Well, that seemed as good an idea as any to Martin.

He poked his head out the north side of the tower and looked down. The avalanche of icy cream had poured from the windows, forming a pink mountain of sugary snow with the tip of the tower poking out from the top. The north side of the mountain hadn't melted yet, and the sloped roofs of the village below were still covered in strawberry goo.

While Martin was distracted gazing out the window, one of the knights tried the knob and realized the door was unlocked. He shushed his companions and quietly slipped into the room. He might have been stealthy enough to sneak up on Martin, but when he crept across the rug, he stepped into the giant hole hidden underneath and fell through the floor all the way to his waist.

Martin climbed onto the desk with the icy cream tub in his hands. The king and the rest of his knights bounded into the study. Martin stepped out onto the window ledge and jumped.

MARTIN FELT HIS stomach fly up to his ears as he fell. His robe flapped in the breeze. He managed to shove his butt into the wooden tub and hold on tight.

SWOOOOOO-OOOSH!

The tub hit the top of the icy cream piled against the north side of the tower and became a toboggan, swooshing down the pink mountain toward the village. Martin's robe thrashed behind him like the tail of a comet.

The king shouted after him, but Martin couldn't hear him over the sound of his own shrieking.

The tub was quickly approaching the edge of the roof.

It was a long way to the cobblestones below.
But the roof sloped upward like a ski jump, and
instead of crashing to the ground, the tub went flying
through the air and landed on a different roof a bit farther
down the hill.

Martin tried to steer the thing, but it was no use; it was
going too fast. His haunches vibrated against the bottom of
the tub, a trail of pink sludge spraying in his wake.

The sled scooted off the second roof, onto a still lower
roof, then landed in the street. The impact jangled Martin's
bones. The tub picked up speed.

"Make way!" shouted Martin. Villagers dove aside as the
sled barreled past.

SMASH!

Martin crashed through a sweet potato stand, tearing
the tangerine taters to tatters.

SMASH!

Martin crashed through a chicken stand. A flurry of fluff festooned his face, but still the tub flew faster. Martin coughed out a feather and wiped egg yolk from his brow. He looked ahead, and his eyes went wide.

A knife merchant at the end of the street was waving his arms in a panic. Martin was headed straight for his cart. Dozens of razor-sharp blades hung from the top, jangling above the chopping block and glimmering in the afternoon sun, ready to slice him to ribbons. Martin ducked his head into the tub and prepared for the end.

The knife merchant dropped the handles of his cart to the ground and fled, which tilted the whole thing like a ramp.

Cowering inside with his hands over his head, Martin heard a thump, a cacophony of clanging metal, and then . . . peaceful silence.

Martin poked his head out from the top of the tub to see if he was dead. He was not. The runaway tub had skated up onto the chopping block, below the dangling knives, launched into the air, and sailed clear over the castle wall.

Martin grinned. He was flying. Soaring through the air. Free as a bird! But only for a brief moment. After which, he crashed into a cherry tree.

SMASH!

The tub broke to pieces, and Martin tumbled through the branches to the ground of the royal forest. He landed with a thud in a pile of leaves.

"Jangus," Martin wheezed.

He lay facedown and assessed his injuries. He was banged up and sore, but all his limbs were still attached. Unfortunately, when he lifted his face from the ground, he discovered something much worse than a broken bone.

SOCOR THE SORCERER had returned from his journey. He sat atop a wagon next to a young girl with dark skin and eyes aglow with purple light. Clearly, she had "it."

Lewis the raven perched on the sorcerer's shoulder and shook his head at Martin in disgust.

"Martin, my boy, what happened?" Socor asked as he examined the castle, which was tinted an unfamiliar shade of pink.

Martin began to sob, and the sorcerer nodded knowingly.

"Come now, calm your mind. Everything will turn out just fine."

The girl helped the ancient sorcerer descend from the wagon, very, very slowly.

Socor approached his weeping assistant and patted his head to comfort him. "I like your new robe." The emerald fabric was sticky with pink goop and splattered with feathers, eggs, and sweet potato. "But it could use a wash."

Martin laughed weakly.

"I had to go," explained the sorcerer. "After generations of searching, I finally discovered a worthy successor." He gestured to the girl. "Martin, meet Shoshana."

Shoshana waved her hand over Martin's robe, and it was suddenly clean. It was also warm and smelled like mint. The raven whistled.

At first, Martin was heartbroken. He thought he'd been replaced by a powerful young sorceress and that Socor would turn him over to King Gary to be thrown in the dungeon or beheaded for the mess he'd made of the kingdom.

But that's not what happened at all.

Socor, in his infinite wisdom, explained that the whole thing was actually his fault. He gathered the villagers in the square, but his powerful baritone voice could be heard throughout the town.

"I should never have left poor Martin without instructions for the harvest celebration," Socor announced to the crowd of unhappy faces. "I expected to return with plenty of time, but I don't move as quickly as I used to back in my dragon-slaying days."

Some of the older people chuckled, but most of the villagers were still pretty grumpy (not to mention pink and sticky).

Martin apologized to King Gary and everyone else in the village. Socor soothed the tension with a spectacular display of dancing auroras that night. No one could stay mad after witnessing the breathtaking beauty of kaleidoscopic colors in the sky.

Rain came and washed away most of the sludge. The sorcerer's assistant was given a mop and a brush to scrub the pink stains from the hard-to-reach places.

When Martin was done with the cleanup, the sorcerer required his assistance. Shoshana spoke three different tongues, but she did not know the language of the kingdom. She needed a tutor for reading and writing, and Socor was busy catching up on a mountain of overdue correspondence.

Martin was happy to help.

THE NEXT YEAR, even though the village had been cleaned up and the icy cream contraption had been repaired, Socor decided to make chocolate chip cookies for the harvest celebration instead of strawberry icy cream. Everyone in the kingdom welcomed the change in tradition, especially Martin.

And since Shoshana was helping Martin with the heavy lifting, he had time to set up a doodle booth to make personalized sketches for the villagers during the festival. People requested all sorts of drawings, and Martin attracted quite a crowd. Spectators huddled together to watch in awe. As Martin's charcoal danced across the page, a fantastic scene would emerge, or a familiar face, and the onlookers would erupt with laughter.

At the end of the day, after everyone had gone for supper and Martin was getting ready to pack up, the washwoman approached him quietly and asked if he might make a drawing of her late husband. Martin agreed.

She described his features as best she could, and Martin examined her children's faces for reference as well. When he handed the washwoman the finished drawing, she stared at the sheet of paper in silence for a long time. The likeness was uncanny. She shook her head, muttered something under her breath, and hurried off without thanking him.

A proud smile crept across Martin's face nonetheless.

He had heard what she said:

"Sorcery."

VI

THE ICE CREAM MACHINE

(the one with the alien space lab)

illustrated by

SEAERRA MILLER

In the deep, inky darkness of space, ten thousand light-years from the nearest star, a mysterious alien scientist constructed a giant laboratory to study the nature of intelligent life across the universe.

The space lab was truly enormous, but from far away, it looked like a slowly spinning gyroscope toy made of Styrofoam.

Three interlocking rings rotated and revolved in, out, and around each other. The inner ring contained the common areas of the space lab: interview rooms, recreational facilities, and a cafeteria. The outer ring was full of rare antimatter crystals that fueled the ship. The middle ring contained specially designed habitats for each of the 347 different test subjects living on board.

Intelligent beings had been gathered from civilizations across the cosmos. One of the creatures had lived on an asteroid trapped in orbit around a black hole. Another had lived on a moon made of gold. But the most recent addition to the great intergalactic experiment came from a planet called Earth. From Cumberland, New Jersey, to be precise.

His name was Phillip T. Washington. He had dark skin

and short, curly hair. He was tall for a human but stood hunched over. His eyes were as green as grass.

Phil was the kind of guy who could fit in almost anywhere. He was quiet, friendly, and easy to talk to. Everyone he met enjoyed his company and then completely forgot about him five minutes later. He had perfected the art of being "normal," which was not terribly different from being "boring." But that was back on Earth.

On the space lab, nothing was boring and everything was far from normal.

For example, most of the other test subjects living on the ship were ten times bigger than Phil. They were all friendly enough, but their razor-sharp fangs, massive claws, and writhing poisonous tentacles did make Phil a bit nervous.

Luckily, the mysterious scientist who ran the experiment put Phil's habitat right next door to the only two creatures on board who were smaller than he was.

First, there was Larf, who stood about as tall as Phil's waist. Larf looked kind of like an uppercase letter H covered in armadillo scales. At the end of each of his limbs was a sticky pink foot with six toes. Larf was astoundingly agile—he could jump and flip off the walls like a video-game ninja. He couldn't see very well and often crashed into things at high velocity, but since his body was armored, he never got hurt.

Then there was Fleebar. Just slightly bigger than Larf, Fleebar was basically a huge eyeball covered in slimy rhino hide. No legs, no arms, just eyeball. She moved around by wriggling her eyelid and inching along like a slug. She had excellent vision but limited mobility.

Larf and Fleebar had been living on the space lab for longer than either one could remember, and though they had come from worlds apart, they had grown to be inseparable. Since Larf couldn't see very well and Fleebar couldn't move very well, they worked together to get around. Larf carried Fleebar above his head, and she directed him where to go. (The mysterious scientist who planned the experiment considered this sort of interspecies collaboration a great success.)

"Look who decided to join us," said Fleebar as Phil stumbled out of his habitat into the hallway one morning, yawning.

"Ugh," said Phil. He hadn't slept well and was in a grumpy mood.

"Good morning, Phil!" said Larf.

All 347 creatures on board spoke a different language, so they had each been issued a universal translation device to facilitate interspecies communication. The device utilized advanced tele-quantum technology, but to Phil, it looked like a cat toy.

The 346 other aliens aboard had installed their translators internally, but the thing was the size of a golf ball, and no matter how hard Phil tried, he couldn't manage to choke it down his throat. Instead, he strapped the thingamabob to his wrist like a watch.

Phil raised his arm to his face and spoke.

"Good morning, Larf." The universal translator made a series of loud cracking sounds. Larf nodded. Phil turned to Fleebar.

"Good morning, Fleebar." Phil's translator emitted a high-pitched screech.

Fleebar blinked. "Good morning to you too, Phil. Now let's hurry, or you're going to be late."

"Not to worry," said Larf as he hoisted Fleebar above his head. "Just follow me, and we'll get there in no time." They launched straight up into the air and out of sight.

Phil sighed, placed his foot against the wall, walked onto the ceiling, and stepped down into the passageway above his head.

Gravity in the space lab did not work like gravity on Earth. All the passageways were round like tubes—Phil could walk up the wall and across the ceiling and, without changing direction, wind up right back where he started. Wherever he was standing felt like the floor, so it was hard to tell up from down. There were doors and passageways that led in every direction. It was very easy to get lost.

Fleebar kept a lookout and gave Larf directions. "Turn left. Turn right. Stop!"

Phil struggled to keep pace.

The journey to the center of the laboratory could be perilous. The hallways were full of monstrous alien creatures rushing about in all directions. Any one of them might accidentally step on, roll over, or otherwise crush a squishy little human without so much as batting a tentacle.

The tiny trio ducked under a flying octopus, barely dodged a tumbling boulder creature, and managed to hitch a ride on the back of an electro-snake (who didn't even notice she had passengers).

When they arrived at the central ring of the lab, they split up to attend their daily interview sessions. That was the main focus of the mysterious scientist's whole experiment: to gather information from the test subjects living on board. Each creature spent a large portion of their time answering questions for the supercomputer. Phil entered a glossy white interview room. Every surface was perfectly flat and impossibly clean. A hazy pink glow spread across the ceiling.

"Good morning, Phillip T. Washington, *Homo sapiens* from New Jersey, planet Earth." The voice of the supercomputer was pleasant, but its English was awkward. "Are you sufficiently rested? Your vital signs indicate fatigue."

"I'm still having a little trouble sleeping," Phil said. "That's all."

There was a rectangular black slab in the center of the room, which shifted shape to take on whatever form might be most comfortable for each species. For Phil (a human), the slab morphed into a cushy easy chair, fully reclined. Phil took a seat, leaned back, and waited for the interview session to begin.

"It is important that you are well rested and alert for your interview sessions," scolded the supercomputer. "Full cognitive participation is vital to our experiment."

"I know, I know," muttered Phil.

He had been asked to explain all sorts of things about life back on Earth. Some of the questions were easy, but others were very specific and made him wish he had traveled more or paid better attention in school. Most of the questions were subjective, though, so there were no clear right or wrong answers.

The supercomputer asked for Phil's opinion on everything—from art to social etiquette to physical fitness. Sometimes, the supercomputer would show Phil abstract images and ask him what words came to his mind. Other times, Phil would have to choose which of two different aromas he found most appealing. For the most part,

Phil felt he had done a pretty good job of answering the questions he'd been asked, but at the same time, he worried that the other test subjects on board were doing an even *better* job.

"Why are yawns contagious?" asked the supercomputer.

Phil thought hard for a minute.

"If a human observes a yawn, it makes them want to yawn," the supercomputer said. "Even hearing the word 'yawn' or reading the word 'yawn'—why does that make humans want to yawn?"

Phil yawned. "I don't know."

The supercomputer pressed on. "Can you explain the annual tradition of lighting pastries on fire?"

"What?" Phil was confused.

"Once a year, a human will gather their companions around a frosted cake, set it ablaze briefly, spew their breath over the food, and then distribute contaminated pieces to everyone in the room. Why?"

"Oh," Phil replied. "I never thought about it like that before. It's just a birthday tradition, I guess."

"But why?"

Phil was stumped. "Can we skip that one for now?"

"Certainly," replied the supercomputer. "What is the appeal of tongue kissing?"

"Uh . . ." Phil was stumped again.

He wasn't sure how to answer any of those questions. He didn't want to say the wrong thing. He hated looking dumb in front of the supercomputer.

"May I be excused early to use the bathroom?" asked Phil.

"Again?"

"I really have to go."

"Fine," replied the supercomputer. *"Terminate interview session in three . . . two . . ."*

Phil slipped out of the interview room and headed down the hall to the elimination station. A kind of gelatinous spider monster scuttled by, and Phil flattened himself against the wall to avoid getting stepped on.

It didn't work.

"Hey!" Phil protested, but the jumbo spider didn't even notice him. Phil wiped the yellow jelly from his shirt and quickly ducked through the door of the bathroom to avoid a humongous fungus with legs bounding down the hallway at top speed.

The "bathroom" on the ship was very simple: a cone-shaped chamber with a safety harness and a hatch in the floor. This ingenious design solved a very complicated problem: 347 aliens have 347 different ways to make waste.

For example, one creature shed all its skin at once, leaving a translucent replica of itself that smelled like cinnamon. Another would simply remove a leg every few days. One creature had to wait patiently for hours until its waste sack exploded with what could best be described as hundreds of blue jelly beans with tails.

For Phil, going to the bathroom on the space lab meant

first getting naked. Most of the other aliens walked around naked (as far as he could tell), but Phil didn't feel comfortable exposing his delicates in the common areas, what with hundreds of gigantic, spiky, acid-spewing aliens poking about.

In the privacy of the elimination station, he stripped off the clothes he had been wearing since the day he left Earth: a green plaid flannel, a white cotton T-shirt, faded blue jeans, black sneakers, plaid boxer shorts, and mismatched gym socks.

Phil folded his clothes neatly and put them in the storage locker. Next, he walked to the middle of the room and strapped himself into the safety harness. The metal buckles felt cold against his skin and gave him goose bumps. He double-checked the straps, inhaled as much air as he could, and reached for the release switch.

When Phil flipped the switch, the bottom of the cone-shaped chamber slid away to expose the vast, cold emptiness that surrounded the space lab. All of the air instantly whooshed out of the room, and Phil's body violently hurtled toward the open hatch below.

Fortunately, the straps of the safety harness snapped taut and prevented him from flying out into the dark vacuum of space. The skin on his cheeks stretched down to his neck, and his bottom lip flapped over his chin from the power of the suction.

Phil relieved himself. Every last speck of whatever came out of him was instantly sucked through the escape hatch and launched into outer space.

When he was finished with his business, he flipped the switch again. The hatch door closed, and breathable gas filled the room. The straps fell slack, and Phil's face returned to its normal shape. He gasped for air.

There was a loud knock at the door—some huge alien who really had to go.

Phil quickly untangled himself from the safety harness, got dressed, and headed to lunch.

MEALTIME WAS PHIL'S least favorite time on the space lab. Everyone gathered in the cafeteria to absorb nutrient fluid and babble at one another through their translators. All Phil heard was a cacophony of slurps, gurgles, squeaks, and roars. It sounded like a symphony orchestra being attacked by zoo animals. He couldn't understand a word of it unless someone had their translator pointed directly at him.

A line of hulking aliens waited in front of the meal dispenser—a large vending machine full of various vats of liquid and tangled hoses.

Each test subject was provided an appropriate portion of nutrient fluid. Some portions were barrel-size, but Phil's looked more like a tube of toothpaste.

Phil waited between a two-ton walking sweet potato and a gargantuan reptilian creature with five eyes. The terrifying lizard stared down at him and licked its lips. Phil tried to avoid eye contact and look as unappetizing as possible.

He often got the feeling that some of the aliens in the cafeteria would rather be eating *him* than ingesting nutrient fluid.

So when Phil reached the front of the line, he quickly retrieved his tube of artificial sustenance and scuttled away from his reptilian admirer.

It was difficult to navigate through the throng of aliens. Phil was far too small to see over the crowd. However, the floor of the cafeteria formed a vertical loop, so all he had to do was look up to see the other side of the room. He spotted Larf doing backflips across an empty table, away from any would-be predators.

"How was your interview session?" asked Fleebar as Phil sat down.

"Not great," admitted Phil. "I had trouble with some of the questions."

"I wonder what they'll discover from all this," said Fleebar, gazing around the room at the wide variety of life-forms. "It's such an honor for me to represent my species. I feel proud. Don't you?"

"I guess so," said Phil.

He uncapped his tube, squeezed out a handful of gray goop, and rubbed it into his face like sunscreen.

The nutrient fluid bubbled and fizzed as it was slowly absorbed into his flesh. It caused a slightly uncomfortable tingling sensation, but it was the only food source available on the space lab. He'd once tried squeezing a drop into his mouth, but it tasted like leather, and when it started to dissolve on his tongue, it felt like licking sandpaper.

"The space pong championship is tomorrow," said Larf as he stuffed a glob of nutrient fluid under his butt sack. "Want to go watch the game?"

"Sure," said Phil.

Larf's butt sack gurgled.

Fleebar rolled around in a puddle on the table, blinking nutrient fluid into her giant eyelid, which created a goopy, sucking sound.

Phil lost his appetite. He decided to head back to his habitat to get some rest.

Since almost everyone on the space lab was eating or otherwise occupied in the central ring, Phil's journey back to his room was easier than usual. He enjoyed a leisurely stroll through the empty passageways, and by the time he got to his habitat, he actually felt relaxed.

But not for long.

Phil approached the door and waited. He gritted his teeth. The motion sensors were not designed to recognize small creatures. Begrudgingly, he waved his hand over his head. Nothing happened.

He waved both hands. He shuffled from side to side and twirled, arms extended. Still nothing.

He walked onto the wall next to the doorway and circled around the entrance, kicking his legs, trying to guess where the motion sensor might be installed. Finally, the door slid open and Phil climbed inside.

On the space lab, each creature's personal habitat was designed to replicate a traditional living environment on their home planet. Phil's habitat looked like a college dorm room back on Earth. To begin with, it had one-directional gravity, which provided a welcome sense of up and down for a human like Phil. There was a simple bed, a chest of drawers, a fuzzy rug, a reading lamp, a mirror, and a wooden rocking chair. There was also a round viewport that looked out onto the stars. The walls were bare except for a single painting of a sailboat.

The only personal possessions Phil had with him were the ones he'd had in his pockets on his last day on Earth: his wallet, a set of keys, a mobile phone (now dead), a red paisley handkerchief, a pocket magnifying glass, a chewed-up pen from a Holiday Inn, and a book of word search puzzles that had all been completed.

There was really no way for Phil to know how much time had passed since he had first arrived on the space lab, but he remembered his last moments in New Jersey as if they'd happened yesterday.

Phil had just finished changing the prices on the sign outside the gas station where he worked the night shift. The birds were chirping, and the cherry trees along the country road swayed in the breeze. From the top of the ladder, Phil could see for miles. There were no cars coming in either direction. He climbed down and treated himself to an ice cream cup from the freezer. Then he sat on the bench out front to watch the sunset.

A sweet song came over the radio.

Jump back, sit back, get back, relax, it's okay.

Phil uncapped his ice cream cup and retrieved the little wooden spoon from underneath the lid. He scraped up a curl of chocolate and popped it into his mouth. It melted slowly on his tongue, and he waited to swallow it.

Crossing his legs and glancing over at the cows in the field across the road, Phil felt totally content. He found the lazy movements of the animals soothing. They were never in a hurry. They didn't seem to have a care in the world.

But then he noticed something disturbing—one of the cows was missing the back half of her body. It looked like she had been sawed right through the middle. Even stranger, the front half of the cow seemed unconcerned and very much alive.

Phil got up from the bench, looked both ways, and hustled across the road to investigate.

As he got closer, he noticed that a hazy pink rectangle of light seemed to be slicing the cow in two. On one side of the rectangle was the front half of the cow, but on the other side, there was nothing. Stranger still, from the back side of the rectangle, he could clearly see the insides of the cow where her body was split in half—bright, slimy guts twitching like something out of a biology class.

His mouth fell open, and he dropped his ice cream cup in the grass. He leaned in for a closer look. The white bones, the red muscles, the dark-purple organs—he could see them all as if he were looking through a full-color x-ray machine.

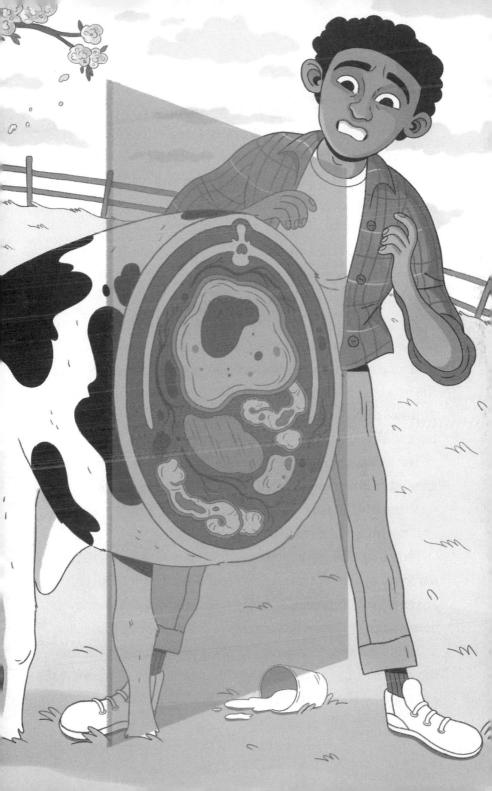

He stepped around the front of the cow and gave it a poke to make sure it was real. The cow mooed. Phil shook his head.

What was in that ice cream? he thought.

That's when the cow took a few steps forward, and the back half of her body reappeared, emerging from the mysterious rectangle unharmed. Phil stumbled backward with surprise. He couldn't believe his eyes. The cow seemed perfectly fine.

Phil cautiously approached the hazy rectangle. It was some sort of laser light. Aside from a pinkish tint, he could see clear through to the other side.

He pulled a pen from the pocket of his jeans. The tip of the pen disappeared as he pushed it through the light. When he pulled it back out, the pen reappeared. He pushed the pen in further. Then he pushed his fingers through too. Phil swore as his hand disappeared before his eyes. It didn't hurt at all.

He reached in up to the elbow and waved his arm around a bit, then stepped back to examine himself. He was fine. He felt fine. The cow was fine too, grazing happily as if nothing had ever happened.

Phil had always considered himself a mildly curious person. Perhaps not so curious as a scientist or a journalist or some great explorer, but curious nonetheless. He enjoyed doing word searches but considered crossword puzzles too difficult. He kept a magnifying glass in his pocket to examine interesting rocks and bugs, but he never bothered to learn any of their names.

It was a lazy curiosity, perhaps. Why look too deep into the water below if you're perfectly happy in the boat? You might fall out of the boat! That was Phil's philosophy anyhow.

But standing in that field, faced with the unknown, Phillip T. Washington felt the responsibility to investigate. He was nervous, and he almost gave up and ran back to the gas station, but a strange voice in his head assured him that everything was going to be all right.

So Phil stood before the glowing pink rectangle, stepped through what turned out to be an interdimensional portal, and walked out onto a space laboratory on the other side of the universe.

"WHAT DO YOU miss most about your home planet?" asked the supercomputer.

Phil felt the skin on his scalp tighten.

"What do I miss most?" he said.

Where to begin? He missed everything. He missed the food. He missed the toilet paper. He missed walking out his door without worrying that something might squash, squish, or swallow him.

Why did he ever step through that stupid portal? Why hadn't he called the fire department instead? He could still be on that bench, watching the cows, instead of stuck in outer space, surrounded by giant aliens with their weird noises and funny smells.

"Phil?" The supercomputer was waiting for him to answer the question.

He had drifted off. He blinked and came back to his senses.

"What do you miss most about your home planet?" repeated the supercomputer.

Phil folded his hands behind his head, leaned back on the morpho-slab easy chair, and took a deep breath.

"I miss the sky," he said. "I miss the clouds and the sun. I miss wind and grass and birds and cows . . . I miss ice cream." He licked his lips and chuckled. "Some ice cream sure would be nice right about now."

"Thank you for your valuable input," replied the super-computer.

WHEN PHIL WAS done with his interview session, he made his way to the recreational area to watch the aliens play space pong. The game was not native to any planet. It was rumored to have been invented by the laboratory's chief architect and scientist, a multidimensional being known as Vromulon X.

Space pong was easily the most popular activity on the space lab. More than two hundred creatures had gathered to watch the final match of the league championships.

The space pong "court" was made of unbreakable glass in the shape of a truncated icosahedron—a massive sphere made of hexagons (the same shape as a soccer ball). Teams of two competed to bounce the hyperball off the walls and into the opposing team's goal. There were no paddles in space pong, and no gravity either, which made game play acrobatic and unpredictable.

The structure itself could rotate around the players, causing the goals to change location. Plus, as the hyperball picked up speed, its swirling colors strobed brighter and brighter. At maximum velocity, it looked like the four creatures inside the glass structure were dancing with a comet.

Phil climbed to the top of the bleachers and sat by himself, away from the rest of the crowd. He felt like being alone.

Greetings, Phil, said a comforting baritone voice inside of Phil's mind. It was Vromulon X, communicating telepathically.

Phil turned to the scientist, who had suddenly materialized beside him in the form of a hovering mist crackling with kaleidoscopic bursts of electricity. He couldn't tell if Vromulon X had a specific face, so he wasn't sure where to look while talking to them. He stared deep into the mist, mesmerized by the flickering spectrum of lightning bolts that seemed to extend for miles within.

"Howdy," said Phil out loud, even though Vromulon X could read his thoughts.

Howdy, thought Phil.

Yes. Howdy, replied Vromulon X. *Are you enjoying the oxygen we have in the air here, Phil?*

Phil took a breath, looked around, and nodded slowly, confused.

Many of the creatures here require nitrogen for respiration, not oxygen, explained the scientist. *Some synthesize helium, and others breathe chemicals that might be poisonous to a* Homo sapiens *like you.*

Phil observed the vast menagerie of aliens that filled the stands.

A precise and delicate balance is required to accommodate the needs of all three hundred forty-seven species, Vromulon X continued. *Slight discomfort is required from each of us so that all of us might live in harmony. Do you understand?*

No, Phil thought.

"Yes," Phil said.

Vromulon X hovered closer.

Your participation in this experiment is very important, Phil, but I am aware that life here is especially difficult for creatures who come from isolated civilizations . . . Uncontacted species tend to consider themselves the center of the universe.

Vromulon X began to glow. *So I have brought you something to help you feel more* at home.

Deep from within the twinkling mist of Vromulon X, a silver box materialized, floated out into the air between them, and landed gently on Phil's lap. It looked like a microwave.

"What is it?" asked Phil. "A microwave?" He eyed the box suspiciously.

No, Vromulon X explained, *it is not a microwave. It is an antimatter quantum telegenerator . . .*

Phil's eyes narrowed, and Vromulon X paused. *It is a* machine *that will satisfy your desires for a taste of Earth. Observe.*

The device activated, and the round button on top began to pulse with inviting red light.

Chocolate ice cream, said Vromulon X.

The machine whirred and sparked, then stopped with a *DING!*

A door swung open, and inside was a small pile of chocolate ice cream.

Ah, yes, said Vromulon X. *When you try it, you may wish to ask for a conveyance. A cup, perhaps?*

Phil's eyes went wide.

Regardless, continued the scientist, *I do hope you enjoy your semi-frozen Earth snack. May this machine bring you happiness and peace of mind.* The door closed, and the red light on the top of the box turned off. *Please arrive rested and on time for your interview sessions in the future.*

And with that, Vromulon X dissolved into another dimension somewhere.

PHIL SPRINTED BACK to his habitat with his shiny new machine. He sat cross-legged on the rug and ran his fingers over the metal box. He pressed the button on top and watched the red light glow. Then he leaned in close and cleared his throat.

"Chocolate ice cream . . . in a cup."

The machine whirred and sparked, then stopped with a *DING!*

When Phil opened the door and peeked inside, he giggled with glee. There was a cup full of chocolate ice cream.

He jumped to his feet and did a celebratory dance. Then he dropped to his hands and knees and marveled at the frosty treat. He was almost afraid to touch it, but eventually he worked up the courage to take a bite.

Phil swooned.

The ice cream was delectable. Creamy and rich and sweet and cold. He ate slowly at first, savoring every bite, but soon he was gobbling greedily, using his fingers to scrape the last bits from the bottom of the cup and scoop them into his mouth. He licked the cup clean.

Phil closed the door of the machine and asked for seconds. It worked! He asked for thirds and fourths. He tried asking for strawberry ice cream, and that worked too! He ordered different flavors: pistachio, butterscotch, and hazelnut. Phil ate so much, he had to unbutton his pants.

That night, he fell asleep in the rocking chair with ice cream spilled on his shirt and a big silly grin on his face.

PHIL WOKE UP in a great mood, though a bit of a mess. His fingers were sticky, and somehow he'd gotten ice cream caked in his hair. He walked over to the control panel by the door and pressed the button labeled DECONTAMINATION MODE.

The artificial gravity shut off, and Phil floated into the air along with his rocking chair, his rug, and his shiny new machine. (Everything else in the room was bolted to the floor.) Sixteen miniature laser cannons mounted to robotic arms emerged from the walls of the habitat and swiveled into position around Phil.

Brilliant green lights exploded from the barrels of the cannons and quickly scanned the surface of Phil's body. All foreign molecules on his clothing, skin, and hair were instantly incinerated. Phil opened his mouth wide to clean his teeth, tongue, and gums. The blasters were so precise, they trimmed the end of each individual strand of hair to ensure that Phil stayed neatly groomed.

When the laser cannons had finished their job, they retracted back into the walls and the artificial gravity gently returned to Earth level. Phil landed on the floor and adjusted the rug. Above him, a cloud of vaporized grime smelled like a tiny burnt fart. An exhaust fan in the ceiling switched on and sucked up the residue. The habitat was squeaky-clean once again.

Phil felt renewed, energized from eating his first solid food since arriving in outer space. He stepped out of his habitat, whistling, and arrived early for his interview session.

"Good morning, Phil. How did you sleep?" asked the supercomputer as Phil took his seat on the morpho-slab.

"Very well!" said Phil. "Probably the best sleep I've had since I left Earth."

"Excellent news," said the supercomputer. "Why do many humans eat pigs but not dogs?"

The day's work had begun.

Phil felt inspired. He provided excellent answers for the supercomputer. He acted out memories and explained how even though doctors said you shouldn't, cleaning your ears with cotton swabs felt really satisfying. He was enjoying himself so much that before he knew it, it was time to break for lunch.

Of course, Phil had no intention of absorbing nutrient fluid ever again. He walked into the cafeteria with the ice cream machine under his arm, feeling newly confident. He skipped past the line for the meal dispenser and didn't even bother searching for the safety of an isolated table or his tiny friends, Larf and Fleebar.

Instead, he took a seat right in the middle of the room, at a table full of large, noisy aliens. A huge sack of slime wheezed like an accordion. A prodigious purple knot jangled like a wind chime.

Phil squeezed in between what looked like an enormous neon seashell and a school bus with antennas. He placed his silver machine on the table. One by one, the creatures noticed it and went quiet.

"Hey, Phil," said a fire being named Blayzar. "What's with the box?"

"I'll show you," said Phil. He leaned in close to the machine. "Vanilla ice cream in a waffle cone."

DING!

Phil opened the door for all to see.

"Oooh," said the aliens in various burps, beeps, and whistles.

"This is a kind of nutrient fluid from my home planet," said Phil, holding up the cone triumphantly. "Try it."

Blayzar reached out his hand to touch the ice cream.

"YAAAAARGH!" screamed Blayzar in pain. "It's so *cold!*" His bright flames diminished, and he clutched his fingers.

"Oh gosh. I'm sorry," muttered Phil. "It's *ice* cream. It's *supposed* to be cold." He cowered before the whimpering inferno. "I guess I should have warned you."

"Are you okay, Blayzar?" asked the purple knot.

"I think so," sniffled Blayzar, cradling his hand. "I'm just very upset right now."

"Let's go," said the knot.

And with that, the aliens packed up their nutrient fluid and left Phil alone at the table with his ice cream.

"Your machine is quite impressive."

Phil turned to see himself reflected in a tremendous floating ball—a mathematically perfect, glistening sphere. Her name was Heather (at least that was what it sounded like to Phil). He had long admired her from afar, and he considered her to be the most mesmerizing creature he had ever seen. When she hovered close, it made the hair on the back of his neck stand up.

"Th-thank you," stammered Phil.

"You're welcome, tiny flesh monster."

"Actually, my name is Phil." He blushed.

"My name is Heather," said the beautiful mirrored sphere.

"I know," said Phil. His eyes darted away. "I mean, nice to meet you."

PHIL COULDN'T SLEEP. He hadn't eaten anything but ice cream for two straight days. His stomach was swollen, and his intestines had gone sour. He lay in bed moaning and tossing from side to side. A trail of melted ice cream led from his pillow to the machine, which sat atop the dresser across the room. Phil had left it turned on, and the pulsing red light began to make him feel dizzy. He had to turn it off, or he'd never get to sleep.

Phil pulled back the covers, swung his legs over the side of the bed, and grunted with pain as he struggled to his feet. With great effort, he managed to heave one foot forward and take a step. He shifted his weight, preparing for a second step, but paused to catch his breath. He was so focused on his destination at the other side of the room, he failed to notice the goopy trail of ice cream he'd left on the floor. His second step landed right in it, and his foot slipped out from under him. He did an awkward split and fell hard on his side. The impact dislodged a hot burp.

Phil crawled to the dresser.

The room was a mess. Ice cream everywhere. Phil's insides were a mess. Too much ice cream. If only the stupid ice cream machine could make something else . . .

He stopped crawling and lifted his head. Maybe the machine could make a different kind of food.

What's the opposite of ice cream? he thought.

"Popcorn," he said out loud.

The machine whirred and sparked, then stopped with a *DING!*

Phil climbed to his feet, using the dresser to steady himself. He opened the door.

Golden, crunchy popcorn spilled out onto the floor. It was hot to the touch. Phil laughed. He grabbed a handful of popped kernels and tossed them into the air like confetti. He laughed harder. He lifted the machine and poured out all the popcorn over his head, cackling like a maniac. Then, suddenly, he stopped laughing, turned around, and threw up on the rug.

Phil had overdosed on ice cream. He was so violently ill that night that his retching woke his neighbors, Larf and Fleebar. But without his universal translator turned on, they couldn't tell if Phil was happy, angry, or sad, so they decided it was best to leave him alone.

After he had emptied his stomach completely, Phil activated decontamination mode. The laser cannons restored the room to pristine condition, and he was finally able to get some sleep.

In the morning, Phil felt much better. He had even regained his appetite. *DING!* He ate a big breakfast of steak and eggs. *DING!* He drank a tall glass of orange juice. *DING!* He thought he might have time for some waffles with strawberries, but three bites in, he realized he was already late for his interview session, so he abandoned his breakfast and dashed out the door.

Thinking better on it, he darted back into the habitat, tucked the machine under his arm, and brought it with him.

THE SUPERCOMPUTER SCOLDED him for being tardy. Phil felt guilty, but as he settled into the morpho-slab, he ordered some nachos to cheer himself up. *DING!*

"Why do humans think monkeys are hilarious?" asked the supercomputer.

Phil grabbed a cheese-covered tortilla chip from the open machine in his lap and munched while he thought.

"Hmm," he mumbled with his mouth full. "What do you mean?"

The screen on the ceiling played a video of a monkey dancing on roller skates. Phil laughed so hard, he choked. A shard of nacho chip slid down the wrong pipe.

"Hahaha . . . Ack! *Gah. Gah.* Hiiiiiiic. Ack! *ACK!*"

Phil wheezed and turned red. He thumped his chest with his fist. He stood and paced the room, trying to work the piece loose. Eventually, eyes tearing, nose running, he managed to clear his throat.

"Play it again," gasped Phil. He closed the lid of the machine and sat back down to watch.

The supercomputer played the monkey video again. Phil was hysterical.

"So good." He could barely catch his breath from laughing. "I wish *I* had a monkey."

The machine whirred and sparked, then stopped with a *DING!*

Phil heard a scratching sound. It was coming from inside the machine. When he opened the door, a real, live monkey clambered out and sat on top of his head. Phil scrambled out of his chair. The monkey jumped onto the floor and hooted.

"Is it real?" Phil asked the supercomputer, gawking.

"*Saimiri sciureus,*" replied the supercomputer. "Sixty percent water, carbon-based Earth life-form."

"Oooh! Aah!" the monkey hollered as it skipped around the room.

"Come back," Phil pleaded. "Come here! Please?" He chased the monkey around and around the morpho-slab and soon ran out of breath.

He offered the machine like a prize. "Wouldn't you like to go back in the box?"

The monkey cocked its head and stared at the human, confused. Phil had an idea. He held up his universal translator and tried again.

"If you get into the box, I'll give you a banana." The device on his wrist hooted a few times. The little monkey nodded and climbed in.

Phil quickly shut the door and rushed out of the interview room.

"I'll be right back," he shouted over his shoulder to the supercomputer.

Phil raced to his habitat with the machine clutched to his chest and the little monkey stirring inside. He shuffled back and forth in front of the door sensors and frowned. The door didn't budge. He set the machine down, stood on top, and waved his arms above his head.

The door slid open.

Phil hurried inside and let the monkey out of the box. It climbed onto the dresser and began to explore the room. It jumped on the bed, scratched at the pillows, and swung from the lamp. Phil was nervous. He didn't know how to take care of a monkey.

"Yah! Yah! Yah!" hooted the monkey.

"What?" said Phil.

"Yah! YAH!" The monkey began to get agitated.

"Right! Oh, right." Phil closed the door of the machine. "Bananas."

DING!

Phil took the bananas out of the machine and tossed them to the monkey.

"Yah," said the monkey gratefully. It happily smooshed a banana in its hand and smeared the paste between its lips. The monkey sprang onto the bed and began to somersault back and forth across the sheets, squishing bananas between its feet and flinging banana bits everywhere. "Oooh, aaah, aaah!"

The little monkey was making a very big mess of the habitat, and Phil didn't know what to do. He smacked his palm against his forehead and collapsed into the rocking chair.

"I wish I had never asked for this stupid monkey," sighed Phil.

DING!

The monkey was gone.

Phil looked around and put his hand over his mouth.

He felt afraid.

THAT EVENING AT dinner, Heather came over to say hello.

Phil was smearing nutrient fluid on his forehead, looking depressed.

"Hello, squishy hairball," said Heather. "Where is your shiny machine?"

"Oh . . . I lost it," lied Phil. It was crammed in the bottom drawer of his dresser. After the monkey incident, he'd hidden it away where it couldn't hurt anyone.

"What a shame," replied Heather. "It was quite beautiful."

"Thank you," said Phil.

"I must go now." Heather turned to float away. "My friends and I are going to play space pong."

"Oh, okay." Phil looked down at his tube of nutrient fluid.

Heather paused. "I'd invite you to play, but I fear you would be badly injured."

Phil faked a laugh.

"Because you are so small and squishy," added Heather.

"Well"—Phil puffed out his chest—"on Earth, I was actually considered above-average height."

"How intriguing," said Heather. "Well, maybe you will join us sometime."

"Yeah, sure. I'd love to," blurted Phil. "But you know"—he gestured at his face dripping with nutrient fluid—"not on a full stomach."

Heather hovered off to meet her friends at the space pong courts, and as she floated away, Phil could see his reflection in her smooth, glimmering body getting smaller and smaller and smaller.

As he walked through the hallway back to his habitat, Phil felt invisible. He got bumped by a large pillow alien with antlers, shoved by a big rolling creature covered in flashing spots, and nearly crushed to death by an enormous pancake that flopped along like a fish in the mud.

"Look out," burped the pillowy one.

"Oops! Didn't see you there," squawked the rolly one.

"Watch it, tiny," whistled the floppy one.

When Phil got back to his room, he sprawled out on his bed and stared at the ceiling for hours. His stomach was growling, and he had a headache.

Suddenly, he thought of a comeback to the floppy pancake who had insulted him earlier. "Oh yeah?" he shouted. "I eat flapjacks like you for breakfast!"

His weak insult echoed off the walls of the habitat, which made it feel cavernous and empty. Even his own room made him feel small.

Phil got out of bed and opened the dresser drawer where he had stashed the machine. It was stuck. He rolled up his sleeves to get a better grip, bent his knees, and yanked as hard as he could.

THWUCK!

The drawer cracked, and the machine broke free. Phil tumbled backward onto the rug.

"Jangus," he blurted.

Phil sat up and pressed the button on top of the machine. He opened the door and shoved his arm inside. He shut his eyes.

"I wish I was big."

DING!

WHEN HEATHER SAW Phil arrive at the space pong courts, she noticed something was different about him.

"You were smaller yesterday," said Heather.

"Yes, uh, we humans sometimes change size," lied Phil as casually as possible.

"How very interesting," said Heather. She hovered closer and paused near his eyes. "These two parts are actually quite shiny."

"Yeah," said Phil as he tried to look at Heather, but she was floating so close, all he could see was a giant warped reflection of his own face.

"You ready to play, or what?" shouted Makrimbus, a huge leathery sheet with two hundred eyes.

"Makrimbus and me versus Heather and Phil," said Ploom as he tossed the hyperball above his four feathered heads.

Phil stepped into the glass structure, and his feet floated up from the hexagonal tile on the floor. The entrance panel slid shut, and the enclosure began to rotate. Phil got dizzy. He paddled his arms to steady himself but found the other three players whirling around him like a tornado. He flailed his limbs and flipped head over heels.

"Stop messing around, Phil," said Makrimbus.

"Zero-zero," announced Ploom. He whacked the hyperball across the court with one of his heads. It whizzed toward Heather, who deflected it away from the goal. The hyperball ricocheted off the walls of the structure and picked up speed, its swirling colors glowing brighter.

Makrimbus wrapped himself around the ball as it zoomed past and brought it under control. He released the

ball to float in midair, then spun his body
and whapped it at Phil, who was still flailing
helplessly in the middle of the court.

The glowing rocket smacked Phil in the stomach and launched him into the wall. He bounced off one angled tile and crashed into another but managed to hold on to the hyperball.

"Are you all right?" asked Heather.

Phil wheezed. The wind had been knocked out of him. He managed to nod.

"Your play, Phil," called Ploom.

Composing himself, Phil grasped the hyperball in one hand, reeled back, and hurled it as hard as he could across the court toward Makrimbus and Ploom.

Unfortunately, the ball slipped from his fingers and went flying sideways, away from where he was aiming.

Fortunately, the hyperball ricocheted off the walls perfectly—*BING, PING, ZING*—and whizzed between two of Ploom's heads into the goal. The glass structure sparkled. Phil had scored his first goal.

"Nice shot, Phil," said Makrimbus.

"Just like I planned it," lied Phil as he steadied himself. He smiled and gave Heather a thumbs-up. Of course, she didn't have any thumbs or any idea what a thumbs-up meant, but she could tell the human was happy.

In the end, Heather and Phil lost the match, but Phil didn't do too bad, considering it was his first time playing and he was just starting to get the hang of the game.

"That was fun," said Heather.

"Why don't we play again tomorrow?" asked Phil.

Just then, they passed what looked like a colossal cater-pillar made of silver confetti.

"Hi, Heather," said the caterpillar.

"Hello, Wymax," cooed Heather. "You are certainly look-ing shiny today."

Phil frowned.

THE NEXT DAY, Heather noticed something else was differ-ent about Phil.

"Your skin," said Heather. "It's so . . . shiny!"

"Oh, is it?" replied Phil. "Well, some days, we humans are shinier than others."

Heather hovered close, and he could see his new metal-lic skin reflected in her mirrored body, which was then reflected back in his new metallic skin.

"Intriguing," said Heather.

Phil's metal cheeks turned red.

He began spending lots of time with the beautiful sphere. They played space pong almost every day, and he started sitting with her at the popular table in the cafeteria. Since Heather was mathematically perfect, she was universally appealing to all species, and everyone wanted to be around her. She introduced Phil to all of her friends.

He actually began to enjoy his time on the space lab. He could walk through the halls without fear of being bumped or slimed or squished.

"Lookin' good, Phil!" said Blayzar as he passed Phil in the hall.

Phil nodded and did a little spin without breaking his stride.

"Nice game today, Phil!" said a hairy pineapple creature.

"You too, Omrey!"

"Hey, big guy," said Fleebar as Phil approached his habitat. The motion sensor recognized him immediately, and the door opened wide. "Long time no see."

"Is that Phil?" Larf asked. "He sounds different."

"He looks different too." Fleebar narrowed her eye at Phil. "Ever since he got that machine from Vromulon X."

Phil squeezed himself through the door to his habitat and curled his knees to his chest to fit inside.

Though he was thoroughly enjoying his newfound size, Phil had a problem. His habitat was now much too small. The bed was only big enough to serve as a kind of tiny pillow. The rug was too small to be much use as a blanket. Phil grunted and huffed as he tried to make himself comfortable. His metal skin clanged against the walls.

"This stinks," grumbled Phil. He wondered if maybe the machine could help.

Phil turned on his side and carefully slid open the bottom drawer of the dresser with his fingertips. He placed the machine in his palm.

All of a sudden, the room around him went black, and he found himself unable to move.

Greetings, Phil, said Vromulon X.

"Gah!" Phil was startled to see the scientist materialize in his habitat. "What are you doing here?"

I have come to retrieve the machine. It's more powerful than I had intended and cannot be entrusted to a primitive life-form.

Phil closed his hand around the metal box. "Primitive? I just—"

No disrespect to human beings, Vromulon X interjected. *You represent a fascinating species. Greedy, petty, and cruel, but fascinating, nonetheless. However,* Homo sapiens *are just one of the possibly infinite forms of intelligent life that exist throughout the cosmos. This laboratory is just one of three hundred forty-seven laboratories that I am currently administering across eleven different dimensions. Tell me: What might happen to the surrounding superstructure if your personal habitat were to suddenly increase in size?*

Phil shrugged.

These experiments require a delicate balance, Phil. My previous attempts to include the human race ended poorly . . . I am afraid I have failed once again. I will now wipe your memory and return you to New Jersey.

"Wait, no!" pleaded Phil. "I'll be good. I won't use the machine on the room or anything else. I'll be more careful. I just want to eat normal food . . . and maybe get a little better at space pong."

Hmm . . . You have been enjoying space pong very much, I see. Vromulon X seemed pleased. *A game of my own design.*

"An excellent game."

Vromulon X paused to evaluate some eleven-dimensional chaos probabilities—calculations that would have taken NASA hundreds of years to even consider.

After analyzing Phil's subconscious mind and reviewing all possible future timelines, the scientist came to a decision.

Very well, Vromulon X sighed. *I will leave you with the machine. But I must warn you, human: Be careful what you wish for.*

"How would you like to switch habitats with me?" Phil asked Makrimbus as they sat down for lunch in the cafeteria.

"Why would you want to switch?" asked Makrimbus. "My habitat is the only part of the space lab where I feel comfortable." He gestured around the cafeteria. "The rest of this place is so weird."

"What did Phil say?" asked Heather.

"He wants to switch habitats," said Makrimbus.

"I don't understand," Heather replied. "My habitat is the only place here that feels like home."

"What does Phil want?" asked Ploom.

"He wants to switch habitats," explained Heather.

"That's a silly idea," said Ploom.

"Never mind," muttered Phil. "Forget I said anything."

"I love my habitat," Heather said to Phil. "It looks just like my home world: a geometrically precise series of ramps and tubes. Smooth, peaceful, and very, very shiny. I miss my planet every day." She lowered her voice. "My greatest wish is to return home once my participation in the grand experiment is complete. I yearn to someday experience—" Heather emitted a pleasant hum, but no words were spoken by the translator.

"What was that last part?" asked Phil. "It didn't translate."

"Oh." Heather paused and hummed again. "It means the experience of total and perfect reflection, during which the distinction between the physical world and the reflected world all but disappears."

"Yeah," said Phil after a pause. "I get homesick too."

He stared at Heather for a while and didn't say anything.

"My planet is a blazing inferno covered in magma and acid rain. The air is toxic, and the ocean is a boiling cesspool." Makrimbus sniffed. "I sure do miss it."

"How about you, Omrey?" Heather turned to the hairy pineapple. "What was life like on your home planet?"

"Gosh," said Omrey, "I've been on this space station so long, I don't think I can remember that far back!"

They translated the joke for everyone around the table, and all the aliens had a good laugh.

Heather hovered near Omrey. "You're so funny, Omrey." She giggled. "Thanks for making me feel better."

———————

THE NEXT DAY, Phil had everyone cracking up at lunch. "And the third alien says, 'Now *that's* what I call nutrient fluid!'"

"Stop it, stop it. I can't breathe!" wheezed Heather, still laughing.

"That's a good one," said Omrey.

Phil smiled.

"Did you know that the nutrient fluid is specially formulated for each species on board, based upon their individual biological requirements for chemical energy?" said Ploom.

"Wow. You're so smart," said Heather. Phil grumbled as Heather and Ploom discussed the finer points of alien metabolisms.

PRETTY SOON, PHIL was funnier than Omrey, smarter than Ploom, stronger than Makrimbus, and faster than Blayzar. The aliens were starting to catch on, but Phil couldn't stop using the ice cream machine to make wishes.

"Phil didn't used to be so strong, did he?" asked Makrimbus.

"I don't remember him being so fast either," replied Blayzar.

"Phil used to be different," said Heather as she floated away. Phil was busy practicing his space pong serve.

He had become unstoppable. No one enjoyed playing with him anymore.

Phil looked around and realized he was alone. "Hey, where did everybody go?"

"You've changed, Phil," said Larf, who was sitting in the bleachers.

"We liked you better before you got that stupid machine," said Fleebar.

THAT NIGHT, SCRUNCHED in his room, Phil lay on his side, petting the little box like it was a kitten. He was nervous. Did everyone know he had used the machine to grow big and shiny and funny and smart and strong and fast, and to become the best at space pong?

Some of his talent came naturally, he convinced himself. The others were just jealous, he decided. But then a terrifying thought crossed his mind: What if someone else were to use the machine to make *their* wishes come true? Phil didn't like that idea at all. It was *his* machine, for him only.

He was suddenly certain that someone would try to steal his precious machine—at any second, some ferocious creature would break through the door to snatch it away from him. Phil clutched the machine in his hands and squashed his body against the back wall, as far from the door as possible. He accidentally crushed his rocking chair in the process.

After a while, he managed to calm himself down. He was being paranoid. He was big and strong now. He could protect the machine against even the most dangerous creatures on board.

Phil opened his hands to admire his treasure. There was just enough light to see his reflection in the metal surface. As he stared at himself, he was struck with a brilliant idea.

What if he didn't need the machine to grant wishes? What if *he* could grant the wishes himself? Then he could destroy the machine and still have everything he ever wanted.

Phil laughed. What a simple plan. Why hadn't he thought of it before?

He smiled and imagined playing space pong with Heather, dancing around her lovely spherical body. They would make a beautiful ballet—huge, shiny, flying.

They could leave the space lab together, return to her home planet to live in mathematical perfection. They would fall in love. They would raise a family! Do spheres have families? Phil wasn't sure, but he was excited to find out. He activated the machine, and the button's red glow made him feel warm.

He held his breath and shut his eyes.

"I wish I had the power to grant wishes myself."

DING!

A FEW DAYS later, Larf and Fleebar came looking for Phil. He had missed three interview sessions in a row, and they were worried about him. Larf knocked on the door, but there was no answer.

"Phil?" Fleebar called from the hallway. "Are you okay?"

Larf tossed Fleebar into the air a few times to activate the motion sensor. But when the door to the habitat slid open, the room was empty.

Phil was gone.

All that was left was some broken furniture and two small, shiny boxes sitting next to each other on the rug.

VII

THE ICE CREAM MACHINE

(the one that hasn't been written yet)

Okay, kid, you've read six of my stories, and now it's time for you to write one of your own.

What will your version of "The Ice Cream Machine" be about? A daring chef creating bold new flavors? A secret government project to create human/Creamsicle hybrids? A hungry ghost? A rock band? Your uncle Doug?

You can write about absolutely anything you want. It could be a sad story, a scary story, a gross story, or a crazy story. This is not homework. There are no rules. You have total creative control.

But if I may be so bold, I would like to share a few tips:

1. **Make a loose plan before you start. Think about what you want to happen at the most**

?

exciting moment of the story and work backward from there.

2. Focus on a character who wants something. It doesn't really matter if they get it. The interesting part is how they try.

3. A story is never finished after the first draft. Monkey around with it for a while to make it better. Take a week off and come back to it fresh.

If these tips are helpful, great. If not, feel free to ignore them completely (you can find others at adamrubinhasawebsite.com). But before I go, here is the one piece of advice that is most important of all:

Write something you like.

You can listen to your friends or your parents or your teachers for feedback, but remember: It's your story. If your story makes you happy, it's a good story.

Oh, and by the way, once you've finished your story, I'd love to read it. Please ask an adult for an envelope and a stamp and send a copy to me:

Adam Rubin
c/o Penguin Young Readers
1745 Broadway
New York, NY 10019

You know what? If you don't feel like writing a story, that's okay too. Maybe you prefer reading them. That's fine by me. I'll make you a deal: As long as you keep reading, I'll keep writing. Hopefully we can do this all again someday soon. Until then, have fun out there.

Your pal,
Adam

Turn Yourself into an Ice Cream Machine

––––––––––––––––

ere's a fun and kind of amazing recipe you can try at home. You don't need any special equipment, and it takes less than half an hour.

In a strong sandwich-size sealable plastic bag, combine:

> 1 cup heavy cream
> 1 ½ tablespoons sugar
> 1 ½ teaspoons vanilla extract
> A pinch of salt

Seal the sandwich-size bag tightly and place it in a very strong gallon-size sealable plastic bag, along with:

$1/3$ cup coarse salt

3 cups ice

Put on some winter gloves to protect your hands from the cold and shake the bags vigorously. This part is easier with some help (not to mention more fun). After about 20 minutes of shaking, the ingredients in the smaller bag will transform into ice cream! It's like a delicious magic trick. Break out the spoons and enjoy.

ACKNOWLEDGMENTS

First and foremost, I'd like to thank you (yes, you) for taking the time to read this whole book and caring enough about whatever the heck was going through my head when I wrote it to look at the acknowledgment pages all the way in the back.

This was my first "big" book, and the writing process was the hardest/scariest I've ever been through. The most important lesson I learned was to spend more time crafting a solid outline before attempting to peck as many words as possible into the computer each day. Because it was a learning process (and I had to start over halfway through), it took me a bit longer than I would have liked, which is part of the reason I have so many people to thank . . .

Heartfelt gratitude to the earliest readers who waded through rough drafts to give me feedback: Josh & Leo, Jared & Martin, BJ, Tia, and Sam. Especially Sam, who is a constant sounding board, intrepid travel companion, and world-class gag man. Early readers are worth their weight in gold. A picture book is one thing, but asking a friend to sift through sixty thousand words that aren't quite finished yet means that person has to be both generous with their time and insightful with their criticism.

My old pal Dan Salmieri was actually the very first person to read the very first drafts of these stories. Dan always knows what's cool and funny, so when he thinks something I wrote is good enough to illustrate, I take it as the highest compliment.

Of course, I'd also like to thank the other five illustrators: Liniers, Nicole, Seaerra, Charles, and Emily. They are a dream team assembled from the four corners of the earth, and the writing in this book seems better because of their terrific pictures. Thanks to John Hendrix, who designed the cover, which is quite possibly the only reason you picked this thing up in the first place. The greatest thrill of being an author is getting to collaborate with such phenomenally talented artists. The second-greatest thrill is seeing your book on sale in an airport.

I wrote most of these stories while living in Spain, and I'd like to thank Cafés El Magnífico on Carrer de l'Argenteria for making delicious cortados that carried me through from sunrise to lunchtime each day. They give you a tiny piece of free chocolate with every coffee.

Thanks to my Barcelona friends for drinking wine patiently while I rambled about whatever I had written that morning: Tati & Karolis, Yorgos, Andrew, Kike & Abi, Julia, Bruno, Andy & Maria, and Seb & Catia. An especial super gracias to my amigos in Madrid: Luis y Ximena, Jorge y Marga, Xavi y Nikki, and Juan y Pepa. Thank you por hacer que España se sienta como mi casa.

Thanks to this international crew of polyglots for their help with translation: Francesco Buscema, Deepa Agashe, Liju George, Gowri Vijay, and Luis Piedrahita.

Thanks to Gabe, Ryan, Max, and Veronica for alerting me to the existence of the word *jangus*. Thanks to Dan & Dave Buck for their grand vision and enthusiastic appreciation of all things curious. Thanks to Kelli, Shiro, Ping, and Fergus for letting me steal their names. Thanks for no particular reason to Noah, Jake, Ben, Derek, Vanessa, Rob, Melissa, Ricky, Laurel, Steve, Sophia, Mark, Corey, Eric, Enrique, Alex, Prakash, Sarina, and Elbaum (even though he didn't read the book after I sent it to him).

As long as I'm on a roll here, I'd like to thank the following entities and organizations for providing encouragement and/or inspiration throughout the years: the Annoyance Theatre, Tannen's Magic Camp, *El Mundo Today* and La Llama, Washington University in St. Louis, Books Are Magic, As Is, Half Moon Bar, Borgo Argenina, the Gathering 4 Gardner, 31 Faces North, *The Stinky Cheese Man*, *The Monster at the End of This Book*, *The Far Side*, *The Simpsons* (seasons 1–10), "Weird Al" Yankovic, Talking Heads, Bob Ross, Monty Don, Neri Oxman, Vulfpeck, Zadie Smith, David G. Haskell, Michael Chabon, Akio Kamei, Dr. Kokichi Sugihara, Ben & Jerry's, Ba-Tampte Garlic Dill Pickles, graph paper, my Mizudashi cold brew pitcher, Harriman State Park, the New York–New Jersey Trail Conference, WFUV, Dr. Bronner's peppermint-flavored soap, and Google Docs. Did you know you can pretty much write whatever you want in the acknowledgments section of your own book?

Speaking of which, I could not have turned my novice scribblings into an actual book without the expert guidance of my editor, Stephanie Pitts, who due to a global pandemic, I still have not met in person as of this writing. Thanks to the whole team at Putnam/Penguin, including Jen Klonsky, Matt Phipps, Cecilia Yung, Tessa Meischeid, Cindy Howle, and Emily Rodriguez. I'd also like to thank my copy editor, Elizabeth Johnson, who made me feel like I was getting my teeth cleaned by laser beams. In a good way. Thanks to Eileen Savage, who designed this whole book, including this page—and maybe she will choose to put a cool little text symbol right here? ♔

Thank you to my agent and co-conspirator, Jennifer Joel, who is the kind of brilliant, high-heeled, no-guff New Yorker every author dreams of having.

Thanks to my mom and dad for indulging the bizarre interests of a weird little kid. Thanks to my nana for proving age is just a number. Thanks to my sister for laughing at all my dumbest bits and occasionally spitting her drink out into the sink in the process.

Most of all, thanks to Temís, who eats Altoids like popcorn and popcorn like a vacuum cleaner. I'm outrageously lucky to have the love and support of someone so adventurous, creative, and fun to look at.

Finally, thanks to all the people I forgot (yes, you). Thanks for being kind and funny and leaving the world a slightly better place than you found it. Gracias a todos.

MEET THE ILLUSTRATORS

EMILY HUGHES is the author and illustrator of the picture books *Wild* and *The Little Gardener*. She also illustrated the Theodor Seuss Geisel Award–winning Charlie & Mouse series by Laurel Snyder, as well as  *Brave Bear* by Sean Taylor and *Everything You Need for a Treehouse* by Carter Higgins.

You can follow Emily on Instagram @plaidemily.

LINIERS is the author of more than thirty books, including the Eisner Award–winning *Good Night, Planet*. He is the creator of the daily comic strip *Macanudo*, which has been published in Argentina by *La Nación*  since 2002 and in English-language collections in the United States since 2014. He received the Inkpot Award for his contributions to the world of comics in 2018.

You can follow Liniers on
Twitter and Instagram @porliniers.

NICOLE MILES is the author of the Eisner Award–nominated comic *Barbara* and the illustrator of *Alley & Rex* by Joel Ross. She contributed illustrations to *Goodnight Stories for Rebel Girls: 100 Immigrant Women Who Changed the World* by Elena Favilli and *Hey You! An Empowering Celebration of Growing Up Black* by Dapo Adeola.

You can visit Nicole at nicolemillo.com or follow her on Twitter @nicolemillu or on Instagram @nicolemillo.

SEAERRA MILLER is the author and illustrator of the Mason Mooney series and the graphic novel *Out There*. She illustrated the first three installments of the Hilda series based on the Netflix original program *Hilda*.

You can visit Seaerra at seaerramiller.com or follow her on Twitter @seaerramiller or on Instagram @seaerram.

DANIEL SALMIERI has illustrated twelve picture books, including the *New York Times* bestsellers *Dragons Love Tacos, Dragons Love Tacos 2: The Sequel, High Five,* and *Robo-Sauce.* He is the author and illustrator of *Bear and Wolf.*

You can visit Daniel at danielsalmieri.com or follow him on Instagram @dansalmieri.

CHARLES SANTOSO has illustrated many books, including the *New York Times* bestseller *Wishtree* by Katherine Applegate and the picture books *Ida, Always* and *This Way, Charlie* by Caron Levis. He is the author and illustrator of *Happy Hippo.*

You can visit Charles at charlessantoso.com or follow him on Twitter @minitreehouse or on Instagram @charlessantoso.

ABOUT THE AUTHOR

Photo Credit: Benjamin Pratt

ADAM RUBIN is the #1 *New York Times* bestselling author of many critically acclaimed picture books, including *Dragons Love Tacos*, *Dragons Love Tacos 2: The Sequel*, *Gladys the Magic Chicken*, *High Five*, *Secret Pizza Party*, *Robo-Sauce*, and *El Chupacabras*, which won the Texas Bluebonnet Award. *The Ice Cream Machine* is his middle-grade debut.

You can visit Adam at adamrubinhasawebsite.com or follow him on Twitter @Rubingo.

Thank you for reading.

Gracias por leer.

Grazie per aver letto.

Takk for at du leser.

पढ़ने के लिए धन्यवाद।